Felony Dementia

Published by Black Hat Books
ISBN: 978-0-615-49072-4
Library of Congress Control Number: 2011910168
Manufactured in the United States of America

Book design by Brion Sausser: www.bookcreatives.com

To all whose lives have been touched by dementia.

PART ONE

April is the cruellest month

~T.S. ELLIOT, THE WASTE LAND

Chapter One

....

The clock on the cardiac monitor glowed 0238. The blue light from the clock face flickered on the bare walls of the room and the blank faces of its occupants. The patient's labored breathing was the only sound interrupting the erratic procession of muted blips counting out his remaining heartbeats.

Recently the breathing pattern had slowed to Cheyne-Stokes, the intervals of apnea or no breathing gradually becoming more prolonged. That was the only change that Tyler L. Harrison, Jr., "Same" to friends and family, had noted in the past twenty-four hours.

Nearly three days had passed since Same made the most difficult decision of his life. He agonized over pulling the feeding tube from his father. Now he sat amid the high tech machines with data displays showing the most minute physiological changes — none of which offered any solutions that could help his father. A parade of doctors had helped Same explore every avenue available, but in the end it had to be his decision alone to end the man's suffering.

Same looked up from the monitor to see the eyes of Dr. Cary Street locked in the same morbid cycle between the cardiac monitor and his father's fading breaths. Street had been the family's doctor for as long as Same could remember and was like a second father. Their families had been so close that Same grew up calling him "Uncle Cary" rather than the "Dr. Street" that his patients used.

Same's brother Mitchell had finally succumbed to exhaustion and lay curled in a chair with Same's jacket for a pillow. Mitch was the product of Tyler Senior's second marriage to a woman hardly older than Same. When the second marriage slid into a cold separation, Mitch's mother had done her best to poison his relationships with Same and Senior, but the boy was much more stubborn in his loyalty than the average nine-year-old.

Same sat uneasily in a patient chair, which struck him as fitting decor for a medieval torture chamber. No matter how he tried to get comfortable, the damn thing simply didn't fit his body. As he readjusted himself yet again, he wondered if his and Mitch's fate was destined to follow that of the withered older man lying in the bed — years of painful deterioration and death long preceding normal expectation.

Same knew about living with his head on the block. For nearly ten years he had known about the gene mutation that would soon trigger in him the same frontotemporal dementia that was killing his father. But as Senior's brutally slow death crept onward, he had begun to worry more about whether that same FTD time bomb ticked within Mitch's small body.

Looking around the hospital room, Same concluded that it was the antithesis of his father's character. It was sterile, cold, and void of anything that would suggest the dynamic, loving personality of his father or the robust life he led before disease struck. Senior had enjoyed a beautiful family and a successful career, the kind of idyllic life you saw in Southern Living magazines. Then some unknown shitty mechanism flipped the FTD switch and ripped it all apart.

His thoughts were suddenly interrupted by a nurse silently entering the room and gliding to the bedside. Same noted that she was a perfect addition to the scene. Her scrubs were starched and immaculate, every strand of her hair was held tightly in place, and her pale face glowed coldly blue in the sterile light. The marketing department should have been delighted at how well she matched the lifeless decor.

She lifted his father's right hand slightly and allowed it to fall back to the bed. The paralysis was among the worst in the long series of symptoms. It had been a slow, creeping death, first the legs to confine him to a wheelchair then the upper body until he was completely helpless. The nurse ran her fingertips across Senior's lips and frowned. Turning to Same, she said without emotion, "His lips are dry from severe dehydration. I'll be back to put something on them."

Same wasn't sure how to take the comment. Was it an accusation that he had made his father's life more miserable by pulling the feeding tube? Should he have allowed the IVs to continue? The doctors said that continuing the fluids would only prolong his life and his suffering.

But nothing they said could help the guilt. The guilt was always there waiting when his mind ran out of distractions. For short periods he convinced himself that he had done what his father would have wanted, but then the guilt pressed in again in waves that couldn't be shaken.

The nurse returned and gently applied a petroleum jelly to his father's lips with a cotton swab. His swollen tongue was protruding slightly from his lips, so she gently moved the tongue to wipe a viscous glob of dark green saliva from the corner of his mouth. When she had finished she turned and offered a smile to Street, who was now methodically flipping the pages of a medical journal. He had long since read everything in the journal, but it was easier than trying to make conversation with Same.

"Is there anything I can get for you?" she asked.

Street looked up to ask Mitch if he wanted anything. The boy was still curled up with his head resting against the coat and wall, sound asleep. Turning to Same he asked, "Any requests?"

Same didn't answer, but simply shook his head, and the nurse departed.

Suddenly Senior's body began a series of retching movements, followed by vomitous spewing from his mouth. He gasped for breath and began aspirating gastric fluid. Street immediately jumped from his chair and instinctively reached for the aspiration cannula hanging on the wall. He opened the suction valve and was moving the cannula to Senior's mouth when he felt a hand on his arm. He turned and looked into Same's face.

Same shook his head. "Please don't prolong it. He wouldn't want it."

Street paused and looked down at his patient and lifelong friend. Closing the suction valve, he slowly placed the cannula back in its resting place.

Same and Street held Senior's hands as his body continued to fight for a couple of minutes. When he was finally motionless, Street took his stethoscope from the pocket of his coat and placed it on Senior's chest. Speaking to himself, he muttered, "There's still a slight irregular heartbeat."

Same turned and went back to his chair, burying his head in his hands. It was only a couple more minutes before he heard Street say, "He's gone."

Same had hated himself for how badly he wanted to hear those words over the past few days. His father no longer had to endure the horror of this torturous death or the indignities of his long descent through dementia. No more waiting to see what infirmity or insult may await him next as his brain slowly degenerated. But with Street's pronouncement, Same couldn't control the tears anymore.

Crossing the room to Mitch, he gently shook his brother awake and gathered him in his arms. Although he had slept for the past hour, Mitch felt the hot tears streaming from Same's face and knew immediately what had happened. He hugged Same around the neck, looked one last time at his father over Same's shoulder, and then ran blindly into the hall.

Same caught up to him just as he approached the waiting area, where Mitch's mother sat with her face locked in a tired and irritable scowl. Mitch saw her, stopped, and turned back to Same. Same dropped to his knees and held his brother until he stopped sobbing. Quietly he whispered into Mitch's ear, "It's okay. I'll always be here for you. You know that you've always been able to call me. Nothing has changed, you call, I come. Now help me out by going to your mom and don't give her a hard time. She loves you."

Mitch stiffened but held on to Same. "Alaina doesn't love me. She said I'm a worthless shit like Dad."

It annoyed Same that Alaina required Mitch to call her "Alaina" rather than "Mom," but the verbal abuse she heaped on the boy pissed him off royally. Hopefully the woman could rise to the occasion and be a decent mother tonight, at least.

Same put his forehead on his brother's and whispered intensely, "Listen, Mitch, don't ever accept that. You're special in so many ways and the best brother I could ever have. And you know your mom loves you too. She gets angry and impatient but she loves you, okay?"

Mitch squeezed Same around the neck until Same gasped something about a fractured trachea. Then releasing his grip, Mitch turned and walked to his mother.

Standing quickly, Alaina reached for Mitch's hand. "Well, thank God it's over. Now maybe we can get on with our lives."

Mitch just stared at her, tears welling in his eyes again. Same could have slit the bitch's throat.

A hand on his shoulder restrained him from doing anything stupid as Mitch was briskly led from the waiting room by his mother. Street had returned just in time after informing the nurse that Senior had passed.

Same leaned back against the painted cinderblock of the hallway, his hands thrust deeply in his pockets and bloodshot eyes staring up at the ceiling. His emotions were so mixed he couldn't think straight, a combination of exhaustion, confusion, and anger.

Street himself was confused about what to say to this man who had just lost his father. Although he'd done it many times in his medical career, this one was personal. He decided to take a stab at practicality. "Same, let me drive you home. Are you ready to go?"

"Ready to go?" Same exploded. "Isn't there some more fucking paperwork that needs to be done? Isn't that what these hallowed halls are for, paperwork, shuffling paper and not doing a damn thing for the people who really need it?"

Street stepped back in shock. He knew his young friend was stressed. He had struggled with his father's illness for years and had agonized watching a dynamic man disintegrate before his eyes. Street reached a hand out to calm him, "Same, that's a bit preposterous and you know it."

Same pushed off the wall and stood face to face with Street, "Preposterous? Preposterous? I'll tell you what's preposterous, Uncle Cary. It's preposterous that nobody is interested in this disease. Hell, nobody gives a rat's ass about FTD. And why is that? Are not enough people dying? Is it not fashionable enough? Did we run out of pink ribbon screaming about breast cancer from every damn light pole in the city?"

Street grabbed him by the shoulders. "Stop it, Same. This isn't helping anyone."

Same snatched away. "Oh, easy for you to say, Doctor. So did you help him? He loved you. He trusted you. But when that drug trial got cancelled in San Francisco all you did was sit back and watch him die."

Same stabbed a finger into Street's chest. "It's so easy for you to talk. You don't have it in your genes. You don't have to wonder whether you're going to wake up one morning walking down the street ass-naked. Are you going to get your face slapped making a pass at a stranger? Are you going to be able to talk at all? Are you going to sit around day after day, week after week waiting to see which part of your brain melts next? No, I'll tell you what you're going to do. You're going to skip around free as a flying falcon to the ripe old age of ninety."

Street was shaken by the assault, but knew it wasn't personal. He waited in silence until Same finally let his finger drop away from his chest and leaned back against the wall. Finally, he said quietly, "Same, I'm not letting you push me away. We need each other. I loved your dad like a brother and there was nothing I could do when the UCSF trial was cancelled. I shared laughter and tears with your dad, and we did argue about his treatment, but we never lost respect for each other. I love you and your brother like you are my own children. I'm here when you're ready."

Street turned to move toward the waiting room. He almost made it to the entrance when he heard Same behind him. He turned to find the face of his young friend screwed up in anguish. Suddenly Same reached out with both arms and pulled Street to him.

They stood silently in the cold fluorescent glare, clinging to each other for support as the tears poured down. The nurses had witnessed this sad scene a hundred times and walked quietly by as the business of the hospital flowed on.

When the crush of emotion had past, they finally regained their composure and stood back. Arms around each other's shoulders, they walked quietly to the parking deck.

Chapter Two

Downtown Richmond, Virginia, was deserted at 4:00 in the morning. Street drove along Main Street before bearing left onto Old Osborne Turnpike. As he approached Rocketts Landing he lifted his foot from the accelerator. He had been to Same's condo many times, but he was never sure which entrance to use. He looked over at Same, who seemed to be sleeping deeply.

Without opening an eye, Same said, "First entrance, Uncle Cary."

Street chuckled, "I should know better than to count you out."

He pulled up to the parking garage gate and pushed the opener attached to the sun visor. The gate silently rose and Street pulled into Same's spot near the entrance.

Neither man spoke until they were in the condo. Same flipped a couple of switches and the long hall came alive. Street stood in the gallery, halfway down the hall, shaking his head. "You know, no matter how many times I come to your place I'm still awed by the beauty of it." He continued on down to the living room and stared at the view of the city along the James River. "That view is magnificent, even at four in the morning."

Same smiled. "I enjoy it any time of day, but it's more impressive at night. I often wonder what the hell I'm doing in this place. It's twenty-one hundred square feet, and it seems even bigger. When I started working for H&B, I told myself that a lawyer working for one of the biggest law firms in Virginia ought to live in a place that looked the part. I figured I didn't have to worry about living to retirement age, so why worry about saving?"

Street didn't comment on Same's fatalism, but walked over to the bar in the library. Glancing over his shoulder he asked, "I'm going to indulge in some of that Talisker single malt. May I fix one for you?"

"Drinking your breakfast, eh? Your patients will smell it on you."

Street laughed, "You forget what day it is. It's Saturday and I'm not on call. If you'll have me, I'm going to have a drink or two and then hit that bed in your guestroom."

"Then by all means, make it on the rocks."

Same went into his bedroom and shortly emerged wearing a long-sleeved t-shirt and gym shorts, a pair that had miraculously survived since his undergrad days. He referred to them as his drinking shorts and by God he needed a drink right about now.

Street handed him his scotch on the rocks and raised a toast, "Here's to Tyler L. Harrison, Sr."

Same lifted his glass and then took a large swallow. They sat in overstuffed chairs across from each other, neither man wanting to look into the eyes of the other. Silently they watched the outline of the city as the whiskey slowly eased the edge from the events of the evening.

Finally, Same rose and asked, "Refresh that for you?"

Street handed him his glass, reached for a pillow from the sofa and stuffed it behind his back. When Same returned Street took the offered glass. "Thanks."

After watching the ice in his glass melt for a minute, Same finally spoke up, "Uncle Cary, you're the only person I can say this to, but I'm scared." Same paused to swirl the amber liquid in his glass for a few seconds. "My family tree is being pruned so damn fast it won't be long before they're down to the roots."

Street still wasn't quite sure which route to take with Same. He suspected it was going to be the wrong one no matter what he said, but decided to try a little hope this time. "Have you heard anything from the University of Pennsylvania?"

"Yeah, actually I got a letter yesterday just before I went to the hospital. It looks like I'm in. There's a lot of paperwork to fill out and it's all still very vague. It sounds like the drug they're testing has shown some promise in animal studies."

"Well, that should make you happy. So far the results haven't exactly been promising for the Alzheimer's drugs that have been tried."

Same snorted, "Now there's an understatement. Donepezil and Memantine only slowed degeneration in four percent, and no one showed improvement. This new drug seems to stop degeneration in the animal studies, but all that does is freeze you in your current state. Assuming this new trial can actually get to Phase II without more cancellations, we'll basically just be walking around like zombies for the rest of our lives."

Street swallowed a reply. There wasn't much use trying to argue about it tonight. Finally, Same shook his head. "Damn, listen to me. All I'm doing is spoiling our scotch. Think it's time we put an end to this miserable day."

He rose and went to the doors leading to the terrace. Street could see Same's reflection in the glass doors. It was obvious that the tears had started again. There was nothing more the doctor could say at that point. He carried their glasses into the kitchen and set them in the sink.

Finally he called out to Same, "I'm turning in. Try to get some sleep."

Same looked over his shoulder. "Good night, Uncle Cary. Hope you know I didn't mean all that crap I said at the hospital. Thanks for everything."

He turned off all the lights, unlocked the terrace doors and went outside. It was a chilly early April night with clear skies and brilliant stars in every direction except where they were suppressed by the lights of downtown.

He felt drained, but his mind wouldn't stop churning. Why? Why can't there be some answers for this thing? The researchers knew the mechanism for the disease but no one seemed closer to an actual treatment than they were ten years ago.

He settled into one of terrace chairs, his head resting on the back. He could see the faces of those in his family who had died from FTD, and those who he knew carried the mutant gene. Naturally, his father was at the top of the list. But his father had a sister who had died very young at thirty-five, leaving behind two children who were now in their forties and possibly beginning to exhibit behavioral symptoms. His grandfather probably had it, although that diagnosis hadn't been available when he committed suicide before Same was born. There was also an aunt and two more cousins who appeared to have avoided the gene. He dreaded finding out Mitch's status.

A genetic screen had confirmed that Same shared the same mutation as his father. His mother had given him the nickname "Same" when he was still a preschooler, saying he was so much like his father that they were like the same person. Looks like she was more right than she realized, he thought. He dozed off wondering if, at age thirty-two now, he would have enough time left to see Mitch through college.

A dog's bark in the distance stirred him and he awoke with a chill. The sun was breaking, casting a golden glow on the river below but providing no warmth. He brushed at the dew on his shorts and went inside. Slowly he managed to brush his teeth, then stood for a few minutes in a hot shower before collapsing completely nude on top of his bed.

Chapter Three

....

Cary Street exited the taxi at the Medical College of Virginia at Marshall and 11th Streets. As he started up the steps to MCV's Sanger Hall he ran a hand across his chin. His face felt like a wire brush. He contemplated dropping by his office to catch a quick shave, but decided not to be any later than he already was.

He quickly entered the building and took the elevator down to the basement. Whenever he visited he was taken aback by the starkness of the place. The yellow-block walls were still shiny but showed their age. The place was scheduled for a complete renovation and he hoped it would do away with the morgue ambience.

He was about to enter the neuropathology autopsy room when he heard a gurney being pushed from the refrigerated storage at the opposite end of the long hall. Street held the swinging door open for the attendant and gurney to pass through. He followed behind them to the autopsy room.

At the center of the room was a stainless steel work table with a slanted surface to facilitate drainage into a large stainless steel sink. Eviscerated organs were handled on work spaces to each side of the sink. A workbench against the right wall held a microscope fitted with a camera that allowed photographs to be downloaded to the computer next to the scope. The long wall was lined with glass front cabinets, its inner shelves filled with white containers where the brain specimens from past autopsies were stored for research and teaching.

A heavy formalin odor hung over the room and scratched at Street's eyes as he entered. When his eyes cleared he saw Dr. Cassandra Brush approaching with an extended hand. "Good morning, Cary. We haven't seen you down here in some time. I heard you were coming in."

Brush was Director of Neuropathology and was known for her savvy, no-nonsense demeanor. She had only been at MCV for a couple of years but had made a name for herself. The residents both feared and admired her.

Street went over and shook Brush's hand. "Good to see you, Cassie. What are you doing here on a Saturday morning?"

Brush pointed at the gurney. "The next case. Middle-aged man with a lot of strange symptoms who died last night. I heard you were coming so I thought this one must be special too."

"He is special, but not as a medical mystery," Street said as he shook his head. "He was special to me, as a patient and a close friend. I expect we'll find evidence of frontotemporal dementia."

Brush could see the pained expression on Street's face. She wasn't happy with a friend participating in an autopsy, but decided to proceed without comment.

She turned from Street to the resident. "Dr. Cary Street, this is Dr. Robert Brafferton, our chief resident. He'll be doing the post. Dr. Brafferton, Dr. Street."

Brafferton extended his hand, "Guess I'd better be on my best behavior with my boss and an attending watching me!"

Street laughed, "Don't be too reverent. Tyler Harrison wouldn't want that. His family is known for its black sense of humor."

"That's cool," said Brafferton. "Let's get started."

The three physicians stepped back into the anteroom to don protective gowns and masks. When everything was set, Brafferton picked up a scalpel and made an incision from behind the right ear across the back of the scalp to the left ear. With some difficulty he managed to pull the scalp flap forward over the forehead. Then with a bone-saw he opened the skull. Finally, with the aid of a retractor, he removed the cranium. With minor difficulty he severed the brain stem and lifting the brain from the skull, he placed it on the table.

Turning to Brush, Street asked, "May I take a closer look?"

"Certainly."

He quickly grabbed a pair of gloves, not realizing how tense he was until he struggled to put them on. Brush noticed his hands shaking, but bit her tongue.

Taking a deep breath, Street lifted the brain and rotated it to see the front. He found the expected atrophy of the frontal lobes. Slowly continuing to rotate the brain, he also noted surprisingly extensive degeneration in the temporal lobes as well.

Suddenly the shaking of his hands intensified and his vision began to blur. As he reached for support, the brain slipped from his hands and hit the table with a loud, wet slap, sliding across the work surface until it knocked over several empty specimen bottles.

Street was mortified. He felt the other doctors' eyes boring into him as he quickly retrieved the slippery oblong that formerly housed the essence of his friend. Forcing a crooked smile, he joked weakly, "Well, Tyler always enjoyed bowling. I guess he wanted to get in one last frame."

Brafferton was aghast, but Brush calmly came to Street's rescue, "I think the Harrisons' sense of humor has rubbed off on you, Doctor. Perhaps Dr. Brafferton should continue?"

Brafferton snatched the brain from Street as if a nurse had just dropped his baby. He carefully repositioned it on the work surface and picked up a large knife. His eyes locked disapprovingly on Street, he said, "Now back to the autopsy. Let's see what the ventricles look like."

As expected they were markedly enlarged. "Are we doing a fifty-fifty on this specimen?" he asked Brush. He then turned back to Street, "I'm not talking about a raffle."

Brush shot him a look that would etch glass. "Yes, Bob, a fifty-fifty. The donation form stipulated specimens from one half go to U. Penn and UCSF. The other half will be frozen for future studies. Obviously, Mr. Harrison knew what he wanted."

Street had seen all he could handle. He had confirmed the FTD diagnosis with his own eyes and could answer any questions that Same may have. He quickly thanked Brush and Brafferton and beat a hasty retreat before his friend's brain could be hacked in half. Brush gave him a quick pat on the shoulder, but Brafferton just stared at him as if he had wiped his mouth with the tablecloth. Fierce territorial protection was nothing new in medicine.

Chapter Four

....

While Street was still clearing the formalin from his lungs, Same awoke to the smell of the coffee the doctor had left brewing in the condo. Rolling out of bed, he forced himself to assume his Saturday morning automaton personality. Every Saturday was condo day. He went about the ritual of cleaning and straightening in exactly the same sequence; strip the beds, start the laundry, clean the kitchen, run the vacuum. Take a coffee break with the newspaper and then begin folding the laundry.

It was while he was folding his underwear that he suddenly stopped short. He realized he had folded the same pair of shorts three times, getting the edges even. He could see his father's obsessive-compulsive behavior, one of the first symptoms of FTD.

Same stared at the stack of clothing for a few moments, then shook his head and quickly gathered up the rest of the clothes into a bundle. He stuffed folded and unfolded clothing into the dresser drawers, as if this pathetic gesture would ward off the disease.

He refilled his coffee cup and walked out on the terrace. Through the brisk, clear air he was able to see his office building in the Richmond skyline. A stronger breeze came across the terrace and his drinking shorts couldn't keep the goose bumps from his legs. He took a big swig of coffee, dropped to the terrace floor, and snapped off fifty push-ups. He made a mental note to go for a run sometime during the day. It had been nearly a week.

Finishing his morning chores, he quickly polished off a generous portion of tuna salad with celery, pine nuts, and egg. To get his mind off disease and death he decided to go to the office. It was hardly a place for reflection, and that was exactly what he hoped to avoid. At least he could see what had been accumulating on his desk over the past few days.

The walk to work never took more than thirty minutes, and on a Saturday afternoon there was little traffic to slow his arrival at the offices of Hustings and Billings at Riverfront Square. Coming to work for H&B was not an easy decision. In law school Same had envisioned joining the legal department of an environmental nonprofit to do battle with greedy corporations despoiling the landscape. But an internship during his second year had opened his eyes and he realized that many of these nonprofits were not exactly altruistic. Then H&B offered him an obscene amount of money to join their corporate and securities group. More than the thrill of the money itself, it was Mitch's presence that sealed the deal, as Same had come to realize that Mitch's care would likely end up being his responsibility.

Same waved to the weekend security guard as he entered the main lobby. Decked out in rose and cream marble, the lobby always impressed him with its thirty-foot ceilings and general grandeur. He pushed a button at the elevator bank and a door opened. As he started in he abruptly came face to face with a beautiful woman. Same laughed, "Sorry, Julie, didn't mean to run you down."

Julie Welford was a junior partner who had taken Same under her wing as his assigned mentor during his first year at the firm. Their relationship had grown into one of mutual respect and trust. Although Julie was only a few years older than Same and was constantly fending off advances from both single and married lawyers at the firm, Same had never considered even inviting her for a social drink. They had become more like brother and sister, and besides she had been dating a guy Same had come to respect.

"Hey there, kid," Julie replied. "What are you doing here? I thought you were out with your dad. How's he doing?"

Same considered for a few seconds. "Actually, better. He suffered a lot this past week and he finally passed away last night."

"Oh, Same, I'm so sorry. Is there anything I can do?"

Same smiled, "Thanks for asking, but I think Mitch and I will be all right. After being at the hospital most of the week, I just wanted to think about something else for a couple hours."

Julie nodded. "Well, seriously, Same, just whistle if there's anything I can do."

"Will do, thanks, Julie," said Same with a wave as he let the elevator door close. He realized he was going to have to deal with a lot of these encounters over the next few weeks. As genuine as Julie was, he dreaded the barrage of polite condolences he would have to endure from others at the firm.

He stepped out on the sixteenth floor and wandered into his office. As his computer booted up he stared at the stacks of paper for his current projects. It all seemed so mundane now.

Corporate and securities work was usually fairly tedious. Particularly for the big mergers and acquisitions, a trained monkey could dig through the vast stacks of documents to perform the "due diligence" his clients needed. He was obsessive in his work, always reminding himself that when one does "due diligence" he usually finds a John Dillinger. But few of the hundreds of hours he billed on the big transactions really mattered to the client, and the net effect of any hours that did matter was to make some very wealthy people a little bit wealthier.

He stood and looked from his window toward the upper James River. As he followed the riverbank he noticed an egret far below, feeding her hungry chicks and then hastily flying off in search of more food. It was not too different from firm life. There was always enough work to keep the associates constantly billing throughout the month. Stuff a little work down the throats of each of the clamoring clients, then try to get back in time to satisfy them again before the clamoring got too loud or they tried to leave the nest. That was the game at H&B and by damn he was good at it. He was one of the firm's most profitable associates and was on track to make partner if he kept playing the game.

Senior had played the corporate game, and played it well. He worked for the same bank his entire career and had moved quickly up the ladder until FTD shook him loose. On Tuesday Same would lay him in the ground, by then cremated *sans* brain and with no real family or friends in attendance. The game didn't seem much worth playing if that was the prize for winning.

Chapter Five

....

Tuesday arrived quickly. Relegating the funeral to the back of his mind had not been difficult. There were mixed emotions, as usual, and he knew it would be difficult but a relief at the same time.

On Monday he'd worked out the details with an Episcopal priest. It would just be a simple interment at the grave site. No need for chairs — Senior's erratic behavior had long since pushed most people away.

Same had dreaded dealing with Alaina, but it had been unavoidable. On Monday afternoon, he called and asked to speak with Mitch, but he knew Alaina would be listening on the other line. Mitch picked up the phone and sounded surprisingly upbeat. "Hi, Same. What's up?"

"I was about to ask you the same thing, big guy."

"Oh, nothing much. Just in the middle of some homework."

"Man, they never give a guy a break, do they?"

"You can say that again. You'd think that when your old man dies, they'd give you a day off. But Alaina said, 'Off to school with you.' Can't you hear her saying that?"

Before Same could answer, Alaina shouted into the phone, "Mitchell, you watch your tone, young man…"

Knowing how quickly it could go downhill, Same interrupted, "Alaina, I'm just trying to talk with Mitch about the funeral arrangements."

"Well, I have some thoughts about that, too," replied Alaina testily.

"I'm sure you do, but when you left Dad you pretty much forfeited those rights. Now Mitch, how does this sound? I talked with the priest and we'll just have a quiet graveside service. You know, with just a few of his friends and us."

Alaina was silent and Mitch asked quietly, "Will Uncle Cary be there? Does he have to be at the hospital?"

"Of course he'll be there," Same replied.

"I will be there as well, Same, whether you want me there or not," hissed Alaina, frost on every word.

"I'm sure you will," Same retorted. "It's a public event and I know you love those."

Hurrying to cut off any reply, Same continued, "Mitch, I'll come by and pick you up at noon. We'll grab lunch and get to the cemetery by two. Sound good?"

"Sure. See you tomorrow."

Before Alaina could interject anything more, Same said goodbye and quickly closed his cell phone. His main concern was that Alaina would make a dramatic spectacle at the service. In terms of drama, Alaina could be Oscar-worthy.

At eleven-thirty on Tuesday morning, Same closed the file he was working on, grabbed his jacket, and went out to his secretary. "Carol, I'm off to pick up Mitch and then to the service."

Same shared Carol Stillwater's secretarial services with Julie and two other associates. She was a godsend. A corporate legal secretary for over forty years, she knew considerably more about the nuts and bolts of practicing corporate law than any of the associates she assisted. There were associates at the firm who fed their own egos by treating their secretaries as if they were too stupid to join the lofty ranks of the licensed legal profession. But Same knew better. Carol was his right hand and they worked closely as a team on most of his projects, which was a big reason why the partners had quickly trusted him to manage transactions on his own.

"Right, I'll see you there," Carol replied.

"That's awful sweet of you, but you really don't have to go."

"Had you rather I didn't?"

"No, no, please do. I don't want you to feel you have to, but you're probably the only one here who actually met him." On his way out he suddenly stopped and turned. "Actually, it will mean a lot to me to have you there. Thanks so much."

Mitch was waiting on the front walk when Same drove up. He climbed in and fastened his seat belt. "Dang, I would've thought you would have rented a big black limo for this. Dad would be disappointed."

Same was taken aback. Then he saw the smile on Mitch's face and reached over to tussle his hair. "All right, you had me for a second. Your sense of humor is as sick as mine."

They both were laughing as they pulled away from the curb. When they arrived at Hollywood Cemetery after lunch, Same was pleasantly surprised at the number of people from his office who had come. Several of the staff and associates and even a couple partners were quietly chatting amongst themselves. As they reached the group, Mitch was quickly smothered in hugs from Julie and Carol as Same shook hands and accepted awkward condolences from the others.

It was a beautiful, crisp spring day with leaves and flowers just beginning to appear in earnest. Hollywood Cemetery was at its spring best. A few daffodils remained and azaleas were ablaze with blooms of white, pink and red. Same found himself fervently hoping that Mitch's young mind would internalize this image of new life and renewal and associate it with his father. If the cold, blue light of that damn cardiac monitor was his defining memory, the boy was going to need some counseling.

The crowd parted as the two brothers approached the gravesite. They walked to the head of the small grave where a mahogany urn rested on a small pedestal. The priest walked to the opposite side and began the service. He followed the ritual from the prayer book and gave a nice homily, though a bit longer than he and Same had agreed upon. He touched on most of the high points Same had provided about Senior's life and thankfully ignored all the stuff related to FTD.

When the service ended most of those assembled came forward to shake hands with Mitch and Same. Some offered words of sympathy and others just had that awkward look that Same was beginning to know well.

As they headed back to the car, Mitch suddenly squeezed Same's hand tightly. Same looked up and saw Alaina walking slowly away. Her shoulders drooped and she was slightly unsteady on her feet. As much as he disliked her, Same knew Senior's decline must have been hard to cope with. As he watched her unsteady gait, he suddenly realized that he actually felt sorry for her.

Alaina expertly quashed any budding sympathy when they finally caught up to her. As she turned and put her hand on Same's arm, he knew immediately what was coming. She was always like this when she made excuses for getting rid of Mitch.

"Sweetie," she said pitiably, "Would you take Mitchell with you for a bit? This has all been so much and I just need a few moments right now."

Same suspected most of those moments would be used digging through the safe in Senior's study and calculating how much she would get from the estate. He was glad to have some more time to be with Mitch after the trauma of the past week, but hated knowing that his brother would feel rejected my his mother yet again.

Looking down, Same realized Mitch wasn't feeling rejected at all. In fact, he looked positively ecstatic.

Relieved, Same replied, "Sure, Alaina, I'd be happy to take him. He can stay over and I'll get him to school. We'll drive by later to pick up his books."

Alaina's eyes burned with resentment at Mitch's obvious preference for Same's company, but she said nothing.

Same turned to his brother, "Mitch, you have a house key?"

"Sure do."

Without further comment they turned to Same's car. "Then c'mon kid, let's go grab a coffee."

Chapter Six

....

Mitch always loved getting coffee at the corner Starbucks near Same's condo. Even though Same made him order decaf, he felt grown up and it was one of the few places where he would usually open up to Same about his life.

They placed their order — medium coffee, black, for Same; small decaf, black, for Mitch — and grabbed their usual small table on the sidewalk outside. Waiting for his decaf to cool, Mitch stared into his cup and chewed his lip. Same started to speak but then realized Mitch was on the verge of an important question.

Mitch took a small sip of coffee and glanced around. Finally his eyes zeroed in on Same. "So is that," he said hesitantly, "is that how we're going to die?"

Same wasn't quite ready for this question. He had planned something of a response for "What happens to Dad now?" but didn't see this one coming. Perhaps he should have, though. By the time Mitch was born, their father's degeneration had progressed to the point where he never showed much interest in the boy. There were no father-son catches, no sporting events, no fishing trips, no long talks like Same had enjoyed. Dad would just stay in his study, reading his magazines and recounting the contents of his safe. There was never much of a bond between the two; to Mitch he had been mostly an odd, quiet old man shuffling around in the study. Then after his parent's separation, he had rarely seen Senior at all.

Same thought about giving him the nine-year-old version, but decided to lay it all out. Mitch had been forced to be independent from a very early age, and he was mature well beyond his years. He would have to find out sometime, and this coffee shop had always been the spot where they had come to be completely open and truthful with each other.

"Well, let's start with what you know. You know that Dad had a disease that was gradually slowing down his brain."

"Right, FTD."

"Exactly, and FTD stands for frontotemporal dementia. There are a bunch of different kinds of dementias, all of which involve various parts of the brain. In Dad, it started in the frontal and temporal lobes, hence the name. Those parts of the brain control behavior, so it made his behavior very different from other adults. He would sometimes do things that people considered weird or rude without realizing what he was doing. The FTD also made it hard for him to remember certain words, and eventually it spread to parts of his brain that controlled very basic things like walking and moving his eyes and swallowing. When he couldn't swallow anymore, he couldn't eat enough to keep alive, and that's why he died."

Same felt his throat constricting as the unavoidable guilt washed over him again. He took a heavy swig of hot coffee and the burn helped bring him back under control. Mitch showed puzzlement, but somewhat eerily, no signs of emotion.

"So what causes it?" he asked.

"Well, there are different things that can cause the disease, but in Dad it was something called the tau protein. The body makes the tau protein for lots of purposes, but Dad's body made the protein wrong, so it stuck together in little clumps. Until he was around forty years old, his body could handle those little clumps. But then they started building up in his brain. That's what caused the disease."

Mitch was listening with rapt attention, and Same could almost see the wheels churning furiously inside his precocious, developing brain. "Okay, so these little taus make clumps, the clumps build up, and the brain starts degenerating?"

"Um, yes," said Same, startled, "degenerating is exactly the right word."

"So," Mitch continued, with the first sign of anxiety, "Alaina said that FTD is from genes and so you and I are going to catch it too. Is that true?"

Same expected nothing less from Alaina than to exaggerate Mitch's prognosis in order to scare the boy. "Not really," he said. "First of all, it's not something you catch from someone else's germs, like a cold." Same pressed on quickly into the hard part, "Now, Dad did have a particular gene that caused his FTD. And he did pass that gene to me as well. There is a fifty percent chance, one out of two, that you also got the bad gene from Dad rather than a good gene from your mom. You can be tested when you are eighteen and find out, if you want."

Adding a little firmness and volume to his voice, he concluded, "Now, you asked whether we are going to die from this. The answer to that is no. A lot of doctors and very smart researchers are working right now on medicines that solve the problem. There could be several hundred thousand people in the United States who have FTD, so the doctors are moving quickly to help all of us. They have tested the medicine on animals, and all they have to do now is show that the medicines work on people too. Then there will be a cure for me, and for you too if you need it."

Mitch seemed relieved, but followed up with one more question. "So who do they test the medicines on?" he asked, more curious than anxious now.

"Well, me for one," Same replied. "I volunteered to be one of the people who tests them. Next week I'm going to Philadelphia to be in a test called a Phase II trial. There are other tests being conducted around the country, so in just a few years we should have a cure."

Mitch seemed okay with this response, and Same gradually steered the conversation on to more cheerful subjects. They spent the rest of the afternoon walking along the river, and as darkness began to fall Same drove them back to Alaina's house. Same stayed in the car while Mitch popped in to retrieve his books. As they pulled into the condo garage Same's resolve was hardening — the cure may well come too late for him, but this boy would not die of this disease.

They spent the evening across the kitchen table. Mitch would fire over questions about homework and they had the usual spelling quiz that Same insisted on whenever Mitch stayed over. After packing Mitch off to bed with a book, Same finally sat down and spread out the hefty questionnaire from U. Penn. They seemed to want to know everything about him except the shape of his toes. Same sighed and went to fetch a pen, the Talisker, and his drinking shorts.

Chapter Seven

....

Mitch went back home the next evening and the rest of the week passed quickly as Same forced himself to get reorganized at the law firm. With the floor cleared and the desk organized, the cleaning crew finally had a chance to actually vacuum the carpet and dust the furniture on Friday night. By the time he arrived late Saturday morning, the office once again resembled the sharp, clean, sophisticated space he had admired when he first joined the firm. He would have taken a few more minutes to enjoy it had he known the décor would be fouled by immense swaths of blood spatter by afternoon.

He now surveyed the neat stacks in front of him as the notepad where he marked time for hourly billing stared blankly back at him. Recording and billing his life six minutes at a time had become a hated ritual. He suddenly straightened, startled, as his office telephone rang with the quick, staccato ring of internal calls.

"Tyler Harrison," Same answered.

"Same, it's me, Carol."

"Carol, what are you doing here?" Same replied. "Do you have weekend duty?" Two of the secretaries manned the main reception desk on the sixteenth floor every weekend. There were hours to be billed on weekends too, and someone always had a need for a secretary to process some last-minute document.

"Yes, but no time to chat, dear boy," she said quickly, "Alaina is dragging Mitch down the hall as we speak. She wouldn't wait for you to come down."

Same suddenly heard Alaina's sharp voice getting nearer as she berated Mitch for walking too slowly. With a sigh, he said, "Okay, thanks Carol, I hear them. Hey, can you come get me with an urgent phone call in about five minutes?"

"You got it, boss," she said, and Same hung up just as Alaina stormed into his office. She was clutching a document in one hand, and dragging a red-faced Mitch behind her by the other.

As she came through the doorway, she released Mitch and began shaking the document. "Just what is this shit?!" she screeched. He was used to seeing her agitated but she was throwing a truly award-winning tantrum today.

"I don't know," said Same, trying to inject a calmer tone. "Why don't you and Mitch have a seat and you can tell me?"

Alaina was too far gone to even consider sitting down. Mitch shrank back against the wall to get some distance from her as she stomped her foot. "It's his will, you ass, and you know it!" she shouted. "Don't play me for a fool. Did you put him up to this?"

Same tried again to defuse the situation. "I didn't have anything to do with his will, Alaina. Another lawyer here drafted it about a year ago and I've never seen the document. Did you find it in his study?"

"Yes, aren't you surprised that he gave me a key? He trusted me, not like some people. It was in his safe." She waved the paper again, "This shit puts you in charge of everything. My ass you haven't seen it. It has your damn smirking face all over it."

It didn't surprise Same in the least that one of the first places Alaina had gone after Senior's death had been Senior's home. Frankly, he was surprised it had taken her so long to break into the safe. Whatever was devised in the will, Same wasn't betting on Alaina leaving any cash in the safe to join the property in the estate.

Same tried again to gain control. "Alaina, I promise you, I have not seen this document. Why don't you let me take a look and we can talk about it?"

She paused for a moment considering whether to believe him, then flung the will on the desk and turned her back on him. Swallowing his amusement at her petulance, Same picked up the document. It appeared to be a properly executed last will and testament. He was not surprised to see that it was only three pages long. His father absolutely hated long legal documents, and would have insisted on brevity in his will. Fact was, Senior not only hated legal documents, he had little use for lawyers in general. That had led to a few interesting conversations when Same had announced his law school plans.

As he read, he quickly understood Alaina's rage. The document named Same as executor of his father's estate. Referencing a premarital agreement with Alaina that had kept all of their preexisting assets separate, the will devised all of Senior's property to a spendthrift trust with Same as sole trustee and Alaina and Mitch as beneficiaries. The corpus of the trust went to Mitch on his twenty-first birthday. Basically, the trust would provide for Alaina and Mitch's basic living expenses until Mitch turned twenty-one, but they would have to come to Same to get the money and Mitch would end up with most of the estate.

As he finished the document, Same couldn't help a broad smile coming over his face. You had to appreciate the sheer mischief of a man forcing his gold-digging bitch of a second wife to go to her adult stepson for money. Same hoped the old man had been able to take some pleasure out of this secret in the last year of his life, but the fact he'd given her a key showed the dementia was in control.

It was quickly apparent, however, that Alaina was taking no pleasure from it. "Oh, this is funny to you," she fumed, "Same and Senior having one last big laugh together."

Alaina paused for a moment as Carol quietly appeared in the doorway, then she snatched the will from Same's hand and sputtered, "Well, let me tell you something, mister. I'm not going down easy. I'm getting a big, fat rich lawyer and getting this piece of shit will thrown out. If I go down it will be with your…," she paused to think of an appropriately hurtful image, "…it will be with your smug little face under my ass."

Same had never heard her use this language in front of Mitch, but he knew that it wasn't uncommon. Between his growing anger, the pressures of the past week, and Alaina's mangled insult, he just couldn't restrain himself. Suddenly, he burst out laughing.

"Alaina," he said, "the only thing going down will be you on that big, fat lawyer to pay the bills you'll owe him. Take whatever cash you're going to steal from Dad's safe and let that be enough. I'll make sure you and Mitch have plenty to live on."

"Damn you, you … condescending little prick," she shot back. "Damn you and your worthless father and your snot-nosed brother and your whole disease-infested family." She held the will up and furiously tore it in half.

Perhaps invigorated by the tearing, or perhaps realizing that the tearing had no affect on the will's validity, she made the worst mistake of her life. Dropping the torn will and pushing all of her weight back onto her left foot, she swung at Same with a long, arching left hook.

Same saw it coming from a mile away. Quickly bending backward, he watched her sharp diamond engagement ring go whistling harmlessly in front of his eyes. Not exactly a practiced pugilist, Alaina was quickly carried forward by the errant blow. She tried to catch her momentum by stabbing her left foot in front of her, but her expensive leather boot slid on a piece of the torn will. She careened forward and sideways, arms flailing, until her momentum was finally interrupted by the corner of the desk.

Same had always hated that corner. He loved the modern look of the furniture, but whoever had designed a desk with such sharp corners had obviously never worked in an office where he or she had to carry around boxes of papers. Same regularly wound up with bruises on his thighs from carelessly walking into the edge of the desk while his mind was occupied with work, and he was occasionally tempted to take a power-sander to it when no one was looking.

Alaina was really most unlucky. As she fell she just missed her hand on the edge of the desk and caught the corner directly between the bridge of her nose and her left eye. Same heard a sharp crack as the wood pierced the sinus cavity and drove through the infraorbital wall of the eye socket, severing muscle and nerves. Alaina's left eye popped out like a golf ball being chipped onto the green, landing in the middle of Same's desk and rolling to a stop against his keyboard. Momentarily it looked like she was going to be left hanging by her head from the corner of the desk, but her body began convulsing, throwing her back onto the carpet.

In the movies death always happened so quickly and cleanly. The deceased would be fatally wounded by a single bullet and immediately drop motionless to the ground, or if it fit the plot better, could say something poignant or critically important before their last breath eased away. This was not Alaina's lot.

Wood or bone had obviously pierced the large vessels at the base of the brain. Blood first sprayed, and then steadily pulsed from the immense gash in her face. Alaina, her one remaining eye wide open, flopped and squirmed on the freshly-vacuumed carpet. Carol, Mitch, and Same all stood absolutely motionless, totally frozen by the ludicrous impossibility of the scene.

As Alaina began to make an unearthly choking sound, Carol finally revived and moved into action. Grabbing Mitch, she pulled him out of the office. "I'm calling 911," she yelled, "you help her."

Same fell to his knees beside Alaina. Help her with what? An immense amount of blood had spread over the carpet, the desk, the wall, the papers, everything. Put pressure on the gaping hole in her face? Do CPR and pump more blood from her heart out through her eye socket? Horrified, Same could only kneel and stare as the flopping slowly subsided, the bleeding slowed to a trickle, and he was left kneeling in a pool of congealing blood with Alaina's motionless body, her wide, staring right eye, and the mangled, oozing hole where her left eye used to be.

The ten minutes that it took for the paramedics to arrive seemed like seconds to Same in his shocked state. They moved him roughly aside to get to Alaina, then quickly started an IV and began CPR. But they all knew that she was dead.

Chapter Eight

....

After the paramedics had rushed out with the body, still going through the motions of CPR, Same wandered slowly into the hallway. Mitch was huddled with Carol at the secretarial station outside his office, and a small group of lawyers and staff had begun to gather in a murmuring huddle. Same began walking toward Mitch and Carol until a look from Carol made him stop. Looking down, he saw that his pants and shirt were soaked in blood.

He tore off his shoes, pants, and shirt. Wiping his hands as clean as he could on the back of his shirt, he threw the clothes back in the office. Now wearing nothing but boxers and a t-shirt, he walked over to Mitch and took his brother from Carol's arms. Mitch was motionless, staring at the floor. Same could feel himself shaking and squeezed Mitch tighter in an effort to disguise it.

In a thin but strengthening voice, Mitch quietly reached out to comfort him, "It's all right, Same," he said. "It wasn't your fault. It was just an accident."

Same looked down at the thin figure of his little brother, amazed by the gesture. He had just lost both of his parents in the space of a week. While neither was ever a loving parent, they were all the close family he had, other than Same. He could see and hear that Mitch was deeply affected, but Same took it as a tremendous testament to the boy's inner resiliency that he was able to put on a brave face to support his big brother.

 Loud voices approaching down the hall shattered their brief moment together. From around the bend strode a huge bull of a man in an obviously expensive grey wool suit, followed closely by two uniformed police officers. As he approached, he bellowed in a vaguely British accent, "Is this where the lady was killed?"

Same stood up straight and let go of Mitch. "Uh, yes, she was right in here," he said, moving toward his office. "Are you a police officer?"

"Detective Richard Jones," he said, with a broad smile and an emphasis on the detective. "And who might you be?"

"I'm Tyler Harrison," Same replied. "The lady was Alaina Harrison, my stepmother. This is her son, Mitch, and my secretary, Carol."

"Well, I'm delighted to make everyone's acquaintance," Jones said sarcastically. "Now, you're the bloke that killed her?"

Same was caught off-guard by the accusation. "Uh, no, not exactly. She fell and hit her head on the desk."

 "Not exactly, huh? We heard there was a fight and a lady was hit in the head and bled out. So did you 'not exactly' hit her head into the desk?"

Same was beginning to get the feeling that Detective Richard Jones was not going to be on his Christmas card list this year. He started to make a smart reply but Carol interjected. "I made the 911 call," she said quickly, "but I didn't say there was a fight. All I said was there was an argument and the lady fell and hit her head."

"Ah," said Jones, with a nod. "Of course you did. Now how about you little fella," he said, pointing to Mitch. "What's your story for what went down?"

Same stepped quickly up to Jones. "His mother just died in front of his eyes, you ass, how about a little sensitivity?"

He should have known Jones would be the type to love provoking a confrontation in the middle of someone else's tragedy. Jones put a thick finger in the middle of Same's chest and moved in until his nose was nearly on Same's forehead. With a big smile and breath that reeked of coffee and fish, he said, "If you want to buck up to me, little man, you may want to wear a little more than your skivvies and you better be ready to go the distance."

Suddenly Mitch spoke up to defuse the confrontation. "I can talk," he said sharply. "It happened like they said. My mom tried to hit Same and she missed and slipped on a piece of paper and hit the desk."

Despite Mitch's explanation, neither man had yet budged. "Right," said Jones, breathing coffee-fish into Same's face. "Same, huh? What kind of hippie name is that? So, Same here doesn't like your mum very much, does he?"

"No, he can't stand her," said Mitch. Same winced, and Detective Jones smiled even wider with his rancid teeth no more than four inches from Same's eyes. Mitch suddenly caught on. "But neither can anyone else."

"Right," said Jones again. Never losing his evil grin, he reached an arm sideways to motion one of his men toward Same. "One of you move this little fella out of my way and let's go see the damage."

Same allowed an officer to hold a hand on his chest as Jones and the other officer walked in to inspect the office. Standing in the hallway they could clearly hear the first few coarse comments about this one being a "bleeder." Same asked Carol to take Mitch down to reception, where there were a couple of couches they could put to good use while they waited for Jones to finish his melodrama.

Just as Mitch and Carol disappeared toward the elevators he saw Julie come running down the hallway from the stairs.

"Oh my god," she said, out of breath, "I just heard what happened. Is Mitch okay? Are you okay?"

"I guess we are. Mitch seems all right for now. I just need to get these cops out so I can get him home."

"You bet," she said, straightening up. "Say no more."

Julie marched right into the office without a moment's hesitation. "Excuse me gentlemen," she said sharply, "may I see your warrant to search this office?"

"Don't start with me, lady," Jones bellowed, "this is a crime scene. I don't need a warrant. Davis!" he yelled to the officer standing with Same. "Please get this lady out of here."

Davis and Same both made their way to the doorway.

"You touch me and your ass will be sued back into the Stone Age," Julie hissed. "You have no probable cause to believe that a crime has occurred here. Mr. Harrison has an expectation of privacy in this office, you have no warrant to search it, and there are no exigent circumstances here to provide you with an exception to that requirement. So leave. Now."

"Okay, bigshot," sneered Jones, "Nancy-boy in his skivvies here gave me consent. How do you like that for an exception to your precious warrant requirement?"

Same chimed in from the doorway. "I hardly gave consent, Detective. But I now revoke any such consent. So as the lady said, leave. Now."

Detective Jones thrust his square jaw and his coffee-fish breath in Same's face for the second disgusting time that afternoon. Same wondered if he deliberately neglected oral hygiene for the sole purpose of intimidating the citizens unfortunate enough to come into contact with him.

"Okay, boy-o," he said, "we'll let you and your pit bull girlfriend here have some alone-time. But just don't be leaving town in case we need to talk to you after the medical examiner takes a look at your lovely stepmum."

In one of the more interesting legal tactics Same had ever seen, Julie grabbed a box of files and slammed it down next to the detective's feet. Jones didn't move, but merely swiveled his thick neck toward her. Climbing onto the box until she stood a good three inches over the detective, she leaned in to assume the same position he had taken with Same.

"Mr. Harrison will go wherever he pleases until you undertake a legal process to confine his movements, such as, perhaps, getting a *warrant*. Until then, as your people say, sod off!"

The detective laughed to cover his retreat as he and his men began moving toward the elevators. "All right, sweetheart, you win." Pointing to Same, he said loudly for the benefit of the crowd in the hall, "I'd watch yourself around that one, though. He may not look like much in his drawers, but from the amount of blood in that office, I'd say he's got a real mean temper around the females. We'll be back for you, Mr. Same, I wouldn't worry too much about that."

Julie was still standing on the box of files as the elevator door closed behind Jones. As Same turned back towards her, he couldn't resist beginning to clap. A few others in the murmuring crowd joined in and Julie took a slight bow before jumping down.

She came up to Same and wrapped her arms around him. "Go home," she said, "and give that little boy a big hug for me. I'll take care of the partners and the office and everything."

Same started to protest but he knew she was right. As tough as Mitch was, he needed his only remaining family right now. He started to gather up his clothes.

"Go wash your hands before you get Mitch, and leave the clothes to me," said Julie. "They're ruined, and Mitch doesn't need to see all that. Besides," she said with a wink, "that detective didn't give you enough credit for how you look in your drawers."

Same needed that little touch of humor to get him moving again. "You're an angel," he called out to Julie, as he headed toward the bathroom. "I owe you big time."

Chapter Nine

....

When dawn came Monday, Same had already slipped onto Interstate 95 for the four-and-a-half hour trip up to U. Penn. Mitch was safely in the care of Dr. Street and seemed to be doing fairly well, all things considered. He was slightly in shock Saturday afternoon, but began coming around on Sunday. There had never been much love lost between he and Alaina and the manner of her death seemed to make more of an impression on Mitch than the emotional loss. It was somewhat bizarre to Same, but once Mitch had convinced Uncle Cary to explain how Alaina had died in technical terms, the boy seemed better able to process what had happened.

Same had almost cancelled his appointment to stay with Mitch, but if he lost his slot in this trial there was no telling when he might get another chance at a treatment before the degeneration started. If he couldn't get treated, Mitch would just be subjected to this same tragic cycle all over again. Finally, it was Mitch's insistence on Sunday afternoon that Same continue on the trip that convinced him to go.

For a desperately needed shot of life, Same had reserved for the trip a brand new Tesla Model S, which Mitch thought was "so cool." The rest of the country had yet to catch on to car-sharing, but for Same it was a no-brainer. One of the advantages of his expensive condo was that it put him within reasonable walking distance of the office. Only needing a car for a couple local trips a week, the hourly car-sharing fee was way cheaper than owning a car, and he loved being able to pick a vehicle that fit the errand or just suited his fancy.

The Model S purred along almost silently. All electric, its three-hundred-mile range was more than enough to take him to Philadelphia, where he would charge the vehicle overnight before his return. The Model S hadn't begun regular selling to the general public, but several car-sharing companies had been selected to test it in their fleets. Same had reserved one as soon as his acceptance into the U. Penn study was confirmed. He loved the smooth, powerful acceleration, and the money he saved in gas covered most of the increase in the rental fee.

As the Model S slipped silently through the early morning fog, Same's thoughts turned to the day ahead. One of U. Penn's leading researchers had developed a drug named Nanotine, which was designed to break apart tau protein aggregates. The drug had showed remarkable effectiveness in eliminating aggregates in nonclinical animal testing. Phase I trials on a few non-FTD patients suggested that the drug was safe in humans, at least over the two months of the trials.

Now they were on to Phase II where eighty subjects — some without FTD, some actively displaying symptoms, and some pre-symptomatic — would take Nanotine over a period of twenty-six weeks. It was to be a randomized, multi-center, double-blind, placebo-controlled trial. The primary goal was to determine whether Nanotine was safe in long term treatment, but they also hoped to discover whether it was effective in slowing the rate of cognitive and behavioral decline.

According to the literature from U. Penn, Same would be busy through the morning and early afternoon with a battery of tests to establish a baseline of brain function. He would be interviewed by three different researchers to assess his verbal, emotional, and cognitive functioning. Then they'd break out the scanners, and he'd get a PET, an MRI, and an EEG. Over the twenty-six weeks there would be six additional visits and frequent phone calls.

Same mused that if the FTD didn't kill him, all the radiation from the scans surely would. Knowing he was going forward with the study anyway, he had purposefully skipped over the risk disclosures, and he now wondered what the increased cancer risks from brain scans would be. Whatever they were, they probably weren't as much as the risk that a chemical intended to break apart tau aggregates would also break apart other protein groups that were vital to any number of bodily systems. At any rate, the cancer would probably take longer to develop than the FTD.

But what the hell, he thought. Whatever the risks, if this was the only way to access treatment before he started his own decline, and to develop a cure for young kids like Mitch, then there was really no choice. He just couldn't stand the thought of generation after generation of his family continuing to march down the same sad, inglorious path.

In his father's case, it was an unusually slow process. Senior had been a remarkably outgoing, vibrant young man by all accounts. He married young and rose quickly up the ranks of a sizeable regional bank until he was their chief of security at thirty-five. In charge of planning and execution of security protocols at over a hundred branches from Maryland to the Carolinas, he travelled extensively during the workweek and considered visiting with the local employees to be one of the highlights of his job. He also dropped in on the bank's investment analysts regularly, and he learned from them how to execute a disciplined, professional financial strategy that resulted in a personal investment portfolio that rivaled the bank's top executives.

In hindsight, one of his first symptoms may have manifested in his early forties when he began cutting down on branch visits. Senior rationalized that his subordinates needed more experience in the field, but his behavior soon became more and more erratic and reclusive. He was finally fired at forty-seven when he began spending significant bank funds on experimental gadgetry without any real application in the bank's branches. Increasing hostility toward his colleagues had left him with few friends, and he left after nearly twenty-five years of service with only a couple handshakes and half-hearted pats on the back.

On the day Senior left the bank, Same remembered coming home from high school to find his father sitting hunched over at the kitchen table in the dimming light of a winter afternoon. Same's mother had left the year before so there was only Same and Senior left in the house, but they rarely saw each other with Same's busy schedule.

Staring out the window, Senior told him the news. Same stood slightly in shock. Maybe it was just the dimming light, but he had been so preoccupied with his own life that he hadn't noticed just how old his father had begun to look. Senior's eyes hadn't moved from the window, and he continued slowly, "I'm just not sure what else there is left for me to do. I don't know that there's much use for me around here anymore."

Same stood motionless, unsure what to say. Was this a cry for help? Was his father talking about suicide? He knew that his grandfather had killed himself, so he was shocked that his father would even think about it. He first grasped awkwardly at a straw of humor, "C'mon Dad, you know I need you for the weekly laundry."

The comment seemed to slip by Senior, who never let his eyes leave the window. Same knew he could do better. Digging deep to force himself to express the emotions he hadn't voiced in years, he said, "Dad, you know I still want you around. I love you. To hell with that job. You don't like working there anyway. You've got piles of money. Take some months off to travel and play some golf. Shit, retire already and go hiking every day."

Senior didn't respond and didn't move his eyes, but he gave a couple slight nods. Same ordered a pizza for dinner that night and gradually picked up dinner preparation and most of the household chores. Senior never worked again, but didn't pick up a hobby either, unless you considered regular trips to the bar at his country club to be a hobby.

Same headed an hour away to the College of William and Mary the next fall. He was surprised when Senior came down to campus one afternoon with a young woman. Alaina was chipper and chatty and gorgeous in a new dress he had just bought her. They took Same out to dinner at the Trellis, an expensive and delicious little restaurant filled with similarly wealthy parents taking their starving student progeny out for a treat. Same was relieved to see a little spark in his father's eyes again, and when he learned that Alaina was the bartender at his father's club, he thought why not? Good for him, let the old man have a little fun. He didn't quite expect that fun to lead to the altar.

Years filled with athletics, partying, and the occasional class slipped by all too quickly, and Same found himself at home less and less. When he did make it home, Alaina was almost always out with friends. He would usually find his father alone in his study reading an endless stack of investment journals and reviewing and recalibrating his investment portfolio.

During Same's junior year, Senior had a wall safe installed. After that he could often be found counting and updating an inventory of its contents, which consisted mostly of stock certificates and a disturbing amount of cash.

It wasn't until Same's second year in law school at William and Mary that Senior was finally diagnosed with FTD. Dr. Street had remained one of Senior's only friends and over the years had been pushing him to see a psychiatrist for what he thought was deepening depression. When Street came over to the house one Saturday afternoon to drag Senior out for a round of golf, Alaina showed him in to the study and he found Senior halfway through recounting a stack of nearly $100,000 in hundred dollar bills. At Street's insistence, Senior spent the afternoon on the couch of a psychiatrist rather than the links, and a few weeks later the specialists at U. Penn confirmed an inherited mutation in a tau-related gene on chromosome seventeen.

The physical symptoms didn't manifest until approximately a year before his death, but from there his decline was fairly quick. He began to show tremors, his eyes refused to focus, his walk became a shuffle, and the once-vibrant man was in the end reduced to a withered, nonresponsive shell, with only an array of plastic tubes keeping him alive.

Same felt the tears coming again and shook his head to clear away the haunting images. He straightened up in his seat, turned the radio up loud, lowered the windows, and breathed in the wet morning air. He would not be going down that path. If the drug trials killed him, then fine. If he had to do it himself, that was okay too. But no one he loved, and definitely not Mitch, would ever have to pull the tube from him.

Chapter Ten

....

The morning mist cleared just in time for commuter congestion to slow things to a crawl north of Fredericksburg. By the time Same could see the soaring spire of the Marine Corps Museum, it was bumper to bumper. He considered switching over to Route US-1, but knew at that point he'd probably lose more time with all the traffic lights.

Going through the Harbor Tunnel outside Baltimore, Same glanced at the clock on the dash and was pleased to note that he was right on time at three hours. He reached Philadelphia at four hours and the GPS smoothly guided him to 3400 Spruce Street. He'd been instructed to park in the Penn Tower, which joined the Hospital of the University of Pennsylvania, known as HUP. On the third level there were two adjoining open spaces. Same unabashedly parked diagonally across the two. Selfish? Yes. But did he give a damn? Not today.

He made his way over to HUP and found the place somewhat overwhelming with soaring ceilings and brown marble-clad columns. A blue banner was affixed high on a wall declaring that U. Penn was in the Top Ten in the nation. That was a comforting detail, at least.

Getting directions at the information desk, he weaved his way to the third floor of the Gates Building where the Neurology Department was located. Ordinarily patients were seen in the clinical setting, but he'd been instructed to come to a Dr. Greenburg's office. Finding Greenburg's office, he entered and was greeted by a woman with a broad, welcoming smile.

"Good morning. You're Mr. Harrison." The way she said it was not a question.

"Uh, yes," replied Same, surprised to be recognized. "My fame must have preceded me."

The receptionist laughed, "I have ESP. Seriously, we don't schedule four patients for each ten minutes. I'll tell Dr. Greenburg you're here."

"You mean there's no more paperwork?" he asked jokingly.

She stopped and turned back to Same. He could swear she blushed as she said, "Uh, you can do that later." She stepped into a hallway and was out of sight.

Before Same could take a seat a door opened and a man in a white lab coat stepped into the waiting room. "Mr. Harrison, I'm Dr. Greenburg. Please come in."

He shook hands with Same as he held the door. When they reached his private office, Greenburg gestured to a chair and then perched himself on the corner of his desk. The room was Spartan, but comfortable. If certificates guaranteed the man was an expert, Same was in good hands.

Greenburg appeared to be in his fifties with curly salt and pepper hair and deep-set green eyes. He had one of those smiles that immediately gave reassurance. That his tie was askew and files were stacked everywhere, Same interpreted as a good sign. He obviously wasn't compulsive about appearances, so hopefully his interest in FTD didn't stem from his own affliction. It was never good if your doctor went demented in the middle of your treatment.

When Same was seated Greenburg said, "I hope your trip up I-95 wasn't too horrible. It's never good."

"No, it was okay. Crowded, but I expected that."

"We tried to call you several times this morning, but your phone must not be on."

Same pulled his Blackberry from the clip on his belt. "You're right. I wanted some peace from work email while I drove and forgot to turn it on. Is there a problem?"

"As a matter of fact there is." Greenburg paused and looked uncomfortable. "Our study has been closed down."

"What do you mean, closed down? It just started. Have you filled your patient quota?" Same was immediately in a sweat.

"We're not sure what's going on yet. Early this morning we received notice by courier that our approval has been reconsidered. I've been reading over the notice for the past few hours and can't quite explain it."

"But who can shut the study down? Did the University pull the rug on you?"

"No, they weren't aware until I called them. The FDA sent the notice. It says little more than that they are rescinding their approval for the next phase of testing. It doesn't make any sense at all."

Same was speechless. He simply sat and stared at Greenburg. This was the heartbreak of his father's cancelled drug trial all over again, only this time it was his own death sentence. From what he had read Nanotine could have offered real hope.

Greenburg could see Same's shock and tried to ease the blow. "I'm terribly sorry you came all this way for nothing."

"No. No, I won't accept that. There must be something you can do."

Same hated the pleading tone in his voice, but it wasn't too much of an exaggeration to think that his life could hang in the balance of this drug trial.

"Trust me, Mr. Harrison. If there was something I could do, I would. I've hired the people to carry out this work and we have the money, but neither the drug company nor the university is going to move forward without FDA approval. The FDA has slammed the door on us."

Same stood and started for the door. As he reached the door he stopped and closed his eyes. Taking a deep breath to regain control of himself, he slowly turned and walked back to his chair. Forcing calm into his voice, he asked, "Doctor, I would be extremely grateful if you would walk me through the process that led to this point."

Recognizing Same's sincerity, Greenburg stood and walked to the window. Looking out the window with his hands thrust into the pockets of his lab coat, he began to lay out the discovery process.

"There's been a lot of recent activity around this disease, but we thought we'd really hit the jackpot with Nanotine. Quite a while ago we started working with the Chemical Genome Center at the National Institutes of Health to find a new class of compounds that would act as inhibitors of tau protein clumping. Our people over at Drug Discovery actually did the work. We wanted to find chemicals that would prevent formation of the tau fibrils. If we could stop fibril accumulation in the brain, we could treat a whole genre of neurodegenerative diseases."

He turned from the window to face Same. "We succeeded. We found two hundred eighty-five compounds that met the criteria we had set. We focused on those called ATPZ's, and then juggled the chemical structure to make them more efficient. Albax Pharmaceuticals worked with us to prepare the drug for clinical trials. Preclinical and Phase I clinical trials went through without a hitch and we were approved for Phase II. We started recruiting patients and had the entire infrastructure in place. Every indication was that we had unequivocal approval from FDA to move forward."

Greenburg walked behind his desk. Picking up a letter on formal-looking stationary, his voice became bitter, "Then this crap arrives this morning and puts us out of business."

When Greenburg didn't continue, Same prodded, "And that's it?"

"I've been on the phone with the CEO of Albax. He's outraged. They've invested millions already. He's never seen anything like this from the FDA."

"Something is screwy here," Same said through gritted teeth.

"There is one more thing. Albax called me back a few minutes before you arrived. They just learned of a separate Phase I trial that was shut down late last week. That strikes me as very scary."

Same rose from the chair and took Greenburg's place at the window. Senior's trial had been cancelled only a few months ago, and now two more were shut down without explanation. Was someone with a friend on the inside trying to corner the market on FTD drugs? Was there some simple explanation and he was just being paranoid? Paranoia was another behavioral symptom of FTD.

Greenburg's voice interrupted his wandering thoughts. "Is there anything else I can tell you?"

Same turned from the window and shook his head. As he extended a hand to Greenburg he said with a smile, "Don't trash your infrastructure, Dr. Greenburg. I happen to know a good lawyer with a keen interest in digging up exactly what's going on."

Stopping short of the door, Same thought he'd give it one last old college try. "By the way, you don't happen to have an extra case of that stuff lying around that you'd like to get rid of, do you?"

Greenburg laughed, "Afraid not. We haven't even received the trial shipment. So, I can't tell the bandit where to steal it."

"Was afraid of that. Hang in there. I'll be in touch."

Back in his car, Same squeezed the steering wheel until his hands hurt. He reached to switch the Tesla to life and was immediately greeted by a chime warning him of low battery charge. "Jesus Tap-dancing Christ," he said aloud. He'd forgotten that he planned to charge the beast during the day's testing.

Chapter Eleven

....

A call back to Greenburg's office got Same to building maintenance, who directed him to a 440 volt outlet at the bottom floor of the garage. As the Tesla's QuickCharge feature did its work, Same reached down and reclined the backrest. He took several deep breaths and gradually relaxed his body. He slowly immersed himself in imagery of walking along the beach at Emerald Isle the previous summer. After thirty minutes he opened his eyes again, now calm and focused. He brought the backrest upright, reached for his phone and dialed Street.

After he relayed the morning's events to an incredulous Street, Same disconnected the Tesla's charging cable and thoughtfully began the trek back down I-95 to Richmond. His first contact had to be Sally Watson, the Executive Director at AFTD. The Association for Fronto-temporal Degeneration had been like extended family to Same during his father's illness. Their care giving advice had been invaluable in preparing him for the extensive support Senior would need in his final couple of years. They had always had time for his calls and questions, and if they didn't know the answer they were quick to find it. Unfortunately, the one answer they still hadn't found was an effective treatment.

On Tuesday morning at 8:00 am sharp he was dialing the number.

The receptionist, Elisa, answered with her usual cheerful greeting.

"Hi, Elisa, it's Tyler Harrison. Is Sally in?"

"She sure is. Hang on"

Sally came on the line, "Hi, Same, how are you?"

"Fine, Sally, you?"

"I'm fine. We were so sorry to hear about your father. How is Mitchell doing?"

"Oh, he's doing well," said Same, deciding not to mention Alaina for now. "He's a tough little nut. He seems to have taken it in stride. Actually, Sally, I'm the one who needs help now."

Sally was stunned. Same was really young to start showing symptoms, but it wasn't unheard of. "Same, don't tell me you too already!"

Same laughed, "No, thank God, it's not that. Well, not that directly. I was scheduled to start as a subject for that new protocol at U. Penn."

"Hasn't it started? I thought you were in."

"I was. Got news for you, the whole study has been cancelled."

"What do you mean cancelled? Phase I had amazing results!"

"I know, but FDA just pulled their approval for Phase II and no one seems to know why. I take it you haven't heard anything?"

"Nothing."

Same filled her in on his trip to Philadelphia and his conversation with Greenburg.

There was shocked silence from the other end of the line. Finally she said, "I can't believe this. We had high hopes and a big research grant invested in that drug."

"You're not the only one with high hopes. I think I was at the top of that queue. Do you think you can find out anything about what's going on at FDA?"

"I don't know, but you can bet I'll be making a few phone calls as soon as we've finished. I'll hit a few contacts at FDA and let you know what I find out tomorrow."

"Thanks, Sally. You're the best."

"We'll see. Give my love to Mitchell."

Same hung up the phone and got to his feet. He was starting to feel a slim ray of hope. There obviously weren't any answers yet but at least some wheels were beginning to churn. There was going to be no lying down and rolling over this time.

It was early Wednesday afternoon when Sally called. As soon as he heard her voice, Same knew it wasn't good news.

"We got nothing, Same. Talk about the royal runaround. People I've known for years shuffled me off to someone else. Finally I called a guy who's an assistant to the director. He couldn't have been more blunt and basically said to stay out of this or else."

"He actually told you that?"

"Not exactly, but that was the message. I don't know anyone else to call. It's all kinds of bizarre. Short of going off the deep end and using your dad's hundred grand for cash bribes to get information, I'm at a loss for where we go from here."

Same thought for a minute. He had hoped Sally's contacts would turn up answers, but based on the cryptic notice to Greenburg, he guessed he shouldn't be surprised that the FDA was being close-lipped. "Well, thanks for asking, Sally. I'll let you know if I turn up anything else."

"Same here. We'll talk soon."

Sally leaned back in her chair after she hung up with Same. She was highly annoyed at being brushed off without explanation with such a promising treatment on the line. She wheeled around to her computer and began to type.

When she finished she had captured the essence of her calls to the FDA. She quoted correspondence from U. Penn describing the promise Nanotine held in treating FTD. If satisfactory answers were not forthcoming within two weeks, she would be forwarding all of this information to legislative contacts and a close personal friend at the Philadelphia Enquirer.

The Director of the FDA's Center for Drug Evaluation and Research got the honors as the formal addressee, then she entered two of her senior FDA contacts, followed by Greenburg. Adding Same for good measure, she hit send with a dramatic sweep of her arm.

Perhaps a little rash, she thought with a smile, but why not stir the pot a bit?

Chapter Twelve

The next morning Same was literally shaking with nervous energy. Pounding a couple Red Bulls with his cereal had probably been a mistake. He decided on a run to the office and set a new personal record for the two mile distance. He showered and changed in the H&B gym, exchanging greetings with a couple of the other early risers.

After his disappointing conversation with Sally, he'd spent the remainder of the previous afternoon calling various numbers at FDA. After three hours all he'd discovered was that it was possible to talk with six people and learn nothing. The "contact us" number on the website led to a voicemail system that seemed to endlessly loop through irrelevant recordings.

When he finally got a live voice, Same explained that he'd like to speak with someone in public relations.

"In what regard," asked the voice on the other end.

"Well, I'd like to start with the relationship of FDA to the Department of Health and Human Services."

"Just a moment, Sir, I'll transfer your call."

The phone clicked and Same enjoyed a thirty-second jazz loop over his speakerphone for the next fifteen minutes. Finally, another voice cut in, "Hello, how may I direct your call?"

Same sighed. "You're with FDA public relations, right?"

"No, Sir, this is the general information line for Health and Human Services."

"I was on the line to FDA, how did I get you?"

"I have no idea. Can I help you?"

"Apparently not," Same snarled as he slammed down the phone. He started all over again and was shuttled to four different people before someone was willing to talk with him. When he explained that he wanted to speak in person to a breathing individual about drug trials, applications for trials, and the general process for handling requests, he was told he should send an email through FDA's web portal and the proper person would contact him for an appointment.

Before he could be blown off with another faceless email address, Same hung up. All night he stewed over how to get to someone with actual answers. The customer service face of FDA seemed to be carefully designed to screen the decision-makers he wanted to talk to from inquiries by irate members of the public such as himself. Finally, he resolved to just walk in. Society had grown so accustomed to making inquiries through technology, maybe there would be fewer layers of protective red tape if he showed up in person. He'd spend Thursday knocking out as much as possible at the office and head to Washington early on Friday. Thursday would give him a day to cool off as much as anything.

Having learned his lesson the previous morning, dawn on Friday found Same with his usual cup of coffee in hand and the Red Bull stashed safely in the fridge. After he got Mitch off to school, he headed for the Amtrak Station on Staples Mill Road. He had considered driving since the FDA was actually in Silver Spring, Maryland, but then settled on Metro and cab.

The morning rush was over by the time he arrived on the Metro red line at Cleveland Park. As he rode the escalator up to street level, he glanced over his shoulder and froze. About ten people back was a man in a blue blazer. He could have sworn he saw him at the shoeshine stand back at Union Station.

Get a grip, he thought. Just because he's coming the same way doesn't mean he's following you.

Out on the street, Same headed to the closest corner to hail a taxi. With his peripheral vision he followed the blue blazer as it slowly moved away down the street.

"You're not as important as you thought," he mumbled to himself as a taxi pulled to the curb.

The cabbie made a left on 16th Street NW, continued past Rock Creek Park and they were soon at White Oak in Silver Spring. The driver made no attempt at conversation and that was just fine with Same. When they arrived, Same paid the fare and walked to the main entrance.

As soon as he was inside he was accosted by security and scanners. He cleared the metal detector with little more impediment than the usual hostile glances. His briefcase captured some attention, but after a cursory inspection a bored guard wordlessly pushed it down the conveyor belt for Same to collect. Another guard then directed him to the security office where they would give him a visitor's pass and call someone to escort him to the proper office.

He had begun to think his plan might actually be working when the guard in the security office demanded the office he was visiting.

"I'm here to see someone in public relations," said Same, affecting a cheerful smile.

The guard's face remained impassive. However, he reached for his phone and punched a few numbers. After a few seconds he turned back to Same, "They say they need to know who you want to see."

"May I speak with the person on the line?"

The guard shrugged and handed the phone to Same, turning his attention back to the video clip of a dancing cat paused on his computer screen.

Here goes nothing, thought Same. "Hello, this is Tyler Harrison. I spoke with John yesterday and he said I could come up today. I'm from Richmond."

Same couldn't believe his luck. The voice on the other end asked, "John Sampson? He's out sick today."

"Yes, it was Sampson. Well, is there anyone else available?"

"Sure. Tell me what it's in reference to and I'll try to find someone."

"Look, this is a bit awkward over the security phone after John had me come all the way up from Richmond."

There was a long silence, then the voice said quickly, "Okay, I'll be down in a couple minutes."

"Thank you."

Same handed the phone back to the guard. "They're on their way down," he said smugly. The guard just shrugged again and handed Same a visitor's badge before turning back to his video.

A few minutes later an awkward, boyish-looking man popped out of the elevator and headed for the security office. He appeared to be about six-four, but couldn't have weighed more than 150 pounds. "Mr. Harrison, I'm Donald McCausley," he said as he drew near.

The two shook and McCausley invited Same back out into the lobby. When they reached the middle of the lobby, McCausley turned and asked, "How may I help you?"

"Are we going to stand here in the lobby?"

"Until I find out what you need, yes."

Same found himself thinking that for a toothpick with acne, the dude was pretty assertive.

"I need some information on why approval for a drug named Nanotine was recently pulled in the middle of trials."

"I wouldn't have that kind of information, Sir."

"Then would you take me to someone who does have that information?"

The little fart had the audacity to laugh. "Sir, do you realize what you're asking? You walk in off the street and simply ask for confidential information and expect someone to reel off stats or whatever?"

Same came closer to McCausley. "You know what, it may be funny to you, but that's precisely what I expect."

McCausley backed up a step. "That isn't going to happen. If you will give me your contact information, I'll be glad to have someone send you the information that's publicly available. Of course, you can get that information yourself with a couple clicks on the web."

Again Same was in his face. He had told himself that he was going to remain cool and polite, but McCausley's condescension had thrown all that out the window. They both knew very well that the FDA didn't post shit online. "Listen, Donny. You probably haven't been working long enough to have the pleasure of paying income taxes. But as someone who pays your salary, I'd appreciate not being jerked around anymore."

This time McCausley stood his ground. "Sir, I'm going to ask you to hand the visitor's badge to me and then leave or I will have security handle the situation."

Same backed off and the two stared at each other for a moment. Suddenly, over one of McCausley's thin shoulders, Same spotted the man in the blue blazer walk through a door on the far end of the lobby. His face froze. A cold tingle ran down both arms into his hands.

McCausley saw Same's expression and turned to follow the direction of his eyes. "What's wrong now?"

"Nothing," said Same, shaking his head and directing his eyes back to McCausley. "I just thought I saw someone I knew."

"Could be, a lot of people work in this place."

McCausley held out his hand. "Badge, please."

Same scrambled to think. If blue blazer was here, something was definitely up and he was definitely *persona non grata*. The smart money was on a careful retreat and rethinking of his strategy. As he reached for the badge, the guard in the security office poked his head from the door and yelled in the direction of the two men, "Donald McCausley?! Call for you!"

Same handed over the badge and watched McCausley walk quickly to the security office. He knew he should leave, but curiosity kept him rooted to the spot. He never was very good at playing the smart money.

He could see McCausley arguing into the phone and gesticulating toward him. After a couple minutes he finally hung up the phone. With a curiously pale expression on his face he approached Same. "Still here, huh? Trust me, you need to go. Now."

McCausley pointed toward the door. Same was intrigued by the man's anxiety after the phone call. He decided to press his luck a bit. "I tell you what, McCausley. I know you don't want a big scene here in your lobby, so I promise I will promptly leave." The immensely relieved look on the man's face told Same he was close to something. Too bad for McCausley the relief wouldn't last long.

Same suddenly dropped to a sit on the polished granite floor. Crossing his legs, he looked up and continued, "But not until you go back to that phone and tell the person you were talking with that I will sit right here until he asks me to leave face to face."

McCausley's face turned red as he began to catch the stares being cast in their direction from around the lobby. "Christ," he said quietly, turning on his heel, "You're a real douche-bag."

Same let the insult slide and smiled in satisfaction as McCausley walked quickly back to the security office. Looks like public embarrassment was his button, thought Same. He gave another smile and wave to two guards who had begun slowly moving toward him from the security screening checkpoint.

McCausley's second conversation was much quicker. Shortly after he hung up the phone, another red-faced man emerged puffing from the elevator and walked straight to Same. Obviously a paper shuffler, his build was exactly the opposite of McCausley's. Same couldn't help but chuckle at the image of the irate pear and bean-pole combination in front of him.

Ignoring McCausley, the pear said sharply to Same, "I assume you're Tyler Harrison."

Same stood and extended his hand. The man neither took nor acknowledged it. "Mr. Harrison, I have already called the police and if you are not off this property by the time they arrive, they will arrest you for criminal trespass."

"Wow, you go straight for the jugular. And you are?"

"My name is of no concern to you. Now leave."

He turned and Same made the mistake of reaching out for his arm. The guards were on him like fleas on a dog. The man looked at Same with steely eyes. "Add assault on a government official to the list."

Same knew better than to push any further. He looked at the man's departing back and said loudly, "I will get that information."

As the elevator closed Same turned to the guards and lowered his voice. "Guys, I'm through. I'm out of here."

Faces still expressionless, the guards released their grip and Same walked quickly out the door.

Chapter Thirteen

....

That evening Same sat brooding in his home office long after Mitch had finished his homework and headed off to bed. Suddenly he heard soft footfalls behind him and spun around to face them.

It was only Mitch, standing in the doorway. "Dude, are you okay?" asked Mitch.

The concern in his voice caught Same in the gut. "Uh, sure, why?"

"You're all wired and it's two in the morning."

Same sighed. "Yeah, sorry, man. Just stressed over work stuff. What are you doing up?"

Mitch yawned and then smiled, "I thought I heard something. It must have been that squeak in your chair. Go to bed, Same. You haven't been sleeping much lately."

Same laughed at being ordered to bed by his nine-year-old brother. "I'm fine, but you're right, as usual. I'm off to bed. See you in the morning."

He slept fitfully that night. The rest of the weekend he spent running around with Mitch, but he couldn't stop spinning his wheels about how to break through the red tape at FDA. On Monday morning he got Mitch off to school and took his time strolling into the office.

On the way in he considered again whether he should play by the rules. He had scoured the agency's website over the weekend and noted with amusement the clear instructions for Freedom of Information Act requests for more detailed information. While he hadn't ever helped a client with a FOIA request, he had been around the practice of law long enough to know that whether he was entitled to the information or not, if an agency didn't want to disclose information it would require a team of lawyers and years of litigation to pry it out of them through FOIA. Spending several more years descending into dementia was not on his to do list, so he would have to skip the formal requests and find an actual human being who had the information.

When he arrived at his office door, his purposeful stride was suddenly arrested by a mountain of a man in a faded varsity letterman jacket. "James!" cried Same, genuinely delighted. "How are you? How long have you been here?"

James Lance was actually Same's very first client. He was a computer science undergrad and an All-American defensive tackle at William and Mary while Same was in law school. Same enrolled in the Entrepreneurial Law Clinic during his last year at the law school, and James was assigned to him as a pro bono client. After a short stint as a hacker in high school, James had quickly recognized that it was ultimately a more lucrative and sustainable career choice to play for the other team. He had developed a sweet little program during his sophomore year at W&M that tracked attempts to hack through the complex firewalls erected by the big banks. He had no money to hire a real lawyer, so he had come to the law clinic for help with a non-disclosure and licensing agreement before testing his program with a regional bank.

Lance had stuck with Same thereafter as he built a security consulting business with twenty employees and a client list that read like the Fed Chairman's speed-dial list. Over the past year Lance had tired of managing the business, and a couple months ago had asked Same to draw up plans to sell ownership of the company while retaining an advisory and part-time consulting role for himself. Unfortunately, Same hadn't made much progress with everything else going on, and he didn't have much for Lance in the way of an update.

Before Same could begin to make apologies, Lance cut him off, "I've just been here a few minutes, Same. Carol brought me in here while she went to call you. She told me about your father and step-mother. I'm really sorry, man."

"I appreciate it, James," said Same. "You know we'd been marking time with my dad, but my stepmother was just a horrific accident out of nowhere. Not to freak you out, but it happened right here on this corner of the desk. Mitch was here for the whole thing."

"Well, you let me know what I can do. I still have those Redskins season tickets. You think Mitchell would want to go see a game?"

"I know for a fact that he'd absolutely love it," Same replied. "We're definitely going to take you up on that. But I need to get moving on your transition plans first. I'm sorry I'm so far behind on that."

"Hey, it's nothing. Things at the company are just humming along in cruise-control. You get to it when you can focus again. That's not why I'm here anyway."

Same was relieved that Lance wasn't anxious about the ownership matter, but made a mental note that he needed to move that file to the top of the list. They both looked up as Carol returned with two cups of coffee. Carol patted Lance on the shoulder as she departed. "Two creams and two sugars, dear," she said. "Now if you'll pardon me, I'm needed upstairs with Ms. Welford."

After Carol made her exit, Lance smiled and said, "You know, sometimes I wonder how much of my legal work is actually done by Carol rather than you."

"Only the harder parts," laughed Same. "She's worth her weight in gold. If I ever hang out my own shingle, she is my first hire at double her current pay. I'm not exaggerating when I tell you that she knows more than most of the lawyers here."

"I believe it," said Lance. They sipped their coffee and Lance reached into the breast pocket of his coat. He casually pulled out a USB flash drive and tossed it across the desk to Same. "This is a little program I threw together a couple weeks ago. I was just thinking about all the push-back to the social networking apps that harvest and distribute information about the GPS location of your phone. So I wrote a little code over lunch that basically scrambles your location, except for emergency calls. A buddy of mine at Google thinks they'd part with a couple hundred grand for it, but I want to get it protected before I start shopping it around. You think one of your patent guys can start working on a software patent?"

"You bet," said Same. He held up the USB drive and laughed. "James, you never cease to amaze me. You can make a couple hundred grand over lunch and you still wear that old worn-out jacket."

Same's laugh quickly died as a booming voice cut through from the door to his office. "A couple hundred grand over lunch? Just what are you boys up to?!"

The grinning face attached to the voice was none other than Detective Richard Jones. Jones had gone all out today and was dressed smartly in a navy pinstripe suit with a white shirt and red power tie. It still didn't look as though he had gotten around to brushing his teeth, though. A pretty, blushing secretary named Emily from the H&B front desk was stuck behind him in the doorway. "Excuse me, Mr. Harrison, but Mr. Jones said that you were expecting him?"

Same rose from his desk. "I was actually not expecting Detective Jones," he said coolly. "Detective, as you can see I am currently in a meeting with a client. If you'll please follow Emily back to the lobby, I'll be with you shortly."

"A client, huh," said Jones, eyeing Lance with suspicion. "I thought you didn't do criminal work?"

Apparently a 6'4", 280 pound black man with long, braided hair didn't fit well with Jones's conception of a corporate client. Not that Jones was alone. Same would bet quite a few of the partners, passing Lance in the hallway, would peg him as part of the cleaning crew rather than one of their best small corporate clients. Richmond still had one foot firmly rooted in the Old South.

Lance rose to his feet and Jones suddenly looked a bit startled as the size of the man became clearer. "Detective," said Lance, extending his hand. Jones took Lance's hand and immediately regretted it. Lance held him firm in a grip that stopped short of assault but dared the detective to show pain. "My name is James Lance," said Lance calmly, "and I engage Mr. Harrison to provide legal counsel with respect to my information technology business. Your intrusion has interrupted our conversation, and I would remind you of Mr. Harrison's request to leave."

The smile was now gone from Detective Jones's face as he finally dislodged his hand from Lance's grip. "Easy does it, gents," he said. He removed an envelope from his jacket and tossed it across the desk toward Same. "I won't disrupt this party any longer. I just came to drop off a copy of the medical examiner's report. Everything's in there except the toxicology reports. They will take another couple of weeks, not that we think anything will show there. You probably didn't force-feed her drugs. Looks like the ME couldn't find any foul play, so you're off the hook for now."

As Jones turned to leave he pointed at the flash drive that Same still held in his hand. "Now don't you boys be getting up to any dirty business with whatever on that little gadget is worth a couple hundred grand. I don't want to have to make any more calls around here."

Same swallowed a retort as the detective turned and followed Emily down the hall. Same started to explain but Lance cut him off again with a wave of his hand. "No need, my friend. I read all about Jones in the paper a couple months ago. Richmond PD has paid out nearly $300,000 to settle civil suits against that asshole, but they keep him on because he somehow seems to have an uncanny knack at solving high-profile crimes. Having now seen him in person, he sure is a piece of work, I'll give him that."

Jones had spoiled the jovial mood for both of them. After a few more notes about the software patent Lance finally stood to leave. "Let me know about that Redskins game," he said finally, "or anything else I can do for you guys."

"You got it," said Same. "I'll be in touch shortly."

After Lance had departed, Same sent an email to the firm's top intellectual property associate. He then closed his door, pulled up the FDA website, clicked the phone on speaker, and renewed his assault on the FDA red tape.

Two hours later he was still nowhere. He shut down his computer and headed out to lunch.

Chapter Fourteen

....

For the rest of the week Same forced himself to push the FDA out of his mind. Work, sleep, exercise. Running to work was routine and three visits a week to the gym were mandatory. Mitch started tagging along to the gym and Same noted with satisfaction that his brother's confidence continued to rebound from the loss of his parents. He tried to convince himself that with people like Dr. Greenburg around, there would be another drug along soon.

On Friday morning, a week after his futile trip to White Oak, Carol popped into Same's office with a very quizzical expression. "Same, there's a guy on the phone who won't give me his name, but says it's important that he speak with you. I told him I wouldn't put him through without a name, but he said it involved your concern about a drug." She smiled and asked, "You expecting a call from your dealer?"

Same laughed, "Yeah, but I told him never to call the office. Go ahead and put him through."

Carol departed and Same picked up the phone as it rang. "This is Tyler Harrison."

A clipped Indian or Pakistani voice spoke rapidly, "Mr. Harrison, I have some information that I believe would be of interest to you."

"Oh, and what would that be?"

"Not over the phone. I'm on a pay phone and have only a minute. It involves your interest in a certain drug. I will meet you in Washington at noon tomorrow." He proceeded to give Same directions.

"Okay, I'll be there," said Same. He started to ask the voice for a name but the phone went dead.

"What was that all about?" asked Carol.

Same sat, almost trance-like. "I'm not sure, but it looks like I'll be going back to Washington this weekend. Can you find an Amtrak reservation for me arriving by eleven tomorrow morning?"

"You got it."

To Same's utter amazement, Amtrak arrived early at Union Station on Saturday morning. Same had worn jeans, sneakers, and a hoodie, hoping to mingle in with the tourists. He slipped his point and shoot camera in his pouch-pocket and hit the street. He was paranoid enough to spend some time looking into store windows for a reflection of the blue blazer or any friends, but there didn't seem to be anyone following him.

In the distance he spotted the Smithsonian Castle. There was no rush; it was only 11:15. He crossed Independence Avenue and casually strolled through the gardens next to the castle. As he looked at the flora he focused on his peripheral vision but still couldn't find anyone following.

Turning left to 20th Street, he crossed the mall to Constitution. The American History Museum was to his right. He casually entered and strolled into the gift shop. At 11:55 he wandered up the stairs to the Star Spangled Banner display. A young, giggling couple and a family of four were the only fellow patrons.

As directed by the "voice," he stood near the entrance and viewed the awesome sight before him. The banner was there in all its glory. Distracted by the beauty and emotional power of the display, he was startled to discover that someone was quietly standing next to him.

"Don't turn around, Mr. Harrison. Continue to enjoy our flag."

Same obeyed. "I hear the same voice, but who are you?"

"Who I am isn't important." The man stood about three feet from Same until the young couple and the family moved off to the next display. "We can talk freely now for a moment."

Same turned and looked at the man. He appeared to be Indian, about five-seven and dressed in jeans and a brown tweed sport coat.

"Why all the secrecy?"

"Trust me, you want to be discrete. You were at White Oak a week ago seeking information on Nanotine. Let's say that I am peripherally involved in that project. I'm here because our normal procedures at CDER, the Center for Drug Evaluation and Research, were circumvented in rescinding approval for Phase II trials. I have the same last name as one of the assistant directors and was accidentally copied on an email from the director talking about the timing of the termination. I'm not sure what it is, but something very odd is happening."

Same interrupted, "I don't understand. Why did they shut everything down?"

"I don't know, but you and your friend Sally Watson have certainly caused great consternation among my superiors. We were all recently reminded of the confidentiality and communications policies and your names were specifically listed as persons making suspicious inquiries outside of authorized channels. If I were you I would be very careful. In the meantime you will find some interesting documents in an envelope I am leaving for you. Perhaps they will help your investigation."

Before Same could say anything more, the man turned and walked quickly away. Same spotted a manila envelope where the man had been standing and quickly moved over to place his foot on it as two middle-aged women entered the exhibit. Collecting the envelope while pretending to tie his shoe, he then straightened and started writing on it as if taking notes.

He waited another five minutes before moving to the exit. It took all his willpower to avoid ripping the envelope open, but he forced himself to visit three more galleries before leaving the museum. His last stop actually captured his attention momentarily. It was Julia Child's kitchen. It was so perfect he almost expected to see the famous chef bent over before her oven.

Finally he left the museum and walked slowly back to the mall. He wandered to a food stand and bought an obscenely priced hotdog with a healthy portion of chili slathered on top. At least his wallet would be lighter if he had to run for it, he thought with wry amusement.

As he leaned to take a bite, he was so engrossed with trying to avoid wearing the chili on his shirt that he failed to notice a man in a park service jumpsuit edge close to him. Suddenly he felt the envelope being snatched from under his arm. He wheeled to see the man already two steps away and accelerating quickly.

Same had just begun to tense to give chase when a woman stuck out her leg and tripped the thief. He hit the ground awkwardly on his side and the envelope slipped from his grasp. Rolling over quickly to his stomach, he reached for the envelope, but Same was on him. Same stomped his foot on the outstretched hand and felt a crunch as one or more fingers shattered into the pavement. The man screamed and rolled to his back clutching his mangled hand to his stomach. With his other hand he reached into the pocket of his jumpsuit.

Same didn't wait to find out what he was reaching for. With nothing else at hand he slammed his hot chili-dog into the man's eyes just as the woman hit him with a stream of liquid from ten feet away. Again the man screamed and began scraping at his face with his good hand. Same assumed he was down for good, but with a surprisingly nimble move he aimed a kick at the side of Same's left knee. The knee buckled and Same hit the ground rolling. By the time he reached his feet the man had scrambled to his feet and had a sizeable jump away from them.

Same limped a couple steps after him before giving up the chase. To hell with it, he thought. Don't want to run into whatever's in that bastard's pocket anyway.

He turned back to his fortuitous ally. She was probably fifty, short and stocky with a serious but friendly face. "Thank you so much," he said. "That was really brave of you."

"Well that guy just came up and grabbed your stuff and took off," she replied. "I wasn't about to let that happen."

"Thank you again. What the hell was that spray?"

She reached into her oversized purse to extract a large spray can. "Wasp spray," she said, smiling broadly. "Burns and blinds like pepper spray but it shoots about twenty feet. I've heard about all the robberies in this city." Her smile widened until she was positively beaming. "I'm thrilled that I actually got to use it!"

Jesus Christ, thought Same. The criminals in this town better watch their ass until this lady goes back home. He held out his hand. "I'm Tyler Harrison," he said.

Laughing, the woman asked, "Any relation to Presidents Tyler or Harrison?"

Same couldn't help laughing along with her infectious good humor. "Nope, just plain old Tyler Harrison," he said. "That's funny. I'm just plain old Martha Wilson from Wilson, North Carolina, and my folks had nothing to do with naming the town. I'm a history teacher but I haven't been here since I was a little girl. I thought it was about time I visited our nation's capitol in person again."

"Well," said Same, "I've just come from seeing the Star Spangled Banner. Have you seen it?"

"Darn tootin'. It's the first thing I did yesterday. Got a lot more stuff planned for today. You gonna call the police?"

Same thought about what his mysterious informant had told him. "No, not much point. The guy's long gone and he didn't get anything. Besides, between the two of us I feel like he's probably suffered enough already. You keep having a great time, Ms. Wilson."

"The name's Martha. I will, and you be careful. That guy seemed to really want whatever you got in that envelope."

"I will and thanks again." Same walked away gingerly, his knee feeling mostly intact, but quite sore. That was only going to get worse over the next couple days.

He limped back to the train station with his head on a swivel. Waiting until last call for a train back to Richmond, he quickly bought a ticket and hustled on board just as the doors closed. He didn't notice anyone boarding with him, but still walked down the train until he found a nearly empty car at the back.

Propping his leg up on the seat beside him, he carefully pulled open the glued flap of the envelope. He withdrew a stack of papers about a quarter inch thick. On top was a two-page document on FDA letterhead with the subject Progress Report: Proposed Process for

Dispute Resolution.

Same quickly scanned the document. It seemed that there were three levels of dispute resolution: an informal process and two levels in a formal process. There were other documents on the same letterhead discussing appeal of adverse accreditation or reaccreditation decisions that preclude certification or recertification. Most of the documents seemed to be written in ancient Cover My Ass legalese, and little could be deciphered from the bureaucratic terminology.

The last page was a letter on FDA letterhead, but the signature line had been cut away. The author stated that he was mystified why the certification process had been terminated. The applicant had complied with all regulatory requirements and the results from preclinical and Phase I trials had been properly submitted. It was the author's opinion that the drug held promise and should be certified for Phase II trials.

Same finished the letter and flipped it over. Nothing else was written on the back. He shoved the documents back in the manila envelope. What the hell, he thought to himself. That's it? All the cloak and dagger for this? The net effect of the documents seemed to be that someone at FDA felt procedures hadn't been followed and was asking questions about Nanotine. But while it gave him a friend, it put Same no closer to any answers. In fact he only had more questions now.

One thing was for sure, he thought as he massaged his knee. He was definitely being followed. And whoever they were, they weren't afraid to get physical.

Chapter Fifteen

On Thursday morning of the following week, Same sat in his office with his head propped in his hands. The week had passed in paranoia and utter frustration. He was certain he had seen blue blazer on several occasions, and was beginning to suspect he may have at least one other tail.

The paranoia might not be so bad under the circumstances, he thought. It may just keep him alive. But the frustration from the FDA dead end was getting to him. His mystery informant had left him with documents that told him little more than that something was wrong. That he already knew. But there was nothing there to build on, no new suggestion for where to take his investigation. And the mystery informant had disappeared into thin air. As nervous as the man was, it didn't seem likely he would stick his neck out to help Same again.

He tried to concentrate on work, but it was next to impossible. The only lead he could see to pursue was the email accidentally forwarded to his informant. If the director was careless with email, maybe he could find something there. But how could he get into White Oak after his first encounter? And even if he got in, then what? He leaned back in his chair and said aloud to himself, "How the hell do you hack into somebody's email?"

Immediately it dawned on him. Quickly he opened the contact list on his computer and found the number. Picking up his office phone, he placed the call to James Lance's office.

"JL Security," answered a serious voice.

"David, it's Tyler Harrison, how are you?" asked Same.

"Great, Mr. Harrison!" said the voice with a good deal friendlier tone. "Should I put you through to Mr. Lance?"

"Please."

Lance came on the line after only a few seconds. "Same! What's new, man?"

"Oh, not much," said Same. "Hey listen, I'm working on your transition plan and I have a few questions for you. You have time for lunch today to talk about it? I'll meet you at your office and we can go from there."

They settled on a time and Same hung up the phone. He would explain his true purpose when they got together in person. His phone may or may not be tapped, but he was starting to think every ounce of his paranoia was justified.

Lance was waiting in the lobby of his office building as Same walked in. They shook hands briefly and headed back out the door to find lunch. Lance was a big fan of sushi, so when Same spotted a small up-scale sushi restaurant with a nice large front window, they ducked in and found a table.

Same purposefully placed his back to the front window and pulled out a pen and legal pad. After the waiter had taken their order, Same leaned forward and got down to business. "James, lunch is on me today. I'm sorry to bring you out here under false pretenses, but I'm actually not here about your legal work."

Lance's expression didn't change, but Same could tell he had his attention. He continued, "Casually take a look out the front window and tell me if you see an average looking white guy, dark grey suit, dark brown hair, just kind of standing around."

Lance took a moment to look and finally his eyes, still expressionless, returned back to Same. "Okay, I got him. He's across the street but he's facing us and has his phone out. Looks like he's texting someone."

"That's my guy," said Same. "I've seen him following me off and on for a couple weeks ever since I started investigating some stuff at the FDA."

Lance kept his face expressionless but his voice dropped a few decibels. "Just what kind of stuff are you investigating, Same?"

Same thought for a minute before he replied. He needed James if he had any hope of following up on the clues left by his source, but he would be dragging his friend into a game that looked increasingly dangerous. Well, he thought, James is a big boy, may as well lay out all the risks out and let him decide whether he wants to take the chance.

"Here's the short version," Same began. "You know my dad had FTD and I carry the same gene that causes that." Lance nodded and Same continued, "A few weeks ago I was scheduled to be in a drug trial at U. Penn to test a drug called Nanotine. It was supposed to be able to freeze the process of the disease. But just before I got there, approvals for Nanotine and a similar drug trial were suddenly pulled by the FDA for no good reason. I started trying to break through the red tape to find answers from FDA and seem to have picked up a tail for my efforts."

"Definitely sounds like you're close enough to make some people uncomfortable," said Lance. "You have any idea why the trials were cancelled?"

"Not yet," said Same, "but that's not all. After I met a pretty chilly reception out at FDA headquarters in Silver Spring, an inside guy tracked me down with some clues about the cancellation. He was bothered by it too, but he seemed scared as hell of retribution from the top brass. He gave me some documents that really didn't turn out to be all that helpful. But he also mentioned that he got suspicious after seeing an email from the Director of Drug Evaluation and Research, a lady named Dr. Alice Mendelson."

"So let me guess," Lance interrupted, "you want me to hack into the email account of one of the most powerful agency directors in the country, a woman who has complete power over pharmaceutical R&D worth hundreds of billions of dollars?"

Lance's expression had turned serious now and his eyes never left Same's as the waiter silently delivered their lunch. Same just nodded sheepishly. When he put it in those terms, perhaps the request was a bit outside the realm of a friendly favor.

Suddenly Lance started laughing. "Shit, man! I thought you wanted me to do something hard! That's almost insulting, really," he said, and deftly wielded his chopsticks to shovel a huge slab of tuna into his mouth.

A wave of relief washed over Same. "Really?" he said. "You think you can do it? But how are you going to hack in without getting caught?"

Lance swallowed the tuna and laughed. "I believe in legal parlance they would call that a trade secret. Don't you worry about it. I'm bored as hell calculating tax withholding, employee benefits, insurance premiums and all that other crap for the business. This is just what I need."

Lance tucked into his plate with the serious concentration of a nearly three hundred pound defensive tackle, and Same momentarily had second thoughts about treating a large and hungry man to lunch at a sushi restaurant. This was easily going to break the week's food budget.

Despite Lance's breezy assurance, he still felt some anxiety mixed with his relief. Lance looked up from his demolition of a California roll and rolled his eyes. "Dude, you need to dig in before I eat the rest of this. I will get the stuff you need. Meet me tomorrow at Morton's Steakhouse for dinner at 7:30. And bring along Dr. Street; I still owe him a steak dinner from when my 'Skins lost to the Eagles in December last year."

He paused, chopsticks halfway to his lips, and smiled a devious smile, "Oh, and you're paying."

Oh good, thought Same, there goes next week's budget too.

Chapter Sixteen

....

Seven forty-five on Friday evening found Same and Cary Street bellied up to the bar at Morton's. The bartender had made several excellent suggestions and Same was nervously swirling a glass of Cabernet Sauvignon while Street slowly tasted an obscure single-malt scotch. As Same glanced toward the door for the fourth time in under a minute, Street laid a hand on his shoulder. "My young friend," he said, "I tell you as a doctor that you're at risk for herniating a disk in your neck, and as the closest thing you have to a father, that if you bruise that wine any more I will make you give it back to the bartender."

Same turned back around to face forward and took a deep breath. "I hear you, Uncle Cary. I'm just nervous. As his lawyer I'm supposed to be protecting James. I hope I haven't gotten him in trouble."

"While we're waiting I've got a little news that should put one segment of your mind at ease."

"Tell me," said Same. "I could use something badly."

"Today I got a phone call from a friend of mine at the Medical Examiner's office. We all know how crazy Alaina had been acting. There's a reason for that."

Same looked at Street like, "Duh."

"No, I'm serious. She was hooked on methamphetamine. The level in her blood was enough to blow the top of her head off."

Same's chin dropped. "That does explain a lot. Wonder how she got started on that shit?"

"Probably to keep those late hours at the country club while she was bartender."

"God, Uncle Cary, Mitch can't know this. There's no reason for him to know. He doesn't have many pleasant memories of his mom, let's not kill what's left."

"I'm with you there. If he never asks, we never tell."

Street took a long pull at his glass and enjoyed the mellow flavor of the single-malt for a few seconds, then said, "Now back to your dithering here, you and I both know that James is absolutely an expert at what he does. He will be here, and he will be fine. You just have to trust me."

"I do trust you," said Same, "and I share your confidence in James, but this thing has gotten some pretty powerful people at FDA noticeably riled up." He took a look at Street's peaceful face as he rolled another sip of the cab around his mouth before swallowing it. "How can you be so calm right now?"

"Well," said Street, "it's partly the blend of wisdom and experience that comes with age." He paused, and continued, "and it's partly that I saw his car drive past about five minutes ago. He's probably just looking for parking."

Same laughed with relief and punched Street on the shoulder. "You bastard!" he said, "I was standing here stewing."

"Quite entertaining," said Street, as he turned to see Lance's frame fill the doorway of the restaurant.

When they had all been seated at a quiet corner banquette and

Lance had selected an Oregon pinot noir for the table, Same could contain his impatience no longer. "Well, I'm immensely relieved that you're still a free man. Any luck with the email?" he asked.

Lance held up a giant palm. "You may find it an interesting story," he said, "but let's wait until the wine gets here."

Same leaned back with a sigh of disgust and Street laughed heartily. The sommelier appeared with Lance's selection and after the appropriate rituals had been performed, Lance finally raised his glass. He leaned forward and in a quiet voice announced, "Here's to our acquisition of the contents of the official email account of one Dr. Alice Mendelson."

"Here, here!" said Street, and raised his glass to Lance's.

Same let out a sigh of relief and joined the toast. He then leaned back and closed his eyes for a moment. For the past thirty hours he had been much more worried for James than when he had gone to White Oak personally, and he promised himself that if there were any more dirty work to be done, he wouldn't be asking anyone else to do it.

Street clapped Lance on the shoulder. "So let's hear it, Mr. Lance. Pray tell."

Lance leaned forward and began in a low voice. "After Same and I met for lunch yesterday I did a little poking around the FDA system. They've actually got surprisingly decent protections. The intellectual property involved in these drug trials is worth untold billions, so I imagine they've invested pretty heavily to protect against corporate espionage. So, good for them."

The waiter arrived with fresh bread and all three helped themselves as Lance continued. "I did find a couple routes that probably would have worked, but it looked like I would have to leave a trail. I could have disguised where the trail led, but my preference was to hit them without them realizing it."

Same and Street nodded and Lance looked down as he buttered his bread, "So I decided to go on-site."

Same's wine glass froze halfway to his mouth. "You went up to White Oak?" he said, the anxiety returning with full force.

"Mother Mary, relax, Same." Lance turned to Street and asked wryly, "Dr. Street, will you work with Same on his relaxation and breathing techniques? To borrow from the Brits, his knickers are in a constant twist."

"I've got to be honest," said Street, "mine are feeling a bit damp right now. So what happened?"

"The story ends well, gentlemen, you can continue enjoying your wine. So after doing a little research on the facility, I paid a visit to White Oak. I've done my fair share of intentional hacks of secure facilities to test the defenses erected by some of our clients. We almost always find that you can install the best technology out there, but if your people aren't alert, it's meaningless. You remember that Army private who was responsible for all the classified documents on WikiLeaks? We invested huge amounts of money protecting the system from the outside, but he just walked in to access secure systems as part of his daily job, and walked out with thousands of classified documents every day. All downloaded on a Lady Gaga CD that he brought with him to work."

Lance's story was interrupted by the waiter coming to take their order. When he was out of earshot again, Lance continued, "Anyway, I pulled a little stunt that worked at Wachovia last year. The FDA website had the Director out giving a presentation at Johns Hopkins this morning. So I put on my hardhat and grabbed a clipboard, clipped my own ID badge on backwards on my shirt pocket, and just walked around behind the main building pretending to take notes. When I got to the back, I walked until I found a fire exit with the first early-morning smoker on his smoke break."

"You gotta be kidding me," said Same. "He just let you in?"

"No, man, you gotta be a little more subtle than that! I just set my hat down and chatted him up for a while. Said I was charting good routes for a new ultra high capacity fiber-optic line. IT is a pure foreign language to most people, just like whatever kind of chemistry that guy was doing would be foreign to me, so people will believe whatever an IT pro tells them.

"After that guy goes in, I lose the hardhat and clipboard and have a couple cigarettes for the cameras while I wait for the next smokers. That was the hardest part since I don't smoke. The security guards are going to expect people hanging out where the employee smokers usually go, so that's not a problem. And the smokers always feel so pushed around now that they usually band together in an instant brotherhood wherever they work.

"Anyway, the next couple smokers came out before too long and I chatted them up a bit. Said I was a new intern in IT and I was nervous because I was supposed to install an update for Director Mendelson and her administrative staff this morning. When they were done I walked back in with them. They even pointed me the best way to go to get to her office."

"That's incredible," exclaimed Street. "Right in the back door. They don't have alarms on the fire exits?"

"These are all disgruntled PhD's Dr. Street," laughed Lance. "That system was rewired within days of that building opening! The smokers have been pushed out of the buildings and away from the front entrance by no-smoking policies. Most are a little embarrassed by the habit, so it's not surprising that they find ways to sneak in and out the back.

"Once I get to the Director's office, it's a cakewalk from there. I tell her assistant that I'm new in IT and need to install a quick patch to Microsoft Office. I have a flash drive to temporarily copy the contents of their desktop and email in case the patch affects the memory. I bang a few keys and basically just shut down and restart their computers, copying all the data in the process, and all with the assistant standing right there. Then I walk right out the front door."

Reaching into the breast pocket of his blazer, he withdrew a flash drive with a flourish. "Voila! Here we are!"

Lance pulled out his phone, popped in the flash drive, and pressed a few keys. "I took the liberty of searching for Nanotine during the drive back. Only one hit, and it looks like you need to be a doctor or a lawyer to figure out what the hell it means." He smiled. "Fortunately, there's no shortage at this table."

He handed the phone over and Same and Street leaned together to peer at the screen. The message was simple but far from clear:

Dear Ms. Mendelson, we have completed our review of Nanotine pursuant to CMS/FDA MOU 225-10-0010, and have determined it is not reasonable and necessary for the treatment of illness. Please discontinue trials.

The signature line belonged to Elizabeth White, Director of the Office of Clinical Standards and Quality at the Centers for Medicare & Medicaid Studies.

Street and Same looked at each other in silence, thoroughly puzzled. Their steaks arrived as they sat and pondered, and neither man moved for his dinner. Lance was beset with no such qualms and immediately tucked in, occasionally raising his eyes to make sure the thoughtful pair hadn't fallen asleep.

Street was the first to speak. "What the hell is CMS doing closing down a drug trial?" he asked.

Lance looked up from his steak. "Why wouldn't they be involved? Aren't they all part of Health and Human Services?"

"Well, yes they are," Street replied, "but FDA has control over approving whether new drugs or medical devices can be used. CMS makes coverage decisions about whether Medicare and Medicaid will pay for certain types of treatments, but I've never heard of CMS controlling what drugs or treatments can be used in the first place."

Street turned to Same. "You remember the outcry when FDA disapproved Avastin for use in end-stage breast cancer? The drug helped with quality of life for a few months but didn't improve mortality. Everybody knew it would have been approved if it had cost a thousand bucks for a course of treatment instead of the actual $50,000. I wonder if CMS had a hand in that as well."

Same poked at his steak thoughtfully. "I actually remember reading an article about this Memorandum of Understanding when it was signed. Basically, the story was that the two agencies wanted access to each other's data. CMS would use FDA drug trial data to make better decisions about what drugs to cover for what uses. FDA would use Medicare and Medicaid claim data for its ongoing monitoring of safety and efficacy."

Another piece of steak disappeared in Lance's mouth and he pointed his empty fork at Same. "Sounds like they got a little more understanding going on than was specified in the memorandum." He then gestured to their untouched plates. "If y'all aren't going to eat those, you can feel free to pass them over here."

Street and Same declined Lance's invitation and the rest of the dinner was spent throwing around conspiracy theories about why CMS wanted Nanotine shut down before it was even approved. The theories got wilder as successive bottles of wine were uncorked, and by the end of the evening they were speculating about all manner of nonsense, and having a glorious time in the process.

They caught a few glances from the waitstaff as the volume went up, and the maitre d' hustled quickly over with their bill when Street produced his Medicare card and tossed it with a few choice words into the flame of the candle on their table. The bill brought Same sharply to his senses, and he finally called the cab into which they poured themselves for the ride home.

Chapter Seventeen

The two men in the dark blue sedan parked next to the Boathouse Restaurant had grown impatient. A sudden cold front had driven temperatures unseasonably cold, though not quite freezing. The engine was running and the heater was cranked all the way up, providing another point of contention between them. Fortunately, the restaurant was closed on Mondays, which gave them the perfect opportunity with no one around.

Bronkowitz, slouched in the passenger seat, was beginning to sweat. "Look Rolston, turn the damn heat down, I'm roasting."

"You're roasting and I'm comfortable and I happen to be driving this piece of shit, so I guess we got a standoff."

Bronkowitz shook his head in disgust. "We don't have a standoff." He reached over and cut the heat. "You're driving, but I'm the goddam boss here. You're being paid to do a job, not to run a barbeque stand."

"Yeah, one job, not two. I signed on to whack a guy and that's it. Now we're supposed to do some kid too? I don't like it."

"You don't like it? Well that's too damn bad. You didn't seem to mind being handed ten big ones and another ten when it's done."

"Like I said, I got no problem with the guy, but why the kid? Shit, I don't even know why we're doing the guy."

"And you don't have to know. I don't know and if I don't need to know, then you don't need to know. My contact called me, gave me the money and the instructions, and that's it."

"I still don't like it. Who's this contact?"

Bronkowitz looked over. "I'm not giving you my contacts. Just do your job. We'll be protected. The FBI's got our backs."

"Holy shit! I really don't like that. The Feds aren't happy until they screw you over. How come you trust this one?"

"Cause he's got more to lose than we do."

Bronkowitz surveyed the area and spotted a private security patrol. "Cut the engine."

Rolston grudgingly turned the key, zipped up his black jacket, and slouched down in the seat. The security vehicle slowed momentarily and then moved on.

Bronkowitz removed a set of binoculars from the glove box, wiped the condensation from the windshield, and focused on the second floor of the Skyview Condos. Still no sign of life in the Harrison unit.

"What the hell!" fumed Bronkowitz. "It's almost midnight. That kid oughta be home and in bed."

Rolston laughed loudly, "Are you serious? We gotta kill the kid and you're worried about his bedtime?"

"Shut up about the kid. To ease your sensitive conscience, we don't do nothing to the kid unless he gets in the way."

"See, now that makes some sense," said Rolston, relieved.

"Okay, so if you're finally satisfied let's get up on that roof and get ready to do this thing."

"Why wait outside? We'll freeze our balls off."

"For Christ's sake will you stop with the weather? This guy don't have a chick so he will be coming home. Let's get up there before that rent-a-cop comes around again."

They bundled out of the vehicle, opening the trunk for Rolston to remove a large rifle case. Moving to the side of the restaurant, they climbed a service ladder and settled in at the corner of the roof facing the condos. Bronkowitz had identified this spot immediately upon scouting the condo. Visibility into Harrison's second-floor condo would be excellent through the sliding glass doors from the terrace, and the one-hundred-yard range was a piece of cake for someone with Rolston's experience.

A couple of pops like fireworks went off in the distance. Gang kids, thought Rolston. Sounds like I'm not the only one shooting tonight. It was windy but there was no moon, a perfect black night for a job.

***

Same had finished up at the office about eight-thirty and driven over to Uncle Cary's for a late dinner with him and Mitch. The evening had gone well. Same missed the fabulous meals that Millie, Street's wife, had prepared before she died of breast cancer three years ago. But Uncle Cary had found a live-in housekeeper who was not only a saint, but must have learned to be a chef while cooking for St. Peter.

After dinner, Mitch promptly fell asleep watching TV. Same and Street sat in the living room sipping brandy. Same always enjoyed watching Uncle Cary warm the snifters with steam from the espresso machine before pouring the chestnut-colored liquid into glasses. It was the perfect temperature to release its bouquet.

They quickly fell into their usual discussion of who or what was blocking FTD drug trials. No matter how many times they had the conversation Same always came away angry. After Lance's hack last week they now had leads, but still no answers.

At midnight Same roused Mitch and they climbed into a taxi for the ride home. Mitch was sound asleep. Same quietly paid the driver and gently lifted Mitch from the seat. It wouldn't be long before his little brother would be too big to carry, and wouldn't let himself be carried in any event. After wrestling with his keys in the door, Same hit the light switch with his elbow and proceeded down to the gallery, where he dropped his keys on the large circular table.

When the lights came on in the condo Bronkowitz nudged his partner, "Here we go. One shot and we're gone."

"I can see the friggin lights," replied Rolston. "You think I'm blind?" He felt the adrenaline coursing through his bloodstream and began to take slow, steadying breaths as the crosshairs of his scope played over the interior of the condo. It'd be no problem making the kill shot with the entire wall being a sheet of glass. He saw Same enter the room and then turn his back. Rolston aimed for the heart, let his breath slowly ease out, and gently squeezed the trigger.

Same moved to sit Mitch on the kitchen counter to get a better grip. Kid is getting heavier by the day, he thought. Suddenly Mitch stirred and said groggily, "Dude, I gotta pee real bad."

With that warning Same scooped him up and spun around just as the bullet pierced the glass with a sharp crack and then slammed into Mitch. The projectile went through the boy's chest and buried itself in Same's shoulder. Falling to the ground with a gasp, Same rolled immediately on top of his brother.

His shoulder stung like hell, but he didn't want to move. Then he heard a gurgling sound, looked down and saw blood oozing from Mitch's mouth.

"Oh, Holy Shit, Mother of God, No!" he screamed. He looked up and saw the shattered glass and the empty terrace. In the back of his mind he registered that they had just been shot and the shots must have come through from a distance. He looked at Mitch again and saw that he was breathing, but barely.

Staying on the floor he grabbed his cell and dialed 911. In an eerily calm voice, the operator instructed him to cover the wounds with plastic wrap in case there was a sucking chest wound, and to keep blood from accumulating in the mouth.

He quickly ripped off Mitch's shirt. Grabbing a roll of plastic wrap from the kitchen, he circled Mitch's chest and then rolled him on his side. As Mitch desperately struggled for breath, his eyes staring off into space and his hand clutching at Same's arms, Same raked his fingers through the boy's mouth to make sure there were no clots. He forced himself to talk to Mitch in the calmest, most reassuring voice he could as he knelt on the floor, rocking his gasping little brother in his arms.

It was only minutes before he heard a pounding on the door. He ran to unlock it and a rescue team of three emergency medical technicians quickly burst into the condo. As two EMTs began working furiously to stabilize Mitch, the third looked at Same, pointed to his shoulder and asked, "Is that your blood or his?"

"Mine, I think, but I'm okay. Just take care of him."

"They're doing that, but let me take a look at your shoulder." On inspection there was little bleeding. "Okay, it looks like a deep flesh wound, but you'll be fine. I'm going to put a dressing on it. I'll call a second ambulance to bring you down to the ER."

Not a chance in hell, thought Same. "I'm riding with my brother."

"That's not permitted, Sir."

"Not permitted?!" Same exploded, causing Mitch's two EMTs to look up suddenly. "You just try and stop me!"

Same's EMT looked to one of the medics beside Mitch, who was apparently the lead. She just shrugged her shoulders and refocused on Mitch. An IV was started and Mitch was transferred to a stretcher and finally down to the ambulance. The EMTs didn't say anything when Same climbed in the back to hold Mitch's hand.

On their way to MCV ER, Same called 911 again and filled in the details for the dispatcher. He knew it was unlikely they would find anything in the condo or wherever the shots had come from, but there was always a chance.

His next call was to Dr. Street. "Uncle Cary, Mitch has been shot. He's serious. We're en route to MCV ER right now."

In the ER, Same started to protest when a nurse pulled him away to look at his shoulder, but was assured that she would put him in the next cubicle so that he could be near his son. Same didn't bother to correct her. He begged the nurse to leave open the curtain between them so Mitch could see him.

As Mitch drifted in and out of consciousness, Same talked to him continuously with reassurance that he was nearby and that he would not leave him. He thought he caught a faint smile as the boy finally slipped into total unconsciousness.

Street set a new speed record on the downtown expressway. He talked with the residents taking care of Mitch and then came to Same.

"He's going to be alright. You're both very lucky."

"That poor guy, how much more shit is he going to have to endure before he's ten? It's just so unfair. That bullet was meant for me and I turned him straight into it."

Street was calm, but firm. "Same, don't go there. You can't beat yourself up about this. He's stable and he's going to be okay, but he'll need you on your game. You've got to be up."

Same didn't comment. The resident was checking his shoulder and the palpation wasn't a pleasant experience. He was told that there was only the entrance hole and therefore the bullet was still inside.

An x-ray revealed that the bullet was about two inches from the surface and no boney structures had been injured. The bullet could be removed under local anesthesia and then he would be ready to go home.

"I'm not leaving him," Same said, pointing to Mitch.

"Tell you what," said Street. "I'll go talk with some people and get a double room for the two of you. You don't need to be sitting up in a chair all night." Same thought back to the days he spent in the medieval torture chair waiting for his father to die. That was almost worse than getting shot.

Street continued, "They're going to put a chest tube in him, so face the fact now that he's going to be here for a few days."

"Whatever puts him in the best possible position for recovery." Same leaned back on his hospital gurney. "Uncle Cary, whoever shot us knows they missed me, at least. We need to know who it is. Mitch and I are in good hands here. Will you go back to the condo and see what you can find out from the police?"

"Okay, I'll go but I'll be back."

Street squeezed Same's hand and left. When he arrived at Rocketts Landing he found a swarm of police. A shooting at an upscale residence drew them out in squads. Building security had acted quickly to place large sheets of plastic over the broken windows and the cops must have gotten a bargain on crime scene tape, judging by the huge loops of yellow plastic cordoning off the area.

Street spent several hours being shuffled around to various individuals, each of whom seemed to know less than the previous one. Frustrated, he finally returned to MCV at four in the morning and found Mitch and Same sound asleep.

The nurse revealed that after the bullet was removed the resident had slipped Same a sleeping pill. Fortunately, he had assumed it was some sort of antibiotic. With that information Street decided he had done all he could for the evening.

At ten in the morning Street was back in the Harrison boys' room. Mitch was sitting up in bed complaining that he was hungry and they would only give him a little juice. Much to Mitch's amusement, Same was still knocked out.

Street wasn't surprised when the deluge of questions started.

"Uncle Cary, what happened? I don't remember much after we left your house."

"I don't know, Mitch. Apparently someone tried to shoot your brother and you wound up getting the worst of the deal."

"Is Same's shoulder okay?"

"It's fine. They removed the bullet."

"Oh, can I have it?" Mitch asked excitedly.

"Ha!" Street replied. "I knew you'd ask that. But no, the police took it for their investigation."

Quietly Street tried to field Mitch's questions as best he could. He knew so little it was difficult to piece together answers that made any sense.

Suddenly Mitch paused mid-question as Same rolled over onto his left shoulder and shot straight up. "Oh, Christ." He held his shoulder and looked around, disoriented.

Mitch and Street couldn't resist laughing. "Dude, we're in the hospital," said Mitch. "I got shot through the chest and the bullet didn't stop until it hit your shoulder."

Same stood slowly from the bed and tried to hug Mitch. Street grabbed him before he fell over onto his brother. "Easy there, man. Mitch is fine. In fact, I think he's better off than you."

Same held one of Mitch's hands in both of his own. "Mitch, I'm so sorry about this. I..."

Mitch cut him off, "Dude, stop it. I'm going to be out of school for at least a week. My friends are never going to believe this." Turning again to Street, he asked, "Do you think the cops will give us the bullet back when they're done with it?"

Street stood, leaning against the wall, laughing. "I think not, but you can ask. They might give in rather than face an interrogation from you."

"You ain't kidding," said Same, chuckling. His face became serious as he turned to Street. "So what did you find out last night? For God's sake what time is it?"

"It's almost eleven and I'm happy you got some sleep," Street replied. "You might as well have kept sleeping because the police found nothing. They have the shell they took out of your shoulder, but their theory is apparently that it was a stray bullet from a gang shooting that went down about a mile away."

Same snorted, "A stray bullet with enough velocity left after a mile to shatter the glass, go through Mitch, and wind up two inches deep in my shoulder?"

"Richmond's finest at work," laughed Street. "I looked out of your window and the best place to shoot is obviously the rooftop of the Boathouse. Line of sight right into the condo and into most of the living room and kitchen."

"Wasn't exactly thinking about defenses from snipers when I bought the place," said Same.

"Whoever did it was a pro," Street continued. "I finally annoyed the police enough that they sent somebody over to climb up on the roof. There were some scuff marks but no shell casings. They wouldn't listen to me anymore after that."

"Well, I think we both know that there's a federal agency behind this." Same paused for a few seconds. "I'm inclined to write a strongly worded letter to my congressman."

Street burst out laughing and Same started to before the pain in his shoulder brought him back down to earth.

Mitch looked puzzled by their laughter. "So what are you really going to do, Same? Don't do anything crazy."

"Hey, buddy, you know me, I'm a lawyer. Speaking and writing are our tools."

"Yeah, but you're not like most of the other lawyers I know."

"Well, we'll see about that. The important thing right now is that you rest and get well so we can get you out of this hospital as soon as possible."

Mitch yawned. As buoyant as his spirits were, his traumatized body needed rest. "When I get home I think I deserve to stay up later and a lot of other stuff. After all, I saved your life."

Same leaned over and kissed Mitch's forehead. "Even if I agreed it wouldn't be an enforceable contract. Prior services freely rendered are not adequate consideration."

Mitch turned to Street. "I hate it when he does that."

"You and me both, kid," replied Street, "now get some sleep. Same, why don't you come with me and we can see about getting you checked out of here and then you can be a visitor to Mitch."

The two men walked down the corridor toward the nurses' station. When they were well away from Mitch's room, Same stopped and spoke in a hushed tone. "Uncle Cary, I am going to find the cocksuckers who did this and I'm going to end them. We know it's somebody tied up with FDA."

"Look, we've been through this a hundred times. We only have suspicions and speculation."

"No, we had suspicions. Now they crossed the line. Somebody's going to pay, and we know at least two people who are in the chain somehow, the director of CDER and that woman at CMS who sent her the email. Maybe I'll arrange a private interview to see what those assholes have to say for themselves."

"Son, don't do anything on your own. At least go talk with the police."

Same pounded the wall with his fist. "The police don't know shit and they're not going to buy some high-level government conspiracy to eliminate my ass. So, there's not going to be any help there. Please, tell me Detective Jones wasn't there last night."

"No, it was a Detective Lawrence."

"Then that's the first blessing in the past twelve hours. C'mon, let's get me checked out of here."

As the afternoon wore on, the more Same thought about the events of the night and how little faith he had in the local police department, the more threatened he felt. He knew it was ridiculous to stereotype the entire department because of Jones, but that's what was happening.

He pulled his cell from its clip and hit a speed dial number. A business-like voice answered, "Rogers here."

Same smiled, "Calvin, it's your nemesis from the South."

"Hey, what's up buddy? You here in Philly?"

"Nope, calling from Richmond. It's been a while."

"Well, you've been busy raking in the big bucks with that high and mighty law firm. You still happy there?"

"I thought I was on my way, but now everything has turned to shit."

"Sorry to hear that. Anything I can do to help?"

"Matter of fact there is." Same explained the events leading up to the shooting. "Any chance you could ask some questions?"

"Oh, yeah, I can ask questions, but no one up here is likely to know anything about what's going on locally in Richmond. I assume Richmond PD is on it, right?"

Same then told Calvin about Jones.

Rogers laughed, "Same, how come you're able to piss off the most gentle of people? Some things never change."

"You certainly never stop giving me a fair ration of shit," Same replied.

"I have to run to a meeting, Same, but I'll ask questions of anybody I think can help. Let's get together. You going to the homecoming this year?"

"Hadn't planned to, but I'll be there to run interference to protect you from your ex-girlfriends if you're scared."

"Ha! Let's talk about it. I'll let you know what I find out."

***

A week later Same and Mitch were climbing the walls at Street's home. While being spoiled by Street's housekeeper was enjoyable for a few days, Same felt like a hamster in an exercise wheel. His shoulder no longer hurt unless he exercised. Yet he felt more of a compulsion to exercise than anytime that he could remember. He had to be ready for anything if the bastards struck again.

Calvin Rogers hadn't been very reassuring when he followed up. The FBI was officially buying Richmond PD's theory that this was a stray bullet from a gang shooting. Calvin tended to agree with Same's conclusion that a stray bullet from that far away wouldn't have the necessary trajectory and velocity to do the damage it did, but it seemed that without a death or a federal crime, the local bureau had no interest in following up. Same intended to act on Calvin's only advice — keep your head on a swivel and watch your ass.

Street finally put his foot down when Same wanted to double the security on the house. The fact that the home had a monitored security system with closed circuit cameras wasn't sufficient in Same's anxious state. The doctor finally had enough of his paranoia, "Go to Rocketts Landing and put an armed guard in every room if you want, but this is my house and you keep your hands off it. Mitch and I will be just fine here."

Mitch settled it. "Dude, if you keep walking around I swear I'll go out the window. I'm serious, Same. You're driving yourself crazy, you're driving Uncle Cary crazy and I'm thinking about referring you to my school counselor."

At that point Same could only laugh. "Okay, okay, you guys win. I'm out."

"And don't bring any chicks up while I'm away." Mitch buried his nose in the book he had been reading and mumbled, "You're too old for that anyway."

"Hey, I heard that."

Same gave Mitch a gentle hug and left. Finally collapsing into his bed at the condo, he slept like a log for the first time since the shooting.

Chapter Eighteen

Sally Watson hustled through the wet May morning. The wind was way too wild, whipping a light rain into her face. She had taken her usual train ride out from Ardmore to the office in Radnor, and had enjoyed being out of the elements for the short ride.

Take out the wind and the rain and it was a glorious morning. That evening her family would be celebrating her son Randy's sixteenth birthday, and she couldn't wait. He was tall and handsome, despite the goatee he insisted on wearing to add some years to his youthful face. She still thought of him as beautiful, even if he would have died of embarrassment if she used that adjective in front of his friends.

Her family loved birthdays in a big way. Her daughter Madelaine, two years younger than Randy, had helped with the cake the night before. They made it while Randy and his voracious appetite were out at basketball practice.

Her husband Mark had wrapped their gift to Randy. Mark was a big, burly man who had started on the ground floor with a pest control company straight out of high school. Ten years ago he had opened his own business specializing in exotic and larger pests. There were no shortage of idiots out there who would buy animals in their cute infancy and then have to set them loose when they outgrew their cages or tanks.

For a guy with massive hands used to wrestling dangerous animals, he'd done a pretty decent job with the wrapping. It was a huge box containing only a note saying that mom and dad would provide a down payment and co-sign the note on a used car. Mark had steadfastly refused to discuss a car with Randy, much to Sally's chagrin. She didn't think it was fair to tease in that manner, but Randy seemed to know his dad had something up his sleeve.

Sally left the train and went down through the tunnel, around to King of Prussia Road, and then over to her office. The Association for Frontotemporal Degeneration had moved their offices from downtown Philadelphia a couple of years ago in order to have more space and more money to spend on solving FTD rather than supporting the commercial real estate market.

Elisa, their receptionist and jack-of-all-trades, greeted Sally with her usual enthusiasm. "Good morning, Sally! You seem awfully cheerful for this nasty weather."

"Good morning, Elisa. It's Randy's birthday. Maddy and I had so much fun making the cake last night. It's a triple chocolate concoction with a terrifying calorie count. Randy will burn right through it, though."

Elisa laughed. Sally was an avid marathoner and rang in at about 5'3" and maybe a hundred pounds, soaking wet. "Somehow I don't imagine the calories will be hanging around on you much longer than Randy," she said as Sally hung her jacket on the coat rack.

Sally went into her office and noted that she had messages. Coffee first, she thought. I'm going to enjoy the little things today. She went down the hall to the small kitchen area and placed a dark roast cup in the Keurig Maker. In a minute she had her cup of heavenly brew, to which she added a smidgen of sugar and a dash of fake half-and-half.

At her desk she duly applied her signature to a few papers that Elisa had prepared for her. She then flipped through the latest draft of the AFTD newsletter. She had read it cover to cover at least three times, but this was a key vehicle for communicating with the association's various constituencies. It had to be perfect.

She reached for the phone receiver, hit the message button, and entered her mailbox code. The first message had no voice, but she could swear she heard breathing. Creepy, she thought.

She deleted the message and moved on to the next. She sat immobile as the brief message played. Then she screamed at the top of her lungs.

Elisa burst into her office in seconds, followed shortly by Victor Hess, director of marketing. Sally had assumed a ghastly greenish color and they could both see she was in shock. "This is not happening," she whispered, her eyes fixed on the center of the desk.

Elisa grabbed Sally's arm, "What is it? What's wrong?"

All Sally could do was point to the receiver in the middle of her desk. Victor picked it up and listened. He looked at Sally. "There's no one on the line."

Without a word Sally leaned forward to replace the receiver. She hit a couple buttons and the message played on speaker. The first voice was clearly Randy. In a strained but even voice he said quietly, "This is Randy Watson."

There was a pause, and then the message continued with a different voice. "We have your son and he is just fine, for the time being. I must commend you; Randy has acted like a perfect gentleman while in our company. At the moment we require you to do absolutely nothing. Obviously calling the police could lead to tragic results. You will hear from us again at precisely 11:00 this morning." The line went dead.

Victor and Elisa looked at each other in stunned silence. Victor finally said tentatively, "A prank from one of his friends?"

Sally turned toward him angrily. "If that's it I'm ripping somebody's head off. I'm going to his school."

She started to her feet and reached for her coat just as the phone rang. They all jumped and quickly gathered around the phone as Sally hit Speaker. "Hello?" she answered.

A much older voice came over the phone. "May I speak with Mrs. Watson, please?"

"This is she."

"Good morning, Mrs. Watson. This is Eric Borland, the Headmaster at St. Xavier. Does Randy have an excused absence from school for the day?"

Sally slumped into her desk chair. The warning from the message played again in her head. "Oh, yes, I'm sorry Mr. Borland. My mother is quite sick and Randy may be out for a few days. Sorry we forgot to call."

"It's no problem, Mrs. Watson. I'll let his teachers know and we'll have one of the boys collect his assignments. Please accept our best wishes for your family."

"Thank you," said Sally, and quickly hung up.

The three stared at each other. "We've got to call the police," said Elisa.

"Didn't you hear the man?" asked Sally. "He said, 'Do nothing' and that's exactly what we're going to do. But I have to call Mark."

Mark was on the highway to Philadelphia to fetch a python from a basement when he got Sally's phone call. Horns blared and the cages in the back of his truck rattled furiously as he made an illegal U-turn across the median and headed to Radnor. When he arrived he found Sally, Elisa, and Victor still clustered in Sally's office. Sally had a white board out and they appeared to be listing facts they knew from the call.

When she saw Mark, Sally simply held up her hand to stop him. Moving to the phone she called up the voicemail again and all four of them listened intently. When it was over she looked at Mark fiercely.

"Those bastards have my baby," she said in a low voice.

Mark felt she was on the verge of something drastic. "I heard, sweetheart," he said quietly. "But we're going to get him back. We need to stay cool and disciplined right now. We have to focus on giving Randy the best chance for survival. I think that means calling the police."

Sally stiffened, "NO! You heard what he said. The guy on that message was calm and intelligent. This isn't some tweaker looking for drug money, and it isn't some thug. This guy is evil, but he's rational. He has an objective. We play ball, we help him accomplish his objective, we get Randy back, and then we tear that bastard apart."

Mark could see her fists clenched white and the blood vessels pounding in her neck. He held up the palms of his hands. "Okay. Okay. That makes sense. For right now, we play ball." He pointed to the phone. "Let me hear it again."

Sally leaned forward and went through the process of retrieving the message again. When the message completed, Mark couldn't help himself. "Those sons-of-bitches. I should have taken him to school for his birthday."

Sally shook her finger. "No blame. He's ridden his bike to school for years. We had no reason to make today any different."

Mark leaned back against the wall and joined the others in the pointless game of brainstorming on the whiteboard. The time seemed to stretch endlessly, but finally eleven approached.

At exactly eleven, Sally's phone rang. She dialed up the volume, hit speaker, and answered calmly, "This is Sally Watson. Mark Watson is also here."

The same voice from the message suddenly blared from the phone, "Ah, Mr. Watson, good to have you join us. I'm sure your wife can use your support at this time."

Mark cut in, "Let's cut the chat and do this. Is our son safe and what do you want? We don't have a lot of money but we'll give you what we have. We want to make this as quick and smooth as possible."

The voice chuckled and Mark felt a chill crease down his spine. "It's not your money that we want, Mr. Watson. Your wife recently accepted a donation of $500,000 from an individual shortly before he committed suicide. My client has a preexisting, if somewhat informal, claim to some of that money. If you do exactly as I instruct, this matter will come to a satisfactory conclusion for everyone involved."

Sally knew exactly which donation he was talking about. Ben Weatherford was a single, childless man suffering from the final stages of FTD. His lawyer had affirmed that he was still competent when he donated the $500,000, the bulk of his retirement savings, to AFTD for drug discovery research. The story caught major headlines when he stepped in front of a commuter train exactly one day later.

Sally had helped arrange care for Ben for nearly two years before his death. There was no way these people had a claim to his money—they were simply exploiting her friend's publicized death as an excuse to rip off the Association. She leaned in angrily toward the phone, but Mark's arm shot out to grab her shoulder, and he quickly spoke to cut her off before she could inject any emotion into the conversation. "Okay, that's fine. We understand. Now let's cut to the chase."

"Okay, let's do." The voice turned into a snarl, "Your son will die if your wife doesn't do exactly as I tell you."

Mark and Sally stiffened. "Got it," said Sally icily. "What do you want?"

"Weatherford borrowed a hundred grand from my client. My client wants it back. You give us the cash, we give you the boy."

"I don't have that donation lying around in cash and you know it," snapped Sally.

"Oh, I can imagine all the excuses, and I don't care about any of them. You're a resourceful lady, and necessity is the mother of invention. You have until tomorrow at noon to figure it out."

The line suddenly went dead. Mark slumped in his chair and raised his eyes to look at Sally. "Can you pull a hundred grand in cash from the AFTD account?"

Sally stared at the telephone and shook her head. Leaning back in his chair to look at the ceiling, Mark swore softly to himself and ran his thick hands through his hair.

Sally sat mute, her eyes never leaving the phone, as ideas slowly started spilling out of the group. Mark, Elisa, and Victor would bat each around and then discard it as less practical than the last.

After a few minutes their half-hearted effort at brainstorming petered out and the three fell silent again. Her eyes still glued to the phone, Sally finally spoke in little more than a whisper. "I know where to find a hundred thousand dollars in cash." The other three looked up quickly as Sally's eyes finally moved up to meet Mark's. "And judging by the amount of the demand, I'm pretty sure whoever's on the other end of that phone knows it too."

She quickly filled them in on Tyler Harrison Sr.'s cash-hoarding compulsion, his death, and Same's quest for information on the cancelled drug trials. "After talking to Same, I jumped in to investigate as well and sent an email a few weeks ago to the head of the Center for Drug Evaluation and Research and a couple senior FDA people threatening to go public if answers weren't provided." She paused and pointed to the phone. "It looks like this is our response."

Without further comment she reached for her purse and withdrew her cell. She hit a speed dial button and placed the phone to her ear. When a voice answered, she audibly exhaled. "Same, we've got a problem here in Radnor." She then explained the two phone calls.

Same could hardly comprehend what Sally had said. After a long silence Sally said, "Same, you still there?"

He quickly replied, "Yes, I'm here, I'm here. Just pissed. Somebody took a shot at me and Mitch last week. They got Mitch pretty good but he's okay now. I'm so sorry I didn't call to warn you. I thought I was the only one they were after."

"No apologies necessary, Same. I'm glad you guys are all right. This pretty much confirms that this isn't about the money. Somebody's trying to bury Nanotine, and they mean business."

After the initial shock, Same's wheels were finally spinning in line with Sally. Alaina's untimely demise had occurred before she had a chance to figure out how to hide all the cash from Senior's safe, so it was still sitting locked away in the safe in Senior's empty house. Same had put settlement of the estate on the back burner when the Nanotine hit the fan.

Same said quickly, "I've got access to the cash, and I'm on my way. Can someone meet me at the Philadelphia airport? I don't know what flight, but I'll be on the first one I can get to. I'll call you from the airport and give you the ETA."

Same borrowed Carol's car and sped to Senior's house, now dark and musty after having been shut up for several months. He scooped all the cash from the safe into a duffel bag without bothering to count it and made it to the airport with only ten minutes to catch the flight Carol had booked.

Chapter Nineteen

Same arrived in Philadelphia at 1:32, four minutes early. When he emerged from the gateway he saw Victor waiting. Driving up to Radnor, Same pumped Victor with multiple questions, none of which could be answered at that point.

At the foundation Same greeted Elisa, Sally, and Mark in the conference area, where Elisa had moved them to force them to eat lunch. They sat around the small conference table and hashed and rehashed the possibilities. Nobody expected to hear an answer that made sense.

Same glanced out the window of Sally's office toward King of Prussia Road, and suddenly spotted a black sedan idling across the street in a parking lot. There was a man in the driver's seat peering through a pair of binoculars. Same pulled quickly back from the window.

After he had brewed a cup of coffee he returned to the conference table and didn't mention what he had seen. As calmly as he could he said, "I don't think these assholes are kidding and I don't think there's any question that they will harm Randy if provoked in any way. They didn't hesitate to shoot me and in the process nearly killed Mitch. When they call tomorrow I want to talk with them."

Mark looked up, "Same, how will that change anything? This is something that Sally has to resolve in some way. They're blaming her."

"No, Mark, they're not blaming her. It's me. I'm the one who came to Sally asking for her help to find out what was happening at FDA. It's me they want out of the way."

At that moment the phone rang again. Elisa jumped up and ran to answer it. She covered the mouthpiece and whispered down the table, "It's him."

Everyone quickly moved to surround the phone. Sally hit speaker and coldly said, "What now?"

The man spoke in a complete monotone. "Mrs. Watson, your actions are being carefully monitored. It's unfortunate you chose to bring someone else into this. That will only increase the risk to your son."

Same spoke up. "This is Tyler Harrison. Your monitors may want to be a little more careful, particularly your man in the black sedan across the street with his binoculars. Now let's talk about ending this game so everybody gets what they want."

"Mr. Harrison, I can assure you we're not playing a game. We are dead serious, if you get my drift."

"I don't doubt you for a second. Call it whatever you like. I want to make an offer. I want to exchange myself for Randy. You want me and not some kid."

There was a pause on the other end. "Perhaps you'll enlighten me further. How does that further my client's interest in the hundred thousand dollars?"

"Look asshole, we all know this isn't about the money. Put me away in a federal pen for a few years on some trumped up charge. I'm pretty sure you can manage that. Neither AFTD or I will talk if you've got access to me in prison. Your people screwed up by almost killing my brother rather than me. Okay, you get a second chance."

There was momentary silence and then the voice said, "Interesting. I'll get back to you." The line clicked and a dial tone blared into the conference room before Elisa finally hit speaker again.

Same looked at the group and with a big smile, "Well, folks, we got a bite. All we can do now is wait."

Sally came around to Same and hugged him, backed off and looked him in the eyes. "Same, I want you to know how much Mark and I appreciate what you're offering, but there's no way we can let you trade yourself for Randy."

Same laughed, "I don't think you have a choice anymore. I made the offer and I think they'll take it. Besides, Randy has a long life in front of him and I may have a very short one, so it seems like a good deal."

"And what about Mitchell? He needs you."

"You're right there, but if something happens he'll have a good life with Uncle Cary."

"Does Dr. Street know that?"

Again Same laughed, "No, he doesn't. He says he's always the last to know. Let's wait for the next call at your house, though. We don't know when it might be. Elisa and Victor, you guys need to keep up an appearance of business as usual here and be ready to forward the next call to us, as well as running any errands we need. If we separate, they may not have enough people to cover both groups."

Same borrowed Victor's phone to send a quick text on their way out. As they left the office for the Watson's house, he noted with satisfaction that the black sedan was no longer in the parking lot across the street. They reached the house in Mark's truck just as the school bus arrived at the bus stop down the street. Sally, oblivious to the bitter wind, bolted from the truck without her jacket to collect Madelaine.

Before mother and daughter got back to the house, the phone rang. Mark answered it on the kitchen extension, and his face hardened as he handed the handset to Same, "It's him."

The voice on the other end was the same monotone. "Mr. Harrison, we have decided to accept your offer and we see no point in waiting until tomorrow. At eleven tonight you will be at the corner of Grace and Lambert Streets with Mrs. Watson. The two of you will be alone. It will be a simple exchange. We'll release Randy to Mrs. Watson and you will come with us. Do you understand?"

Mark was reading the notes Same was scribbling on a pad. Suddenly he waved his hands at Same and violently shook his head. He grabbed the pen and wrote, "Deserted Warehouse."

Same smiled and nodded. He then spoke into the phone, "Well that's not a real nice place for a picnic."

The voice snapped quickly, "Listen, you're in no position to make any rules."

"That may be true, but I'll tell you this, if anything happens to that boy, you can bet this whole story will be splashed all over the national news. Now you listen. There is a small park on Lancaster Avenue just east of Interstate 476. I'm not telling you where I'm coming from, but when I see Randy on the bandstand in the middle of that park I will walk toward the stand and Randy will start walking toward Sally on Lancaster. When Randy is at the street, I'll surrender my weapon to you."

"Mr. Harrison, you sound very confident. In my experience that can be dangerous. We don't want anyone to get hurt."

"That's thoughtful of you. Do we have a deal?"

"It's a deal."

The phone clicked dead again just as Sally walked into the kitchen with her arms around Madelaine. She stopped short when she saw the serious expressions on the men's faces. As Mark hugged his daughter, Same gave orders, "Okay, Mark, I'll fill in Sally. While I do that, I need you to first call this number and tell them you have a leak in an upstairs toilet and need a plumber as soon as possible. I'll explain later. Then pull up a map of the area on your computer."

Mark frowned, but went to the phone. When he hung up, Same had just finished getting Sally up to speed. Mark looked at Sally and then to Same. "Same, Sally is not going with you. I'll go with you and do whatever you say."

"What's this?" asked Sally.

Before Same could reply, Mark said, "Same told the guy you'd be going with him for the exchange. There's no way I'm letting that happen…"

Sally walked right up into Mark's face. "Just a minute, there's no way you're going to let it happen? Pardon me, but I'm the one who caused all this and if the deal is that I go, then I go." With that she turned back.

Mark started to argue but quickly recognized that it was pointless. He retrieved a laptop and after a few keystrokes they had a map of the park and surrounding roads. Time passed quickly as they discussed the best means of access, and they were startled by a knock on the door about thirty minutes later. Mark answered it and soon ushered a man about Same's age into the kitchen. He was dressed in white coveralls with an Ajax Plumbing logo and the name "Charlie Higgins" embroidered on the breast pocket.

Higgins quickly asked, "Which one of you guys is Harrison?"

Same stood, "That's me."

Higgins smiled and shook his head. "Dude, I don't know what you've got on my boss, but when you texted this afternoon things sure did get shaking at the office."

"He was my only hope. We were at William and Mary together. But let me fill you in on where we stand. We need you to be seen in an upstairs window, then let's talk in the basement."

After Same had briefed Higgins in the basement, Mark walked with Higgins out the front door, where Mark signed some papers on his clipboard before the "plumber" got in his truck and left.

When Mark rejoined the group, he asked Same anxiously, "What's going to happen?"

"Frankly, I don't know. It will be up to Higgins's boss, Calvin Rogers. I have eternal trust in Calvin. He's somewhat of a maverick within the FBI, but that's exactly what we need right now. He'll keep everything quiet and discrete. We'll play our parts and give the kidnappers no reason to do anything crazy, and Calvin will get our backs if anything goes wrong. We won't even carry weapons, but is there any chance you have night vision goggles?"

"I've got a night scope on one of my rifles for beaver and muskrats," replied Mark.

Sally was quiet, but her stomach was in a knot. The more she thought of her son being pushed around by some idiot the more angry she became, like a clock whose spring was being wound tighter and tighter.

Chapter Twenty

Time seemed to crawl as the Watson family waited with Same for the exchange. Finally, at a quarter to eleven, Same announced that it was time to go. Sally and Same left the house in Sally's car and drove several blocks away from the park, then turned right, back left, then left again and around they went.

At exactly eleven, Sally parked at the dimly lit curb on the south side of Lancaster across from the park. Using the night scope, Same gradually brought the bandstand into view. Vision was poor with the light from the street, but he could make out two large individuals and one much thinner individual walking toward the stand from the opposite side of the park. They walked up on the stand and stood under the roof in the deeper shadows.

Same and Sally got out of the car and Same quickly crossed the street. Making sure he was seen, he began walking slowly toward the bandstand. In the distance he could barely make out Randy descending the steps and walking toward him.

When they were opposite each other, Randy held out his hand and Same grasped it. As they passed Same whispered, "Run, Randy, fast." The words were hardly out of his mouth when Randy took off. Same breathed a sigh of relief at the sound of the receding footsteps and forced himself to continue at a measured pace. Gotta go slow, he thought, give Randy some distance.

Randy finally reached the car as Same neared the bandstand. Sally reached out and hugged her son quickly, then handed him the night scope. "Tell me if you can see anything in there."

Randy reported one man on the steps of the bandstand and two back in the shadows. He was just about to report that the single man had reached the top of the steps when all hell broke loose.

The bandstand erupted in automatic rifle fire. He thought he saw one of the men in the shadows fall but suddenly dropped the scope as his mother jerked him down behind the car. It was all over in seconds.

After an agonizing thirty seconds of silence, Sally's cell phone buzzed and she quickly answered, "Same?"

"Yeah, it's me. Is Randy okay?"

She breathed a sigh of relief. "He's with me and he's fine. What happened?"

"We're clear here. It's all over."

Sally and Randy walked quickly to the bandstand. There were two bodies sprawled on the hardwood and a growing pool of blood beginning to drip over the side. The eyes of one of the men were frozen open in shock, and as he felt his mother's arm squeeze his shoulders, Randy knew instantly that the image would haunt him forever.

***

Sebastian Delgado was a real bastard. He was raised by an older brother on the streets of Laredo, Texas, and had worked hard to make his name as an enforcer for a sizeable drug-smuggling operation by the time he was twenty-one. When the FBI finally busted him, he was only too happy to cut a deal to do some of the Bureau's dirty work instead of spending the rest of his life in a cell. Hell, it was basically the same thing he had been doing before, only now he usually had a safe place to sleep at night.

The job in Ardmore had been pretty simple. His controller didn't tell him why he was doing the job, and Sebastian didn't ask any questions. He really wasn't even that scared when the shooting started. He had been in plenty of gunfights before.

As the boards around him disintegrated and the shots ripped through his calf and his lower back, he felt only anger. When the shooting stopped, he was on his back and couldn't feel his legs anymore. The men with guns emerged quickly from under the bandstand and kicked his gun away.

Sebastian played dead, forcing his eyes to stare into the sky in horror as he had seen in some of the men he had killed. The gunmen seemed to buy it, and began to talk in low voices on their cell phones. His gun had fallen too far from his body to retrieve before the men emerged, but the small black hunting knife he kept in his pocket had fallen a only about a foot from his hand. The men had missed it in the darkness. It would be his last act, but someone was coming with him on his trip to hell tonight. He just needed one to come within range.

Out of his peripheral vision he saw the man who traded himself for the boy walk over to meet the boy and his mother at the top of the steps. Suddenly he heard one of the other gunmen approaching him, talking distractedly on his cell phone. This was his chance. He slowly eased his hand toward the knife, then froze as he heard the woman's footsteps running towards him.

Then she was on him. He still wouldn't have been scared except for a brief glimpse into her eyes as she leapt for him. He had killed many people and always tried to look into their eyes to see what they felt. He had seen emotions from terror to acceptance to rage to confusion. But in her eyes was only the emptiness of death.

Sebastian couldn't believe how fast she moved as she straddled him and tore wildly at his face with her fingernails. He struggled to shake her off and suddenly felt fire slice through his right eye as she raked her fingernails into his eyeball. He screamed and reached for the knife with his right hand, clutching at his mangled eye with his left.

He never got to the knife. She was just too fast. The blurred vision in his remaining eye cleared just enough for him to see her holding the knife in both hands, arms raised as high as she could. Sebastian knew death had finally come. She screamed as she drove the knife into his body. The pain exploded from his chest, and as the knife plunged in again and again, he gradually lost track of whether the screaming was coming from her or from him.

***

Between Same and two FBI agents, they finally wrestled Sally off the dying kidnapper after four or five driving thrusts of the knife. As Same hauled her away by the waist, she cocked her arm and with one last immense effort, hurled the knife at the spasming body. The knife missed and bounced harmlessly across the wooden planks, and Sally broke down sobbing on her knees as Randy wrapped his arms around her.

After a few seconds of feeling for a pulse in the kidnapper, one of the FBI agents slowly shook his head. He turned to Same, still huddled with Randy and Sally. "Mr. Harrison, I see no reason to prolong this experience for them. Why don't you take them home. We'll get this scene cleaned up and handle the local cops."

Same pulled Sally to her feet and led her down from the band-stand. With Randy on her other side they walked silently back to the car. Same drove with Randy in the backseat with his mother. When Sally's grip on Randy finally eased enough for him to talk, he asked quietly, "How'd you get out of there, Same? I was sure they were going to kill you."

"I think that was their plan. So happens the agents you saw were waiting under the bandstand. A friend of mine in the FBI helped set it up. When I hit the top of the stairs, I heard a voice telling me to dive off. Then the agents took out the goons."

They were all quiet for a minute as the adrenaline continued to subside. Finally Same spoke again. "Sally, I have to ask, where did that knife come from?"

She spoke in a low, shaky voice. "When we were looking at the bodies, I saw that guy's hand move. Something in me just snapped. I just remember being on top of him and seeing him reach for the knife. I couldn't stop myself."

"Lady, you are a surprise a minute."

"It really wasn't me out there. You don't screw with a mother's children."

When they finally reached home, Sally quietly went upstairs and took a long, hot shower. As the family awaited her return, the phone suddenly rang. Mark answered, then turned to Same, "It's him, and he wants to talk with you."

Same quickly took the phone from Mark. "Harrison here."

The voice on the other end was bitterly cold. "Mr. Harrison, you have a charmed life for a doomed man. Be sure to keep looking over your shoulder." Before Same could respond, the line went dead.

Chapter Twenty-One

Two days later in a small office in Alexandria, Virginia, two men were in a conversation that was heated to the boiling point. Tyler Harrison appeared to be lighting a fire under a lot of people.

Agent Blip Tatum sat behind a typical government-issue desk. He closed a drawer and it emitted a hollow clang; it was empty except for a .45 Magnum and a single envelope. He looked up toward the other man, who sat slumped in a straight chair against the far wall eight feet away.

Tatum spoke, "It seems we've had another screw-up by your people. You said they were the best in the business. This is part of the same group that screwed up by shooting that kid instead of our target. I don't think your people could hit water if they were falling out of a boat."

The second man was edgy. He looked into the cold eyes of Tatum, eyes that could freeze boiling water. "Look, I've done work for you for a long time and this is the only time we didn't get results the first time out."

If it was possible the eyes seemed to get colder. "I'm not concerned with what happened in the past. I'm concerned with the job at hand. I've paid you big money for success, not for screw-ups. Every time your people screw up there has to be another event, and the more events there are, the more opportunity there is for my agency to be compromised. Do I make myself clear?"

"All I'm saying is my people are good. It's no fun standing in the distance watching two very capable helpers being gunned down and butchered. Whoever was out there that night, they weren't amateurs."

"You could be right. But that changes nothing. So here's what we're going to do. I'm going to have to be hands-on with this. Considering the men who went down were connected to you, I want you to take a vacation to that house we bought for you in the Bahamas. I doubt it will be necessary, but we can arrange proof that you've been there for the past couple months. I'm sure I'll need you in the future, but I'm going to put someone else to work on this situation."

"That doesn't fit into my plans right now. I'll be okay here. Even if they identify the bodies, no one can trace those guys to me."

"You're so wrong. I'm telling you that it fits your plans and I expect you to be on a flight tomorrow morning." He opened the desk drawer. It was tempting to use the .45 and end any chance of a connection, but instead he withdrew the envelope and tossed it to the other man.

"Here is your ticket and sufficient money to finalize our contract."

The second man opened the envelope and saw a stack of twenties. He looked again at the cold eyes, "I don't think this finishes our contract by any means. There couldn't be more than a grand in here."

"You know, that comment only proves I've made the right decision. There are two grand in there to cover your travel expenses and that's on top of the very large deposit yesterday in your Cayman account. Now get out of here, I've got work to do."

Tatum watched the other man quietly get up and walk out. He'd known Tatum long enough to know when to fold. Tatum opened the top draw again, withdrew the .45 and shoved it into his shoulder holster. He stood for a few moments until he was sure the other man was gone. He took the elevator to the garage and drove across the Potomac to his office in the district.

***

It had been a week and each day Agent Tatum dreaded going to the office. He knew the meeting would be called eventually, and at 1645 the day before he'd gotten word to be in the division director's office at 0800 the next morning.

When Tatum arrived he was told by the director's secretary to go directly to the conference room. Already at the table were the director and two people Tatum didn't know. The director wordlessly pointed Tatum to a seat opposite the two strangers. The director was at his usual place at the head of the table. Tatum made sure to casually pour himself a cup of coffee from the sideboard to let them know he wasn't afraid of the ass-chewing he was sure he was about to receive.

As soon as Tatum was seated, the director spoke, "This is Agent Tatum. He has been in charge of the specific operations with which you're concerned." There was no introduction offered otherwise.

The man appeared to be stamped "Ivy League Legal." He was about sixty, in a three-piece suit, white shirt, and a bow tie that seemed starkly out of place for this sort of meeting. The woman was in a black pinstripe blazer and an open neck white blouse. They both exuded business, strictly business.

The woman spoke first, "Mr. Tatum, could you encapsulate the status of the Harrison affair?"

Tatum glanced at his boss. "I'm not sure how far I'm to speak, sir?"

The director's face was stone, "You're to speak as though we are alone. Let's just say these two people have clearance you can only dream of."

Tatum looked back at the woman. "Ma'am, we've had a couple of disappointments so far. I'm sure you're aware that there have been two attempts to silence Harrison and his associate Watson and something has happened both times."

"That is what we've been told," said the woman flatly. "Could you enlighten us as to why? It's my understanding that this should have been a simple operation."

Tatum could feel perspiration on his forehead. He wanted to reach up and wipe it but he wouldn't give this iron bitch the satisfaction of thinking she had him on the hot seat.

"I'm making no excuses. The people who were under contract bungled the first attempt and their second was interrupted by some pros. To date we have no idea who killed our operatives."

Ivy Legal spoke, "And now we have the idiot who controlled the bunglers running around talking to God knows who."

"No sir, that's not true," Tatum said. "That individual is out of the country until I tell him to return."

"I'd say that should be permanently," said Ivy Legal. "Now what?"

"I have some ideas, but I'd like to ask a couple of questions."

Tatum again turned to his boss. The boss didn't react other than to hold out his palm as if to say, "Proceed."

Tatum squirmed in his seat and then looked directly at the woman. "You seem to be the lead here, so tell me why we were supposed to take Harrison and Watson out. What have they done?"

Without facial reaction she replied, "This is of no concern to you. Unless the director tells me otherwise I assume you are given an order and you comply with that order. Is that correct?"

Tatum didn't give the director time to answer. "Generally that is true. However, they appeared to have some unknown friends in Pennsylvania and I'd like to know who I'm dealing with."

Ivy Legal leaned over and whispered to the woman, who then responded, "Agent Tatum, I'm not authorized to provide those answers. I will say that it is in the best interests of the United States. Unless I'm mistaken you swore to uphold your duties to defend your country."

Tatum snapped upright, his face glowing red as he spoke through gritted teeth, "Lady, nobody questions my loyalty."

The director stood and came to Tatum. When he felt the director's hand on his shoulder he settled back into his seat. He would obey his boss, but he wasn't a happy man.

Ivy Legal cleared his throat. "A related problem has arisen. We've discovered that another associate of Harrison's may have breached a secure facility and downloaded certain classified communications onto a portable memory device. That device is likely now in Harrison's possession. It would be convenient if that device were recovered at the same time that Harrison is eliminated."

Tatum snorted in disgust. "Okay, I'll take care of both of your problems. This time we'll be a little more subtle and it may take a little more time, but he'll be out of the picture. Now if you'll excuse me I have work to do."

"And what do you propose to do, Agent Tatum?" asked Ivy Legal.

"At this time I'd prefer not to say. I'm sure you wouldn't want your name associated with whatever it is. It might ruffle your cute bow tie."

The director coughed. "Agent Tatum you're excused."

Tatum picked up his coffee and walked out of the room. He headed directly to his office. At the moment he wished he was a drinking man; he could sure use a shot of something right about now. Instead he loosened his tie and sat with his head in his hands, his elbows resting on the desk.

After a couple of minutes he sat back and stared at the ceiling. "I'd like to shoot Harrison right on that bitch's doorstep, or better still, in her bed," he said to himself. He thoughtfully reached for his rolodex and found the number he wanted. A voice answered quickly and he said, "I have another job for you. We'll meet in the usual place tomorrow at two."

Chapter Twenty-Two

Same flew out of Philadelphia the morning after the gunfight in Ardmore. He had agreed with the Watsons that the next step was to lay low and watch their backs. If they all put on a show of being intimidated into silence by all the violence, they might be able to buy themselves enough time to solve this thing. They still didn't know who exactly was behind any of this, and they had nothing solid to bring to the press or the authorities. Hell, they didn't even know which authorities were trustworthy at this point and their only evidence of something suspicious was obtained through the violation of who knew how many federal laws.

With Mitch still safely with Uncle Cary, Same decided to get back into his running routine. Two weeks after Ardmore he was finally able to make it all the way to work without pain in his shoulder and without jumping at any loud noises. Maybe laying low was working after all.

After a brisk run to work early one morning, he was about to enter the elevator when he heard from behind, "Aren't you dressed a little skimpily for court?" It was Julie.

Same looked straight ahead. "Is that the voice of a former friend, one who nurtured me as an infant?"

"You're still an infant in a lot of ways, buddy. Did you have a good run?"

"Yup, it was beautiful down at the river. There was this real heavy mist overlaying the entire thing from shore to shore. What are you up to this morning?"

"Nothing different." They entered the elevator with two other attorneys, reached the 16th floor and left the elevator. Julie reached out and took Same's elbow. "Let's walk down this way."

Same followed. When they were far away from their office, Julie said, "We're supposed to have a new assistant this morning. You were away yesterday."

"Couldn't be helped. Mitch had a check with the pulmonary doc and then I had to get him back in school. Was there a problem? Where's Carol?"

"Carol was involved in a hit and run, Same. She's in Henrico Doctors. Her leg was broken and she'll be out for a month. I called HR for a temp and they said they'd have someone in this morning. That's why I wanted to catch you before you went in and saw a stranger."

Same struggled to stay calm as his heart started racing. Settle down, he told himself, don't get paranoid. Carol has no involvement in this. "Is she okay?" he asked.

"Her husband said she's having some pain but the orthopedist said she'll be fine."

"How did it happen?"

"Don't know, but let's go see who our temp is."

Julie and Same walked down to Carol's desk and were greeted by the new assistant, "Good morning, I'm Molly Rose, your executive assistant."

Julie and Same shook hands with Molly as Same thought, Executive? I've been here a while and I don't have a title. Not bad for the first day on a job.

Molly Rose's appearance fit someone who would assume a title, but more like Miss Universe. She was about 5'10" and had curves upon curves in all the right places. The knit dress she modeled managed to cling to the curves like a sports car on a wet road. The red of her dress was jarring and matched only by her lip gloss. The lips and her heavy green eye shadow made Same suspect she'd be ready when Christmas rolled around.

After introductions were completed, Julie said to Molly, "I have a contract that'll need word processing this morning. Come into my office and I'll give it to you."

Molly jumped to her feet and scampered into Julie's office. Julie stood back to avoid being run over. She turned to Same, "Put your eyeballs back in and snap your jaw back into place. Also, you might want to put on some pants. I think she liked your legs."

Same blushed and looked down. He'd forgotten he was still in running gear. "I'll go shower and change."

"Make it a cold one," quipped Julie as she moved away toward her office.

At about four in the afternoon, Same stuck his head in Julie's office doorway. "Angie, I'm headed home. Going to grab my car, pick up Mitch, and go out to see Carol. I'll finish reviewing the McConnell contract tonight. You want to go?"

"Wish I could, but I'm meeting Bob for a drink and then we're going to the symphony. Please give her my love and tell her I'll see her tomorrow."

The walk home was as pleasant as the run had been in the morning. Summer had arrived and the air was warm, but they hadn't yet hit the heat and humidity of July.

When Mitch started back in school after the shooting, the head-master at St. Christopher's had suggested he stay after school to get extra help to catch up. Mitch had protested that he didn't want to stay with the "detainees," but he didn't put up much of a fuss. He was a good student and had inherited his father's competitive drive. Same hoped fervently that was all he had inherited.

Mitch was waiting in the doorway when Same arrived, and quickly walked to the car. He wasn't up to a run yet.

"What's up, man?" asked Same.

"Nothing," Mitch replied coolly. He managed to buckle his seat belt and nonchalantly look out the window for a few seconds until he couldn't restrain himself any longer. "I got the highest grade on a math test that I didn't even know we were having today!"

"Sweet!" Same exclaimed. "Maybe you won't have to stay extra for that long after all."

"I hope not," said Mitch. "It sucks in there."

"Hey," said Same, changing the subject before Mitch could plead for release. "I'm going to see Carol."

Mitch interrupted, "Isn't she married?"

"Gross, dude. Actually, she was in an accident. Her leg is broken."

"Aw, man, I'm sorry, Same. I didn't know."

"Hey, it's okay; you had no way of knowing. Do you want to go with me or should I drop you at Uncle Cary's?"

"No, I'll go with you."

In the hospital lobby Same bought flowers and handed them over to Mitch to carry. When they knocked on the open door and entered her room they found Carol lying in bed with her right leg elevated and covered in a cast from hip to ankle. While the contraption looked painful, Carol's voice was still cheerful. "Hi, Same, and what a wonderful surprise to see you, Mitchell! How are you?"

"I'm fine. These are for you," Mitchell said as he shyly thrust the vase toward Carol.

"They're beautiful. Thank you so much."

"So how are you doing?" asked Same. "I was off yesterday and didn't hear about this until Julie told me this morning."

"Well, I've got a fractured fibula and a compound fracture of the femur. But the doctor said it was a mess that cleaned up well. I should be fine in six weeks."

"Don't fret about work, it won't be the same but we'll get by somehow. What happened anyway?"

"It was just bad luck, Same. I had gotten off the bus and was crossing the street. The light was red but this guy in a baseball cap was looking down at his cell phone or something and came right through the light and wham. That's all I remember until I was in the ER."

Same shook his head in disbelief. "You sure it was an accident?"

"Well, a careless accident. I could swear I saw the guy texting right as he was about to hit me."

After a few more minutes Same and Mitch said their goodbyes and promised to see her again soon. All the way home Same tried to be light and talkative with Mitch but his mind was still churning. What could they possibly want to hurt Carol for? This had to be just a coincidental accident. Pedestrians got hit by careless drivers all the time, and texters were a positive menace.

Chapter Twenty-Three

On Friday Molly entered Same's office at five o'clock on the dot. She was punctual if nothing else, eight to five every day. "Is there anything else I can do for you before I leave, Mr. Harrison?"

Same laid down the contract he'd been reading for the last hour. Suddenly he saw Molly as if for the first time. She had done something different and yet he wasn't sure what it was. She looked absolutely radiant.

He knew she always dressed on the edge, as if daring H&B's managing partners, but today she had really outdone herself. Her black jersey dress clung to every nuance of curve. Same particularly approved of the plunging neckline. He could have sworn the cleavage wasn't that deep when he had returned from lunch. He couldn't help staring.

Molly was obviously aware of his stare. She repeated, "Mr. Harrison, is there anything else?"

"Uh, no, but please drop the Mr. Harrison."

"I know, but I have trouble calling you Tyler," she said softly. "I don't want to seem forward."

"Please just call me Same. Everyone else does."

Molly giggled. "That's such a funny name. I've heard the other attorneys call you that and I always want to laugh. I hope you don't mind, but it's kind of the weirdest name I've ever heard. How'd you get it?"

Same laughed, "It is a little weird. Are you in any hurry to get home?"

"Well, no. Is there something else you want?"

"There sure is," thought Same, but instead said, "Let me make a phone call. We'll go grab a drink and I'll tell you all about my name. Sound good?"

Molly smiled and ran her tongue around her lips. "I can taste it now." Same didn't miss the gesture or the comment.

He picked up the phone and hit a speed dial button to reach Street's housekeeper, who watched Mitch on nights when Street and Same were both working. She agreed to tell Mitch that Same would be a little late that evening, and Same quickly hung up.

He rose from his desk, walked across the room and grabbed his suit jacket from the back of the door. Opening the outer office door, he allowed Molly to pass. As he slipped his arm in the coat he had a sudden memory of his mother's brother that brought a momentary smile. Uncle Gus had been a Marine, and told Same just before he left for college, "Boy, don't ever shit in your mess kit."

Fraternizing with the staff was definitely frowned upon at H&B, but to hell with that, thought Same. Even the corner partners did it all the time. Besides, it would just be a drink for tonight, and Molly would be gone soon when Carol returned.

In the elevator, Same suggested the Back Fin Restaurant, about a five minute walk from their office. They left the elevator in the lower garage, walked out the back of the building, and crossed the street.

When they entered the restaurant, Same found himself missing the more carefree days when he first started at the firm. The young associates would come here often for drinks after work. The building was a very chic, high-ceilinged, contemporary structure set right on the river. They passed into the bar, which was already a watering hole for a number of lawyers Same recognized, thankfully none from H&B. Same chose a table in a corner as far away from the crowd as possible.

After consulting with Molly, Same ordered a pinot grigio for her and a Talisker on the rocks for himself. He reached up and pulled his tie from his neck. Folding it precisely, he tucked it into an inside coat pocket. "Don't think I'll need this until morning," he thought to himself

He looked up to see Molly appraising him coolly. "It's good to see you relax a little. You've been working so hard ever since I've been on the job and I'm sure it was just as tense before I came. I know you've been worried about Mitchell. How's he doing?"

"Thanks for asking. I was worried when he left the hospital, but I have a family friend who has a full-time housekeeper since his wife died, and Mitch stayed there until he went back to school last week. The housekeeper is actually looking after him now. He likes her and it's taken a lot of pressure off me."

When their drinks arrived, they touched glasses and Molly took a sip. She showcased perfect white teeth with a beautiful smile and said, "Now to lighter stuff. I'm not letting you get away without telling me what I want to know."

"And what is it that you want?" teased Same.

"Well for starters you know what I want, but in the meantime I want to hear about your name."

Same could feel a flush come to his face. He took a swig of his scotch and enjoyed the flow of the fiery liquor. "Oh that. It's a carryover from childhood. My dad had the same name and everybody said we were exactly alike, so my mom started calling me 'Same.' I used to hate it, but now it's all right. You know, my mom hired a woman once whose actual name was Reethyl. Her mother's name had been Ethyl."

Molly leaned back in her chair and laughed. "That has to be true. No one could make that up."

Same finished his drink and held the glass up as the waiter passed by. His drive to pick up Mitch would get a little precarious with two Taliskers, but if he switched to water thereafter he should be able to sober up.

Time seemed to speed by as they talked. The Talisker was working its magic and he opened up about his life. As usual with two people from the same office it was difficult to avoid talking shop. After her second glass of wine Molly leaned forward with a conspiratorial look. "So, I got instructions from Carol to immediately forward all calls about drugs or the FDA. Are you in some big fight with them?"

"First of all," said Same, holding up an index finger, "I'm not in a fight with the FDA. I'm trying to find out why a drug trial, in which I was to participate, has been cancelled."

Molly frowned, "I didn't know you were part of a study. Are you sick?" She reached out and placed her hand upon Same's.

It was like an electrical jolt that ran straight from his hand to his groin. His first instinct was to pull his hand away, but he quickly realized he was enjoying the touch of a woman for the first time in many months. He didn't know how long he had in this life and it would be a crying shame to let an opportunity like this go to waste.

"Yes and no," he replied. Don't scare her off you dumbass, he thought to himself. "I have a gene that might start to affect my behavior in a few years if a cure isn't found. But for the time being I'm free as a bird."

"I understand." She squeezed his hand and then took another sip of wine. "So why'd they cancel it?"

"Shit, who knows. I've got all kinds of clues, but I haven't pieced it all together yet. I'm going to find out, though. I haven't given up yet."

They sat in silence for a moment as Same stared at the table. Get off the depressing FDA shit, he thought to himself, that's never going to get you laid. He was about to order another round of drinks when he felt Molly's hand on his knee. "Why don't we head back? I'm going to have to be going before long."

"Oh, I thought you had the evening free."

Molly looked at her watch. "Time flies when you're having fun. It's eight o'clock."

Same looked incredulous. "You're kidding. We've been here over two hours?" He looked at his watch. "Well I'll be damned. Let me pay the check."

Same took care of the check as Molly excused herself to the ladies room. When they were back on the street Molly slipped her arm through his and leaned her head again his shoulder. "This is such a wonderful evening. I don't want it to end yet."

All kinds of visions danced in his head, and none of them were sugarplums. A combination of scotch and hormones had eradicated the last vestiges of good sense. When they entered his office he didn't turn on the lights. The reflection of the city lights provided the perfect ambience, and he didn't bother to disguise turning the lock on the door.

He pulled off his coat and threw it toward the hook on the back of the door. When he turned, Molly was already on him. His hands caressed her cheeks and he suddenly pulled her to him. At first he brushed his lips lightly over hers. A slight moan escaped from her mouth and then he felt her arms about his waist as her tongue darted against his.

Blindly they clawed at each other's clothes. Her dress fell to the floor and he stopped in surprise when he realized she wasn't wearing panties. Huskily she whispered into his ear, "I want you."

She pressed him against the desk and he felt her releasing his belt and unzipping his fly. As she pulled down his tented whities a brief image flashed through his spinning brain of Alaina, eyeless, hanging from the corner of the desk beside him. He shook his head and the image vanished as he felt her mouth engulf him.

Same felt as if he would explode right there. She sensed his urgency and rose to deeply kiss him again. With one sweep she cleared his desk. She leaned back on the desk and he could feel her high heels against his buttocks.

It was so erotic, dangerous, and unpredictable that it was over in just a few minutes. He rolled to his back on the desk, panting. He felt her move between his thighs as she leaned over, kissed him lightly on the lips and moved away.

He tried to reach for her but she quickly slipped his hand and slid into her dress. Following suit he pulled up his pants. Once he was fastened he walked over to the door and flipped the light switch. He covered his eyes, as much from embarrassment as the brightness of the lights.

As his eyes focused he saw Molly picking up the papers and desk items. He walked over to her and took her arm, "Molly, are you all right?"

She forced a weak smile. "Yes, fine. I just guess this shouldn't have happened. You caught me off guard."

Same was stunned. "I caught you off guard? I thought…"

"Please, Same," Molly interrupted. "Just let me get this mess cleaned up."

Robotically Same started picking up the shuffled and scattered reams of paper. The buzz from the alcohol and the sex had quickly worn off in the harsh fluorescent lights of the office. When all of the papers were at least on the desk, Molly said, "I'll straighten it all out Monday morning. Right now I'm going to the ladies."

Same was standing in the middle of the office as she walked out. He sighed, shook his head, and walked over to pick up his jacket. Real smooth, Same, he thought.

It was nearly ten when he arrived at Uncle Cary's home. He noted that the doctor's car was not in the driveway and concluded he was at the hospital. He took his key and entered the darkened house. Mrs. Davis had gone to bed long ago. He quietly went up the stairs and down the hall to Mitch's room. A dim light came from under the door, so he quietly tapped and then opened the door.

Mitch didn't look up from his computer. "You didn't have to come way out here. You should have just gone on home. I'm about to turn out the light, anyway. Where you been?"

Same crossed the room and kissed his brother on top of his head. "Where have I been? I've just come from the office."

Mitch turned to face him. "Bullshit."

"Dude, watch your language, what are you talking about?"

"You've been with some woman, probably hanging out at a bar."

"Why would you say that?"

"I'm nine, not stupid. You smell like Uncle Cary's whiskey and you've got lipstick all over your face. She must have been a sloppy kisser, looks like she missed your lips a lot."

Same went over to the full length mirror on the closet door and saw Mitch was right. He had lipstick from one side of his face to the other. His shirt tail was out on the left and the scarlet color of his face screamed "Guilty as charged."

He turned back to Mitch. "So I stretched the truth a bit. I did just leave the office, but I had been to a bar with a woman."

"It's whatever," said Mitch, "I don't really care anyway. Just don't get any of that stuff on me."

Same leaned over to hug Mitch and then walked to the door. "Do you need anything? I promise I'll be in early tomorrow."

"No, Mrs. Davis takes care of everything."

On the drive home Same replayed the events of the evening. It was certainly a memorable night, but he was not looking forward to seeing Molly Monday morning.

***

After Same left, Mitch couldn't hold it together any longer. All kinds of visions, real and imaginary, flooded his mind. He was angry and frightened. It was a collage of textures, emotions and colors. The emotion of losing his father and being shot were right on top. The eerie blue in the hospital room and the red of his mother's blood spurting from her head supplied enough color. Yet, the most threatening thought was that of losing Same to some broad.

He turned out his bedside light, rolled onto his side and pulled the bedcovers up to his chin. But the lights in his head couldn't be turned off. He cried himself to sleep.

Chapter Twenty-Four

To avoid any awkwardness, Same decided to get in early on Monday and get everything organized before Molly arrived. He'd get focused and hopefully start to catch up a bit. He walked quickly to work as the sun was rising and took the elevator to his floor.

As he flipped the light switch in his office, he immediately sensed that something was wrong. Friday evening before he left the office, he and Molly had picked everything up off the floor, but it was still a mess on the desk. She had said that she was coming in Monday to clean everything up, but there was no sign she had arrived. Yet the papers were now in neat piles. The cleaning crew knew not to touch any papers in the lawyer's offices, so it couldn't be them unless they had new cleaners on staff.

He walked around the desk and carefully looked through the first stack. It was made up of random sheets pertaining to one of three contracts on which he'd been working on Friday. The second stack was a repeat of the first. It was as if someone had studied the cards and then shuffled the deck.

He inserted his desk key into the lock on the middle drawer and turned it counter clockwise. It wouldn't budge. It was already unlocked.

He quickly bent closer to examine the lock. There were scratches along the edges of the lock and the desk. Somebody had jimmied it. He took a quick inventory of the drawer's contents; it appeared everything was in order. He was about to close the drawer when he had a sudden sick feeling in his stomach. The flash drive with Lance's $200,000 iPhone app was missing.

"Oh, shit," he said aloud.

He leaned back in his chair, took a deep breath and murmured, "What else is going to kick me in the balls?"

Same contemplated calling the police or building security, but decided there was nothing they were going to find. If someone had the ability to evade security, they certainly weren't dumb enough to leave fingerprints. Besides, he didn't want to advertise the missing flash drive until he had a chance to talk with Lance.

He was staring out the window at the rising sun and contemplating his next move when he heard someone enter the outer office. He looked at his watch. Must be Julie, he thought.

He looked up and felt his face flush. Molly was standing in the doorway. He was immediately taken aback by the transformation in the woman. Her hair was tied back into a ponytail, there was little makeup and she was dressed in dark slacks with a tailored white blouse. She was also wearing glasses now.

"Good morning, Mr. Harrison. I came in a little early to straighten things but I see you've taken care of that. Call me if there's something for me to do."

"Thank you, Molly. Has Julie come in yet?"

Molly stepped back through the doorway and looked toward Julie's office then back to Same. "Her door is closed but there's light under the door, so I suppose she is." Molly turned and went to her desk.

"Christ, from blast furnace to deep freeze," Same said under his breath.

He pushed back from his desk and went over to Julie's office. He knocked but there was no answer. He knocked again as he opened the door.

The words escaping his lips sounded far away to him. "Sweet Mary, Mother of God."

Molly spun around and saw Same rooted in Julie's doorway. She hurried over and looked into the office. Suddenly she loosed a horrendous scream. She turned and ran into the hallway with one continuous scream after another.

Several co-workers came running. They asked Molly what was wrong but she could only point toward Same, still standing in shock at Julie's doorway.

Dan Cooley, the corner partner on their floor, came up behind Same. "What the hell is going on, man?" Then he saw.

Julie's body was on the floor with her left leg extended under her desk and the right flexed under the left. Her face was toward the desk and there was a small amount of congealed blood on her upper lip. Her skirt was up over her chest, revealing her lower abdomen and white bikini panties.

Dan slipped around Same and knelt beside Julie's body. He touched her wrist and quickly withdrew his hand. He felt her wrist again to check for any sign of a pulse, but he knew there wouldn't be any. She was cold.

Same came and knelt beside Dan. Julie's face was cyanotic and puffy. There were petechiae on her face and eyelids where tiny blood vessels had ruptured. Dan pointed to the contusions on her neck.

"She was strangled." They had both read enough forensics that they knew the signs.

Dan reached for her skirt and started to pull it down before Same caught his arm. "Don't touch anything. We'd better call the police."

They both left Julie's office and closed the door. Molly was still hysterical and one of the other secretaries was trying vainly to comfort her. Same called 911 from the secretarial station outside and in a few minutes they could hear the muffled sounds of sirens from the street.

Same sat on the floor against the wall of his office staring into space. Julie had been more than a mentor and a colleague. She was basically his best friend. Had he caused her death? Even with all the crap he had stirred up he couldn't imagine how she would possibly be involved. But too many people were getting hurt for this to just be coincidence.

Same heard the voices down the hall and knew immediately that he was about to get kicked in the balls again. Clear above the rest of the voices was Detective Richard Jones. Why couldn't that ass have been on vacation?

In a voice loud enough for the entire floor to hear, Jones asked, "And where is the eminent Tyler Harrison Esquire?"

Same yelled through his open doorway, "In my office, Jones."

Jones entered Same's office with the cockiness of a Bantam rooster. "Ah, Mr. Harrison, I understand you're the one who called emergency services. Is that correct?"

Same sighed, "That's correct."

"And you're the one who discovered the body?"

"That's correct."

"And when did you discover the body?"

"A few minutes before I called you."

Jones smiled even broader as he looked about the office. "You're doing pretty well for yourself. I see the place has been redecorated since your mum died in here."

"It was my father's second wife, not my mother."

"Oh, that's right, your stepmum."

Same was not about to let Jones bait him. "Whatever."

Jones pulled up one of Same's chairs and sat directly in front of Same. "Won't you have a seat, Jones?" asked Same with obvious sarcasm.

"That's Detective Jones, Mr. Harrison. Now, suppose you tell me what happened?"

Let's get it over with, Same thought. "I was working when my assistant came in. I asked her if Julie had come in and she said she didn't know but that there was a light on in her office. I went to her office, knocked on the door and then opened the door. Molly came over and took one look and she's been crying ever since."

"Apparently she cared for the deceased. You seem pretty accepting."

"What the hell is that supposed to mean?"

"Maybe you're getting used to women dying in your presence." Jones picked at his teeth with a finger nail.

One of the medical examiner's people came into Same's office. "Detective Jones, may I speak with you in the hall?"

Jones got up and started for the door. He turned back to Same, pointed and said, "Don't go away."

Same would have laughed under any other circumstance. "Wouldn't think of it."

The detective was gone about five minutes. When he returned he promptly resumed his questioning, "When was the last time you saw the deceased alive?"

"Sometime on Friday, we were working on a contract together. She came here to my office."

"The preliminary observations suggest she died sometime on Saturday night. Where were you Saturday night?"

"Are you saying I'm a suspect?

"Do you think you should be a suspect?"

"Don't be ridiculous. Julie was like a sister to me."

"You have a girlfriend, Mr. Harrison?"

"What do you care?"

"What I'm saying is that the ME thinks there may be semen on the victim. I was just wondering if you were getting any."

Same came up off the floor in a hurry and Jones stood quickly to meet him face to face. "You'd better be sure that that's what you want to do," Jones said with a leer. "I'd love to take you in for assaulting a police officer."

As much as he hated him, Same knew Jones was right. He had to get control of himself. "I'm walking out now. If you want to arrest me on what you've got, now's your chance."

Same moved toward the door but was halted by one of the detective's thick palms on his chest. "One of my investigators is going to ask all the males for a cheek swab for DNA analysis. I'm sure you won't object, will you Mr. Harrison?"

Same stared into his eyes. "Absolutely not, Detective. I have nothing to hide."

Jones's reaction was disappointment. He quickly turned and walked out of the office.

Chapter Twenty-Five

Four days later Same's vain attempts at concentration were suddenly interrupted by the smug, coarse countenance of Detective Jones muscling through his door. Molly fluttered helplessly behind, squeaking something about waiting in the lobby.

"Mr. Harrison," boomed Jones, his smirk now covering most of his impossibly thick face. "So good to see you again. I have the distinct pleasure of informing you that you are under arrest for the murder of Julie Welford."

For a few seconds the shock didn't hit Same, who was still stuck on finding the right words to describe the detective's shit-eating grin. He got somewhere close to an analogy involving a Welsh sheep-shagger and a prize ewe stuck ass-up in a mudpit before the appearance of two of Jones's henchmen brought him back to the moment. As the accusation sunk in, Same heard himself stammering, "For the murder of WHOM?"

Jones nearly burst out laughing. "Julie Welford. Why, you got some more putrid corpses stashed around here?"

Same was faintly surprised that the detective's vocabulary extended to the word "putrid," and thought about congratulating him on the accomplishment of using such a fancy word and insulting the memory of his deceased friend at the same time. A real coup-de-grace for a genuine asshole. Instead he replied, "No, Dick. Just the one. But what do you and your lovely gentlemen friends have on me? Julie was my good friend. I would never hurt her."

"It's not what we have on you, Slick, it's what you put on her. You left your little boys behind." Same didn't think it possible but the sheep-shagging face smiled wider. "Don't you know you should bag it before you bang it? You might catch something that won't wash off. Especially from a fine-looking piece like that. Anyway, the semen on the victim matches your cheek swab. That's about as tight a case as we get. You're going to the big house, tough guy, and I'd plan on staying a while if I were you."

Somewhere outside the door Molly was loudly crying again. Between the squeaking sounds and the heaving breaths Same could make out faint gasps that sounded like "Not Same … not Same …." He felt like he should say something, proclaim his innocence, shout some proof to the contrary, but the utter impossibility of the detective's statement had stunned him into silence. The henchmen lost no time taking his silence as acquiescence and quickly dragged him up from his chair and handcuffed him while Jones basked in the moment.

Being handcuffed and escorted from his office was something surreal out of a bad cop show. One of the henchmen squinted slightly as he read the *Miranda* rights from a card. Same found himself bizarrely noticing that Molly's mascara was streaking as she cried. She leaned on two other secretaries, who made comforting noises while glaring at him as he was led out the office.

Two police sedans waited in the circular drive in front of his office building. One of the officers placed a hand roughly on Same's head.

"Have a seat in the car, please," he said as he shoved his head under the door frame.

Same noted the absence of door handles on the inside of the doors. He tried to lean back but the handcuffs precluded any comfortable position. The officer closed the door and got into the front passenger side. The second officer drove.

Same found thoughts pushing through his head too rapidly to sort and focus. He needed a damn good lawyer. How did that asshole find a match to his DNA? Did somebody rig the results of the test? Did Jones just make it up to trick him into confessing? Goddam it, what the hell was going on here! Was this a mistake or was he being set up? First things first, he needed a lawyer pronto.

The ride downtown in the squad car gave Same time to piece together his next steps. He would be booked and tossed in a cell with a bunch of new best friends. Because it was a Friday afternoon, he would almost certainly be in for the weekend, that much was unavoidable. But he needed a good lawyer, now, to pull together a strategy for the bail hearing. Getting out on bail for a rape and murder charge would be next to impossible, but he would be damned if he was going to go down without a fight.

He thought about the various lawyers he knew. Only the practicing criminal lawyers would be any good on a charge this serious. But most of those guys were largely content to advise their clients to take a negotiated plea, collect their few hundred bucks in legal fees, and move on to the next case. He needed a fighter, someone good, but who wouldn't have a lot of other cases pending. Maybe some young hot shot not too far out of law school, willing to take on the system at full tilt despite evidence that looked bad. Now that he thought about it, real bad.

He had been trying to avoid the conclusion, but he knew exactly who he needed. Annika Tamm. She was known to his law school buddies as the Estonian Snow Queen, but Same just called her Tamm. She was definitely the right person for this charge. Now he just had to convince her to take the case, today.

As they drove up Ninth Street the officer riding shotgun called headquarters to get the requisite paperwork prepared. When they arrived the CCRE was completed and showed no previous criminal record. That form, along with the warrant, comprised everything they would need at booking.

They made a right turn onto Leigh Street and then immediately another right down to the lower level of the Health and Safety building. One look told Same the structure should have been imploded before it was ever finished. Now it was a gray bunker of a building that rained down two-by-two-inch ceramic tiles from its facade like a hail storm. At the rate the place shed tiles it should have been bare years ago.

The officer pulled the car into the lot and swung around to back up to the Sally Port. The gate raised and the car was backed in. They all sat until the gate slowly lowered into place.

The officers took a firm grip on Same's elbows and ushered him into the booking area. Suddenly Same had a new vision of law enforcement. The area was stark, hot, and well worn. The flow of paperwork over the island writing desk had long ago stripped off all of the enamel finish.

Same was taken into a tiny room where a monitor and fax machine sat on wall-mounted shelf. A copy of the paperwork was faxed to the magistrate. On the monitor Same could see the magistrate as she read over the paperwork. She quickly made a few notes and promptly a copy of the commitment order came spewing from another fax machine.

The papers were stamped and a nurse came from her office to complete a medical and risk assessment. The check sheet covered everything from suicidal ideation to itching to exposure to sexually transmitted diseases.

Same was impressed by the inclusive nature of the form, but was not asked if he had any medical concerns. Unless his health took a nosedive he had never in his life considered suicide. Well, maybe not until the last two hours, but he let that pass.

When the nurse blandly asked Same to sign the assessment form, he couldn't let the opportunity pass. Picking up the offered pen, he looked at the nurse and said, "I have a gene mutation on number 17."

The nurse sighed. "Is that where you live? I don't have any need to know that."

"No, that's not where I live. It's a gene in my DNA that will lead to early onset of dementia."

She turned and went over to an officer. Not attempting to lower her voice, she said wearily, "This one may need meds. Let's put him on suicide watch."

Same spoke up, "I didn't say that I needed meds, although that's interesting that you mention that. I said I have a problem that could lead to dementia in the future. God, I hope it hasn't started."

The nurse looked skeptical as Same picked up the pen and made a notation of his condition in the comments section and then signed the form. Shaking her head, she picked up the form and handed it to the processing officer.

Personal property inventory was completed. Same was only carrying $60 in cash, a few coins, and his wallet. Each item was carefully recorded. He was asked to remove his belt and shoe laces.

All the forms were handed to the booking officer, who sat on a raised area behind high counters with two other women. She fed information into a computer and waited to see if there were outstanding warrants or records in any other jurisdictions.

Finding nothing, she handed the forms over to the housing officer with a comment to the processing officer that there were no outstanding warrants or records. The two arresting officers looked relieved and bid their farewell to everyone.

Same was beginning to find the whole paperwork dance amusing in spite of himself. Finally, frontal and profile photos were taken and he was moved to the fingerprint machine. With his sweaty hands, Same was surprised that all his prints came out clear on the first try.

After the photos and prints he was escorted to a telephone and instructed that he had five minutes to make phone calls. He immediately dialed Street to arrange care for Mitch. Street said nothing as Same hit him with the short version of the story. Hearing silence, Same continued, "Uncle Cary, I don't know what the hell you will tell Mitch. He has had enough crap in the past couple months to wreck him for life."

"Same, Mitch is the least of your problems. I'll take care of him, you find a real good lawyer."

"You don't think I did this do you?"

"I don't know what to think, but if you say you didn't, then I believe you. What else can I do?"

"Nothing right now. I'll let you know. Got to hang up and call my lawyer. They only give me five minutes."

Annika picked up after only half a ring. "Tamm here," she barked.

Same paused for a moment. He absolutely hated to be contacting her after all these years only when his life was spiraling out of control. But he needed to beat this case quickly, and she was definitely the one to do it. "Tamm, it's Same," he said finally.

"Same!" she said immediately, "How delightful! How are you?"

Same breathed a big sigh of relief. He could clearly see the smile on her face, and her voice came down the line exactly as he remembered. God, he loved that accent. But there was no time for memories on this phone call.

"I'm in a bit of trouble, actually. I'm sorry I don't have more time on the phone, but I've actually just been booked into an executive suite at the Health and Safety building for a crime I didn't commit. The accommodations and service here aren't up to my usual standards, and I'd like to get out, sooner rather than later if possible."

Now it was Annika's turn to pause. Same thought she might be angry, but when she spoke she was all business. "Okay. You listen to me carefully. You do not speak to anyone about this case until I get there, not the police, not your family, not the guys in the holding tank, nobody. I will be there as soon as I can get out of court."

Same started to say thank you but was interrupted by an earful of dial tone.

Chapter Twenty-Six

....

After he hung up Same was told to follow the processing officer, who unlocked a metal door and guided Same into the holding tank. The room was about twenty feet by twenty feet with two wooden benches affixed to the wall. The lighting was surprisingly bright compared to the booking area.

There were twelve other men in the room. Two stood leaning against the wall and the rest were seated, with the exception of one who muttered while pacing in circles in the middle of the floor. When Same entered, all twenty-four eyes immediately focused on him. Within moments they had apparently appraised him, and their stares reverted back into space.

Not being versed on holding tank etiquette, Same sat on the edge of a bench, leaned forward, and rested his head on his hands. Thankfully, no one spoke. Over the next three hours four men were removed from the population and two were added. Same sat dejectedly and stared at the clock on the wall. It seemed to be a common pastime in the tank.

As he watched the second hand of the clock slowly make its rounds, Same thought back to when he had first met Annika. She made a dramatic entry into his life nearly ten years ago when they both played flag football in their first semester as law students at William and Mary.

The first time Same saw her, she was covering a cocky little bastard from Same's Contracts class. He was the kind of guy with Old Virginia Money written all over his preppy clothes and his big new SUV. He went by "T.W.", and it was no surprise to Same to see his name added to his father's law firm website as T. Worthington Allridge III after law school. Those guys always had to have first initials on the website.

Despite the fact that Annika had five athletic inches on him, T.W. saw his big opportunity in being covered by a girl and kept motioning at the line of scrimmage for the quarterback to hit him with a deep ball. When the ball was snapped, the quarterback dropped back a few steps, found inspiration from some long-lost glory days in high school, and launched a huge, loose spiral deep downfield and well out of range. T.W. pulled up and began jawing and gesticulating at the ex-jock, and few of the other players bothered to continue watching the trajectory of the overthrown pass.

But Same was transfixed. Eyes glued on the ball, streaking downfield, eating up yards with the most graceful, effortless stride Same had ever seen in his life, Annika closed in. With one last incredible leap, she launched her 5'10" frame horizontally, stretched out an impossibly long arm, snatched the ball into her chest, and crashed awkwardly into the turf just outside the back line of the end zone. Face down, she lay still.

Same ran with the rest of the players and spectators toward the end zone. As they crowded around her motionless body, he laid a hand on her back. He felt her struggling to breathe with her chest twitching as if she had rapid hiccoughs. A relieved murmur went through the gathering crowd as she slowly turned over, eyes squeezed closed and arms crossed above her head, and began taking choppy but deepening breaths.

Same couldn't help but notice how sharply her pale, pained features were set off against the blackness of her eyebrows and grass-strewn hair. She wasn't the supermodel that many of her countrywomen were, but Same found himself transfixed by the clean strength of her features, and embarrassed to be thinking about it while she was still recovering. As her breathing slowed, she gradually relaxed and opened dark blue eyes to look up at him with an unnerving directness. Same blinked and mumbled, stuttered something about an amazing catch, and offered her a hand up.

As Annika began to struggle to her feet, T.W. had finally bulled his way into the center of the crowd. He stuck out a pudgy paw and she hauled herself off the ground with help from both. As T.W. lifted with his right hand, he took the chance to pat her rear end with his left and said loudly, "Not a bad play, sweetheart, but you would have had the pick if you'd dragged a foot in the end zone when you caught it. It comes natural once you've played a bit more."

Annika's look froze him in his tracks. She leaned towards him and in a slightly Eastern European accent said quietly, "You touch me again, my friend, and I snap a little limp dick off a little rich prick." Turning to Same she said, "Thank you. Personally, I think that was a nice catch."

Same was hooked. In a couple weeks he managed to "coincidentally" get on the same study schedule in the same section of the library she used, and by the time exams came around they had become regular study partners. The immense pressure of first-semester exams led to several weeks of caffeine-fueled study binges and vodka-soaked post-exam decompression. True to her heritage, Annika appeared to remain unaffected by quantities of vodka that laid Same flat on his back.

It wasn't until they had pushed through the final exam that she finally took him to her apartment and into her bed. After handing in their Constitutional Law final, they had poured a liter of Stolichnaya in a water bottle and gone for a long walk down on the James River. The vodka kept them warm from the early flurries of snow falling on the river bank, and they walked and drank for several miles until Same could barely keep his feet. Annika half-carried him back to her apartment, with only a slight reddening of her eyes and the beginnings of a smile to show that she had killed the majority of the bottle.

They made love in the sparse surroundings of her tiny efficiency apartment. Only 5'7", Same would have felt awkward about the difference in height had he not been good and thoroughly drunk. As it was, he simply relished the pale, clean perfection of her skin and the length of her arms and legs as she wrapped herself around him.

Afterward they lay in her bed watching the snow drift down outside her window in the deepening evening. They talked of her family back in Estonia and the highly disciplined childhood that led to her scholarship offer from William and Mary. Same carefully avoided the subject of his father and Alaina and told stories of the antics of slightly-deranged gymnasts he had trained with in high school and as undergrad at William and Mary.

Through the remainder of their first year and the entirety of their second year, the two were generally inseparable. Same's friends were frankly astonished that it lasted. Annika never smiled and rarely spoke unless called upon to present an argument in class, and then she was precise, methodical, and without pity. Always meticulously prepared, she would regularly embarrass the students unlucky enough to be called upon to oppose her or foolhardy enough to challenge her of their own volition.

She earned the nickname "Estonian Snow Queen" after one particularly humiliating demolition of an unprepared sorority-type forced to argue against her on a hypothetical motion for summary judgment. As the tearful sorority sister made an impromptu, tearful exit from the auditorium to the hushed whispers of her classmates, the slightest flicker of a smile crossed Annika's face. "Finally, Your Honor," she concluded to the professor, "we ask this court to deny the motion for summary judgment and respectfully request that this court consider finding opposing counsel in contempt for her indefensible lack of professionalism." The room erupted in scoffs of disbelief and a few scattered laughs, and the sorority sister cast one last blurry, hateful glance back at Annika before stumbling out of the rear doors.

What the rest of the class never saw, or was permitted to see, was that her hard exterior was only one facet of her personality. Same loved the fact that she allowed him in to see her dry sense of humor and her intense loyalty. He wasn't really sure what had attracted her to him, but was content for the time to enjoy her company as they pushed through law school.

It all began to unravel after Mitch's birth. During their second year, Same got a late-night call from his father that Alaina had given birth to a boy. Senior sounded bizarrely robotic on the phone, and the conversation quickly ended. Same's visit to the hospital ended abruptly when he discovered that Alaina had left him off the approved visitation list.

Only a few days later, Alaina called. She needed to run a few errands, Tyler was feeling tired, and would Same be a dear and babysit his new brother for a few minutes. Same jumped at the chance, and spent one of the most incredible days of his life rocking his tiny, fragile baby brother. While baby Mitchell would not seem to bond with either his mother or his father, there was an instant connection to Same. They rocked and gurgled and snuggled together until Alaina finally returned, arms loaded with shopping bags, later that evening.

After that the calls from Alaina came regularly two or three times a week. Same felt guilty about pulling Annika away from studying for the two-hour round trip and babysitting in Richmond. As Same bounced and rocked the growing boy, he would pass by his father quietly counting his stack of bills in his study. Same hadn't spent much time at home over the past few years, and the frequent reminder of his father's decline was disheartening. He knew that this was his own path, and couldn't see subjecting Annika, and potentially their own children, to this depressing routine.

With her customary perceptiveness, Annika sensed him slowly pulling away. She didn't speak to him about it, but during the spring of their third year she quietly suggested that they find separate apartments in Richmond to be closer to their respective workplaces after they passed the bar. Same agreed, and they faded into a distant sort of friendship.

Over the years since graduation, Same had noted her appearance in the various bar journals that were kept in a tidy stack at H&B reception. She had taken a job in a small criminal defense firm in Richmond. One of Same's law school buddies in the DA's office reported that the Estonian Snow Queen moniker had stuck and the prosecutors knew to look sharp whenever she was on the docket. While over 98% of criminal cases were typically resolved by a negotiated plea deal, Annika had a reputation for forcing trials, and winning. She was a constant thorn in the DA's side.

Same's reverie was suddenly interrupted when a guard yelled out,

"Harrison!" Twenty tired, wary eyes locked on him again as he stood up and approached the door. The guard led him back through the metal door to a small, windowless room equipped with only a scratched stainless steel table and three metal chairs.

Annika was already seated at the table with her notepad in front of her. Just like law school, she was busily taking notes. She seemed somehow to have already gotten through nearly a full page. Based on the brevity of their telephone conversation, he couldn't imagine what they were about. He recalled asking her in law school why she took such copious notes even on material that she had obviously memorized cold. "The mind is a frail and forgetful tool," she said seriously, "unless aided by fierce and unyielding discipline." At the time, Same couldn't help but laugh at her intensity, but he was immensely thankful to have it on his side now.

She looked up as the guard opened the door, and Same was surprised to see how little she had changed since he last saw her six years ago. She kept her long, straight hair in the same simple chignon at the nape of her neck. Her pale features had sharpened somewhat, but they were still strikingly framed against jet black hair and eyebrows. Only a few extra wrinkles formed at the corners of her eyes as she smiled and moved toward him.

"You dumb shit!" she said, hugging him and laughing, "What have you gotten yourself into?"

"I can't tell you how good it is to see you, Tamm," Same replied. "But apparently you hung up on me before you caught the part about me not doing it."

The guard stood staring, taken aback by the sight of the Snow Queen not only smiling, but hugging a client. The guys on his shift were never going to believe this. "Officer Gonzalez," said Annika, releasing Same and turning her attention toward him. "I would like to consult with my client privately, please."

After the guard quickly closed the door, they pulled up chairs across from each other. "Now listen," said Annika, "tell me everything you know, and no bullshit. You know I can read you like a book if you try to hide anything."

Same decided to start from when they had last had a full conversation about six years ago. He briefly told her about his father's decline and death and the cancellation of a trial that he had entered for a potential drug. He described Alaina's horrific accident and the ME's report that cleared him, and his suspicions about Detective Jones's interest in the missing flash drive with Lance's $200,000 software. Then there was the mysterious closure of the Nanotine trials at U. Penn, the call from the nameless insider, Lance's hack into the FDA, Mitch's shooting, and the Ardmore kidnapping. Finally, he described in detail his discovery of Julie's body, the scene in her office, and his arrest earlier in the day.

Annika was expressionless through the whole tale, her eyes never moving from Same's as she flipped pages and scribbled furiously on her notepad. Only when he finally stopped talking did she lift her pen from the paper. He waited as she sat silently, reviewed her notes, and began tapping her pen on her teeth in the same pensive manner he remembered from the law school library.

As her silence stretched into a second and then a third minute, he could stand it no longer. "Tamm, you've got to believe me, I did not touch that woman. She was a good friend of mine."

She looked up and a slight smile crept into her eyes. "Of course you didn't. You don't have the balls for that sort of thing."

Same let out a sigh of relief. How many people could be so lucky to have a friend that would take them on their word without question after six years and a story like this? He counted his lucky stars as she continued, "As bizarre as your account is, and as stupid as you are to try to blindly hack your way into the inner workings of the FDA, it fits you perfectly and I believe every word."

Flipping to a clean page and beginning a formal to-do list, she then began laying out strategy. "Okay, here is what we do in the short term. You will be here until arraignment on Monday. There is a slight chance I can get you out on bail Monday, but you probably shouldn't expect to get out until later in the week. Do you need Mitchell to come stay with me?"

"No. But thanks. Dr. Street took him in."

"Okay, perfect. I have the feeling Cary is going to be a key character witness for us, and Mitchell is the closest you have to an alibi, so I'll go see both of them tomorrow."

Annika made a note, drew another bullet, and leaned forward. "Now listen, ordinarily I would tell a client to insist on their right to remain silent and refuse interviews with the police. In your case, however, I think we can turn the tables on them. I know Jones by reputation. He's effective in a sense, but the enormity of his ego causes him to make mistakes. Based on what I've heard, I'm betting this DNA match is a complete fabrication intended to make you confess."

Same cut in, "So can he just lie like that?"

Annika looked at him, exasperated, "How did you pass first year law before we started studying together? Of course he can, that's one of the oldest interrogation tactics. He can't actually create falsified government documents, so look at any pieces of paper he waves around claiming to be DNA results, but he can definitely lie."

Annika teasingly rolled her eyes at Same's ignorance. "Anyway, he will likely expect you to break down and cop a plea after a few nights in jail. He's also the sort to brag about his investigation, and that could expose some holes in his case, provided I'm not around to make him watch his step. So, I want you to send him a kite Monday morning saying you don't belong in here and you're ready to talk."

Same hesitated to expose his ignorance again but had to jump in. "Okay, but what's a kite?"

"Ah, yes, I forgot you don't sully your delicate mind with the slang of the criminal underworld," she said with a laugh. "A kite is just a note out from a prisoner. Just tell one of the officers that you want to talk to the detective and they'll get you a form. You should expect Jones to interrogate you for a while, but just stay focused on what we're trying to accomplish. We need to know what leads he's chasing and if there is evidence pointing away from you. Most prosecutors are pretty good about giving us exculpatory evidence, but the detectives often fail to give it to the prosecutors. They develop a theory of the case and it's just human nature to chase down and report only the evidence that fits that theory. So we need to get inside Jones's thick skull."

She allowed herself a quick smile. "He might close up if I'm around, but you can play wounded and draw him out. Just stay focused, let him bully you, and see what you can get. Keep strictly away from all of this FDA nonsense, but definitely let Lance's software drop a few times and see if he bites. His reputation is for being an asshole rather than crooked, but we can certainly create some reasonable doubts about him when he's on the witness stand. If we can't find hard evidence of the perpetrator, we may be able to leave a jury with enough suspicions about Jones to acquit you, at any rate."

Annika wrapped up with a couple more bullets and then quickly gathered her things and departed for another court setting. She made Same promise to try and call her as soon as the interrogation was over so that he could give her a precise description of what was said. Same found himself desperately wishing that she would stay a little longer, but after a quick peck on the cheek, she was out the door.

When he got back to the holding tank, only sixteen eyes studied his return. At this rate perhaps he'd have a single for the weekend, he thought. Wouldn't that be lovely.

Then there was that newly familiar noise of a key in a heavy lock, and the door opened and his name was called sharply. Same rose and went out the door. He was guided down a corridor past two cell blocks. At the third his escort said, "Turn to your right, and go into the first cell on your left. This will be your home until the next working day, which is Monday. On that day you'll be taken to the Manchester Court Building for your arraignment."

Without further comment the cell door was closed, locked, and the guard departed. Same looked around at his new home away from home. It wasn't the Playboy Resort. The cell measured about four by eight feet and contained a metal bunk with a piece of plastic-covered foam for a mattress. The folded sheet on top was definitely not 400-count Egyptian cotton. A stainless toilet was the only other furniture. Once Same had christened the toilet, he covered the mattress with the sheet. Decorating was easy and rent was cheap, he thought, maybe this place ain't so bad.

As he sat on the bed he noticed that the place was eerily quiet and hot with no windows. He removed his dress shirt and quickly noted how badly he needed a shower. Anxiety had over-powered his deodorant long ago.

He folded the shirt with each crease exact. He placed the shirt on one end of the bunk, pleased but not satisfied. He shook it out and holding it by the shoulder seams, once again folded it into a precise package. Placing the shirt back on the bunk, he noted an edge of the hem was sticking out. He reached for the shirt again but caught himself.

"Dude," he said aloud, "enough with the shirt."

He sighed, kicked off his shoes and sat back on the bunk with his back against the wall. A few minutes later he fell over on his side and drew up into a fetal position. He saw Julie's body again, and the images of his father and Alaina quickly rolled in. He felt his eyes grow hot but no tears came. Now he knew what despondency felt like.

Chapter Twenty-Seven

Two hours later Same was awakened by a heavy-set guard bringing the evening meal. Same looked at the bologna sandwich and applesauce and his stomach turned. Passively he asked the guard, "What time is it?"

The guard looked at his watch and replied, "Five-thirty. What's the problem? You got a hot date for the opera tonight?" He laughed sadistically and walked away.

Same let the guard's comment slide and managed to eat the applesauce and half of the sandwich. The only truly palatable part of the meal was the water in the large plastic cup. He placed the tray on the floor and sat staring at the opposite wall.

In conversation with himself, he formulated how he would maintain his sanity for the next two days. Mentally he would focus on Mitch, how he would make up to his brother for all he'd had to endure. Same forced himself to think of the good times they'd had, and there had been many. After all he'd practically raised the kid.

When his thoughts returned to reality he knew he had to plan how he would take care of himself. If he was going to survive in prison he had to stay in good shape. Within the confines of the cell he'd have to carefully plan a workout schedule.

He removed his T-shirt and trousers. Using the bars of the cell he went through every exercise he could devise using his arms and legs. Then it was a hundred pushups and two hundred crunches. Finally he ran in place until he was completely exhausted.

The guard returned for the food tray and brought more water. Same requested permission to take a shower but was told maybe tomorrow. He folded his trousers and used them for a pillow. He congratulated himself on his calmness and soon drifted to sleep.

The next two days passed without incident. On Sunday Same requested to make a phone call again. Apparently all the planets were in correct alignment and he soon found himself with Mitch on the other end of the line. The conversation was different than Same had envisioned, consisting mainly of Mitch reassuring him that everything would be fine. "Dude, Uncle Cary told me everything and I know that it's all a lie. You wouldn't have done that to Julie."

Tears came to Same's eyes at his brother's unswerving confidence. "Thanks, buddy. I needed to hear that. Be good and do what Uncle Cary tells you."

"Oh, I will. He lets me do whatever I want."

"Then I'd better talk with him again."

"I'm just kidding, man. You know I know how to behave. Anyway, I love you and I'll see you in a couple days."

As brave a front as Mitch was trying to project, Same could hear the quivering in his brother's voice. The little guy wasn't covering how scared he was. Same knew he had to hang up soon before his voice started shaking more than Mitch's. "All right, love you too, see you soon."

He quickly hung up the phone, turned, and walked back to his cell.

It was a long night of nightmares featuring Mitch gasping for air on the floor of his condo.

The next morning Same and four other men were placed in handcuffs and leg irons with chains connecting the two. By police van they were taken to the Manchester Courts Building on Decatur Street to appear before a District Court judge for arraignment.

As Same shuffled into the courtroom along with the other criminals, his humiliation was quickly displaced by hope when he spotted Annika. The whole process turned out to be largely perfunctory.

After the City Attorney had presented the charges against Same, the judge said robotically, "Mr. Harrison, do you have an attorney to represent you or do you need the court to appoint one?"

Before Same could answer, Annika stepped forward. "Your honor, I will be representing Mr. Harrison."

"Good morning, Ms Tamm. Good to see you again." Then he turned to Same, "Good for you, Mr. Harrison, I would say there is no need for a court appointment." Same noted a faint smile on the judge's face as he continued, "I am certifying Commonwealth v. Harrison to Circuit Court. Trial date will be set as quickly as possible."

Annika cut in quickly as the judge raised his gavel, "Your Honor, I would like to request a bail hearing."

The judge turned to the City Attorney, "Any objection to a hearing in two days?"

The lawyer looked up from another file and shook his head, "No, Your Honor."

"Very well, the hearing is scheduled for Wednesday at two pm. In the meantime, Mr. Harrison, you are remanded to the Richmond City Jail." With that the judge brought down his gavel.

Annika held a thumbs-up as the guards approached Same. He could see more than hear her whisper the words "stay focused" as the guards reached him. He nodded toward Annika, then turned and walked toward the door through which he had entered.

At the city jail, Same was taken aback by the noise and the heat. He was told by the housing officer about his new living arrangements. "Harrison, it's our understanding that you're a lawyer. We don't know if you have done criminal work or not. However, we are concerned with housing you in the general population. Therefore, we're placing you in a separate cell. You will have a cellmate who we removed from the population. He's from out of state so he should have no beef with you." With that she turned and left.

Heavy steel doors slammed behind him as a guard took Same into the cell block. He opened a cell door and Same entered. The other occupant was quickly on his feet.

"Well, it looks like I've got company."

The guard looked at the man and said, "Let's you two get along fine. Okay, Farley?"

Farley laughed. "Of course we will. Right, buddy?"

Same didn't reply. He went to the empty bunk and began placing the sheet over the mattress. When the guards had left Farley slowly sauntered over.

The man had Same beat by six inches and at least eighty pounds. Much of his exposed skin had tattoos, most of which were clearly of the jailhouse variety. But more disturbing were the eyes. He hardly ever blinked and the cold, steel color was unnerving.

Same stood up. "Hey man, I'm tired, it hasn't been one of the best days in my life, and I'm not much of a conversationalist. So let's just tolerate one another."

"Oh, not a 'conversationalist.' You one of them educated types, too good to talk to the likes of me?"

He moved closer to Same, who forced himself not to show emotion. "I'm not judging you. I just saw you for the first time a few minutes ago. You may be a doctor for all I know. What matters is that we're both in this shithole together so why make it worse?"

Farley began to laugh, "Shit, I think I like you. Maybe we can be friends."

Same didn't like the tone of the last comment but decided to let it ride. He wanted away from Farley, but knew not to turn his back at that point. Farley reached out and playfully slapped him on the shoulder before turning back to his bunk.

Several hours later, Same was mentally rehearsing questions and comments he wanted to drop on Jones when a loud bang on the steel of the door made both him and Farley jump. Leering in was the visage of the good detective himself.

"Hey boys!" he bellowed, "I didn't interrupt a private moment did I? I arranged for you two to be bunk-buddies 'cause I thought you might enjoy each other's company. Harrison, get your ass out here for a little chat. I'll let you get back to continue getting acquainted with Farley as soon as we're done."

Jones let out a loud laugh. He mopped his Paleolithic brow with a silk handkerchief and motioned for an accompanying officer to unlock the door. The hanky he slipped back into the breast pocket of a grey striped Valentino suit. Same caught himself wondering about the twisted psychology of an individual who insisted on wearing a suit that probably cost two grand into the heat of this place. Shaking his head, he quickly gathered himself. Game time. Stay focused. Play the game and have the last laugh.

The guard accompanying Jones led the way past a number of cells with mostly dozing occupants. With little else to do, most slept an astounding number of hours a day. Unable to repress his manic boorishness, Jones trailed behind and amused himself by banging on cell doors as they passed by.

They proceeded through several locked doors until they finally came to a tiny, barren room labeled "Interview 2." Four bare white walls contained a space no bigger than eight by eight feet. A small table and two chairs were shoved against the far wall away from the door.

Same slouched into the chair indicated by the guard and noted a video camera mounted high on the wall facing him. The guard remained standing silently by the door, staring at Same without expression. Meanwhile, Jones pulled the other chair uncomfortably close to Same's and loudly adjusted his considerable bulk until Same had to pull his legs slightly to one side to keep their knees from rubbing.

Jones pulled a four by six inch blue card from his jacket and again read Same the *Miranda* warnings now familiar to crime show fans around the country. Same signed the card where he was directed by Jones's thick finger to indicate that he understood his rights.

"Now, then," said the detective, leaning back and delivering what Same thought of as his Happy-Dick grin, "Your kite said something about not belonging in here. Of course, this is where we put the murderers and rapists, so you should be fitting right in."

He reached over and clapped Same on the shoulder. "You're going to be in here for a while champ. We've got a slam-dunk case and there's nothing I can do to help you there. But I have quite a bit of pull around here and down at the state pen. If you help this process move along smoothly, I promise you that I'll make sure you end up protected on the inside, with a cellmate that's not quite as friendly as Farley."

Suddenly Jones leaned in close. Happy-Dick grin changed to Mean-Dick grin and Same was blasted by the stench of coffee-fish breath, interestingly with more of a spoiled-salmon scent today than the usual day-old hot tuna with minced onion. "But if you decide to fuck with me, I will throw you to the fucking wolves. I will put a big juicy target on your sweet little ass and you will be a bitch to a succession of very angry men for the next forty years, if you live that long."

Same decided not to mention that he'd be checking out considerably sooner than that if something didn't come up to treat FTD. He made sure to flinch noticeably away from Jones while the threat was delivered, and was inwardly pleased to see the detective's satisfaction turn his grin back to Happy-Dick and then a classic Shit-Eater. "Okay, I get it," Same said. "I just … well, I mean, I just want to make sure I know what's going on before I make any big decisions. You know what I mean?"

Jones leaned back. "Sure, sure, that's smart. You're a smart guy and you're thinking now. You gotta think through how to make the best of a bad situation. Now I gotta tell you, you don't want to throw this thing to a jury. They're going to see all those pictures of that pretty little white girl laid out dead and raped and strangled on the floor and they're gonna hear from her upper-class, grieving parents and they'll be out for blood. Some of them are going to want to stick the needle in you themselves. You don't want that shit in front of a jury. You want to cooperate, you want to tell us what happened, and there's a chance that you can live a decent life in the state pen and maybe even walk out of there someday. Now that's the smart play here, and you know it."

"Yeah, I get that," said Same, keeping his eyes lowered. "I guess I'm still just on the fence though. I have a good record and a lot of good character witnesses. I have an alibi. Maybe I should take my chances?"

"Chances?" Jones snorted. "In here code for a jury trial is thirteen and a half. Twelve jurors, a judge, and a half-ass chance. For you it's thirteen, and that ain't lucky. You shot your wad on the dead girl. We matched your DNA. Once we got that match we wrapped our investigation and sent it to the DA in a pretty little bow. You have no half-ass chance. Your alibi witness is your nine-year-old brother, and no jury is going to believe that you didn't put him up to his testimony, particularly after the DA gets through ripping him apart. After that the jury is only going to hate you more for making that little boy lie for you."

And so it went. Same would come close to talking, then hesitate and back away. Jones hopped back and forth between Happy-Dick and Mean-Dick, occasionally slamming his fist on the table or pouring his fetid breath directly into Same's face to keep him shaken up. While he was pretty sure he wasn't giving the detective anything useful, Same wasn't particularly elated about anything he was discovering and wasn't too crazy about getting repeated doses of Jones's breath.

He was confident that Jones actually believed he had a DNA match, although that was hardly good news. The fact that the investigation was somewhat unprofessionally terminated immediately upon finding the DNA match could help Annika in her cross-examination, but it also meant there were no leads to other suspects subsequent to the match. Jones didn't react to mention of the stolen software in any meaningful way, other than a chuckling observation that the extent of his legal practice was going to be writs of habeas corpus for the other inmates from now on.

The one interesting fact that Jones did let slip was that their initial investigation turned up no signs of forced entry into the office. For Jones, that was simply another piece of evidence incriminating Same. But Same guessed that made it more likely that Julie must either have known her assailant well enough to let him in, or he was someone who worked in the office or had access through someone working in the office. That was somewhere to start, at least, and he hoped Annika could convince building security to give her access to the entry and exit records without going through the subpoena process.

The interrogation went on for hours. Same had to give Jones credit, he was one tenacious bastard. Finally, Jones packed up and left with the repeated pronouncement that he had enough evidence to make sure Same had an appointment to meet the needle in an execution room. Night had come by the time Same returned to his cell.

He saw his evening meal tray on his bunk and it was obvious that Farley had eaten half of it. Same just took the tray off the bunk and placed it next to the cell door. He ignored Farley's questions about where he had been all day.

After washing his face he removed his orange jumpsuit and stretched out on the bunk facing the wall. He managed to shut out the constant din that resonated throughout the building, but fought sleep. He knew Farley would be coming eventually.

Shortly after lights out Same heard him stirring. He felt vulnerable with his back turned, but decided to wait. He could sense Farley standing next to him and suddenly felt a tap on his shoulder. Farley whispered, "Hey, man, turn over. I've got something here for you."

Slowly Same rolled over. With the faint light from the hallway he could see Farley's penis and testicles hanging from the fly of his shorts. He acted drowsy, yawned, and asked, "What? What'd you want?"

"I want you to suck this like a good little pussy-boy and keep your voice down."

"No thanks, man."

"It's not an invitation. You do it nice or I will break that pretty little face of yours."

"Aw, shit, man," Same said, rolling on his side and sitting up on the side of the bunk. He was staring directly into Farley's erect junk. He took a deep breath and reached out to take the testicles in his left hand. He encircled the scrotum, stretching the testicles gently to his right. Farley moaned and tilted his head back. Same quietly pulled back his right hand and suddenly drove the heel of his right palm into Farley's extended testicles.

Farley screamed and weakly swung a fist at Same's head before going to the ground on hands and knees. Same easily ducked the fist and quickly leapt to his feet. Crouching low and driving through his right leg, he smashed a hard uppercut into Farley's side. He both heard and felt a satisfying crack as two of Farley's ribs buckled.

Farley gasped sharply and Same grabbed him by the jumpsuit and slung him back into his bunk, where he promptly curled into a fetal position. Suddenly Same heard guards running down the corridor and he jumped back into his own bunk.

When the guards arrived with flashlights they saw Same sitting on his bunk and Farley curled up facing the wall, struggling for breath.

"What's going on in here?" yelled one of the guards.

"Don't know," said Same, lifting his hands palms up. "I was asleep. It sounded like he tripped and caught the edge of the toilet."

"Is that what happened, Farley?"

Farley managed to grunt, "Yeah, tripped."

The two guards looked at each other, shrugged and left.

Same waited for ten minutes after the guards left. He eased quietly from his bunk and moved until he was inches from Farley's head.

"Hey!" he whispered loudly, and couldn't help a smile as Farley spasmed and covered his head with his arms. "I call that the ketchup bottle treatment. You even come near me again and I'm going to give you the wine making treatment. That's where I crush your little grapes until there's not an ounce of juice left. Trust me, you'll never get it up again. I'm in here for capital murder, asshole. I ain't got shit to lose."

Farley didn't reply. Same returned to his bunk and within minutes fell sound asleep. Neither felt the need to exchange words for the remainder of Same's stay.

***

On Wednesday the bail hearing went off without a hitch. Annika quickly showed that Same's faith in her was warranted. Her argument to the judge was concise and confident. "Your Honor, Mr. Harrison is a good citizen of this community and has a clean criminal record. He also has a sterling record for ethical representation of his clients as a senior associate with the largest law firm in the city. This case is based entirely on a single piece of forensic evidence which was obtained in the course of a highly unprofessional investigation and which conflicts with other evidence in the case. Most importantly, Mr. Harrison is the sole guardian of his nine-year-old brother, who he would never consider leaving. In short, he is not a flight risk and he needs to be out in order to care for his brother."

"And where is the brother now?" inquired the judge.

"He's being cared for by a friend of the Harrison brothers, Dr. Cary Street."

"I know Dr. Street, you're fortunate to have such a friend, Mr. Harrison."

"I know that, Your Honor," Same said quietly.

"Very well, I will set the bail at $100,000."

The paperwork was taken care of and Same was returned to the jail to retrieve his personal possessions. Annika waited outside the jail and loaned him her car to pick up Mitch.

Same had been in jail for Mitch's last day of the school year. Mitch had enrolled in a summer drama camp that started promptly the next week, so he was back at St. Christopher's in the mornings. Same was delighted when he arrived at the school just in time to catch Mitch walking out of the building. After hugs and fist bumping, they climbed into the car and Same pulled out of the parking lot.

"Sorry I was away, Mitch."

"It's okay. I knew you'd be back," he replied. The voice was confident but from the corner of his eye Same caught the worried look that belied his words.

They rode for a few minutes in silence until Same finally spoke. "Dude, listen to me. There's going to be no more dangerous stuff going on. I'm letting all the FDA stuff drop for now. We're just going to chill and have fun over your summer break. We'll get out of town on vacation whenever and wherever you want to go. In a couple months I'm going to kick this trial's butt, and then we're going to be back to just the two of us doing our thing, all right?"

Mitch sat quietly staring out of the window. Same was beginning to worry when Mitch suddenly turned to him, "Can we go to New

York? I want to see the Statue of Liberty."

Same smiled and breathed a sigh of relief. "You bet your fanny we can."

Chapter Twenty-Eight

Agent Tatum thought things had worked well, up to a point. His people had been following the Watsons' email and telephone, and there was nary a peep out of them. They seemed to have been scared straight. Harrison was out of action and anything he would say would be discredited by the criminal charges. Unfortunately, some moron judge had let him out on bail. Somehow he knew the higher-ups weren't going to be satisfied with that.

Tatum swore to himself as he walked to his boss's office. He just hoped that pinstriped bitch wasn't there. He didn't bother checking with the boss's secretary but went straight to the conference room. His good luck Irish clover must have lost a leaf, because there she sat with her bow-tied boyfriend.

The Director looked up with an annoyed expression. "Come in, Agent Tatum. Have a seat. You've met our guests."

"Believe I have."

No one offered a greeting.

Ivy Legal spoke before Tatum's butt had touched the chair. "Well, Tatum, it seems your elaborate scheme has not worked. Harrison is out on bail and will probably continue to create mischief."

Tatum didn't respond. He simply kept his cold eyes latched on Ivy

Legal. He didn't blink until Pinstripe spoke, then he transferred his glare to her.

She pulled at the lapels of her jacket as an airline flight attendant would adjust her safety belts. "Agent Tatum, the entire situation has grown far more complicated than we anticipated. Your efforts have been significantly less effective than we were led to expect."

Tatum was convinced his career was already over. He turned to the Director, "Sir, are these people here to do my annual performance review? I thought that was in November."

The boss wasn't laughing at his weak joke. "Maybe it's time for an interim review, Agent."

Tatum couldn't help but laugh. "Do what you want, I'm ready to go, but hear me out first." He turned to face Pinstripe and Ivy Legal. "I find it strange that you two are willing to go to such lengths to shut down one poor bastard who's only trying to get a few answers to treat his family's dementia."

Pinstripe's face blanched. She turned to the Director, who only stared at Tatum. Again she faced Tatum, "As we discussed, it's not necessary for you to understand the reason for your assignment. It's your job to execute your assignment."

The agent couldn't suppress his smile, "Yeah, matter of fact I have heard that a few times during my twenty-four years here."

From his peripheral vision Tatum could see the flicker of a smile on his boss's face. Emboldened, he continued, "I'm going to make an assumption here, ma'am, I assume you and your friend are with the FDA. So why all this excitement about Nanotine?"

Ivy Legal quickly replied, "Who said we're talking about Nanotine?

Tatum was indignant, "Don't screw with me. I complete assignments, but I always keep my eyes open and my ear to the ground. I just can't seem to find authorization for these sorts of operations within the mandate of the FDA."

Ivy Legal spoke coldly, "Quite the contrary, Agent Tatum. Since you're so curious, the FDA Modernization Act of 1997 gives the agency great discretion in accomplishing its objectives."

"I thought you might go there," said Tatum, smiling broadly. "It's funny, I was just reading an article by one of your former deputy commissioners. Turns out a number of drugs like Pirfenidone and Avastin have run into newsworthy roadblocks recently. Your people usually seem to prefer long, drawn-out trials to insulate the agency from critics who say your decisions have to do with cost rather than safety. Now you're trying to nip trials in the bud before they even start. From what I've seen, there's no question about Nanotine's safety or effectiveness, and it won't even cost that much, so just what kind of game are you running over there?"

Ivy Legal's face was beginning to lose its ivory tower calmness. "Tatum, unless you've had more education than I'm aware of, I don't think you're qualified to discuss complex pharmaceutical research."

He turned abruptly to the Director. "I don't see anything to be gained by Agent Tatum's continued presence in this meeting. It appears we will have to assume responsibility for this project."

Looking thoughtful, the Director said quietly, "Will you no longer need the assistance of the FBI?"

"We may well require assistance in the future, but for the time being we'll take matters into our own hands."

Tatum was too pissed off by this point to exit gracefully. "You jokers keep playing God over there and somebody's going to send you to answer to him sooner rather than later."

Ivy Legal leapt from his chair and leaned across the table. "Are you threatening us, Tatum?"

"Of course not, pal, I'm not 'qualified' for that. I'm just telling you, these operations are not child's play. Take matters into your own hands and innocent people are going to get hurt."

Pinstripe was now standing too. "Like Julie Welford? Or was she just collateral damage in your brilliant scheme?"

"Look, lady, I didn't order that and I don't know how that went down. Maybe Harrison did kill her." He pointed at the two visitors. "What I do know is you people need to check your egos at the door before you get yourselves or innocent people hurt. Trust me when I tell you that the people you try to eliminate tend to have real strong objections to your plans. Harrison in particular."

As the three stared red-faced across the table, the Director finally rose wearily to his feet. "Well, I think that about wraps things up." Ivy Legal and Pinstripe stormed out in icy silence and Tatum followed shortly thereafter. The Director quietly pulled a flask from the breast pocket of his suit jacket and poured a healthy dose into his coffee. Only four more months until retirement, he thought to himself. The images of his quiet little hunting cabin in Montana filled his head as the combination of whiskey and caffeine slowly eased the pressure in his chest.

PART TWO

Fiat justitia ruat caelum

LET JUSTICE BE DONE, THOUGH THE HEAVENS FALL

Chapter Twenty-Nine

....

Same stared at the ceiling as dawn crept through the draperies of his living room window. The past three months had been a glorious reprieve from the hell of the spring. He had cashed in his accumulated vacation days at work and he and Mitch had travelled up and down the East Coast for most of July and August.

In the back of his mind his trial date loomed, but in the right spot on the right beach he could sometimes go for half a day without thinking about it. Annika had obtained a sample of the semen found on Julie's body and submitted it to a private lab for testing. With the backlog of DNA samples waiting to be tested, she had warned Same that it could be months before they got the results. But whoever had been after him seemed to be content with the stalemate, and Same was fine with that as well. For now, at least.

But now it was time to pay the piper. Jury selection started promptly at 9:00 am, and Same had set his alarm for 6:30 to make sure he had plenty of time to get himself and Mitch ready before Uncle Cary picked them up for the short trip to the courthouse.

There was no need for the alarm though; Same had been awake for hours. Mitch was curled up on the couch beside him. They had watched the first Rocky movie last night. Mitch had fallen asleep before it ended and he could beg for a "double feature" with Rocky IV. The fourth was always their favorite. Instead of carrying him to his bed, Same had just pulled a couple blankets around them and finished the double feature himself.

When the second movie was over he closed his eyes and soaked in the peaceful, rhythmic rise and fall of his brother's breathing. This is what it was all about. This two-person family was what he was fighting for. This kid deserved to grow up with a family and a chance to prove his merit. To Same that was all a person really deserved from this world, and he was going to do his best to ensure that Mitch got that chance.

Mitch finally stirred as the alarm began to beep in Same's bedroom. As he opened his eyes he popped up almost immediately. "I fell asleep," he said, disappointed. "We didn't even get to watch Rocky IV."

"Dude," said Same, "You've got all the lines memorized anyway. You can probably recite the entire thing while you sit through all the boring jury selection stuff this morning."

Mitch put on a shocked expression. "Boring? Are you kidding me? Annika says jury selection is one of the most critical parts. She said I need to look professional in my suit and sit as close to you as I can and pay attention so I can take notes of how each potential jurors looks at you so we can decide which ones to strike."

Same couldn't help but smile. That clever, clever girl. Softening the jurors' hearts through strategic placement of the defendant's bright-eyed, dressed-up little brother in close proximity to the defendant, who was his last remaining family after the tragic deaths of both his mother and father. A jury trial was nothing if not an elaborate show, and Annika was undoubtedly a brilliant stage-master, letting no opportunity pass to swing the emotions of the jury to her side.

Mitch and Same quickly showered, dressed, and wolfed down breakfast. They tried to kill time by flipping through the morning paper, but when Street came to pick them up he found them standing down on the street ready to go. He leaned slowly out of the driver's window of his dark metallic blue 2010 Porsche Panamera. "A little antsy this morning, boys?" he said.

Mitch practically bounced into the front seat and Same slid quickly into the back. Street glanced at his phone and said absently, "I've just got to pop round for a couple errands before we get to the courthouse."

"Uncle Cary, we can't!" cried Mitch, looking at his watch. "It's 8:00 and Annika said we should be there by 8:30 sharp or we might get stuck in the line getting into the building and be late!"

"Ha! Got you!" Street chucked him on the shoulder. "I just wanted to see if a person could actually jump out of their skin. You got pretty close, and I think your brother back there was about to wet himself."

Turning to look at them both, Street said seriously, "Now listen, from what I've seen Annika is one of the best defense lawyers in the business. But four brains are better than one. We need to stay calm and focused and contribute what we can. So keep your eyes and ears open and don't let anxiety get in the way of your concentration." He paused a moment to let his words sink in, then turned forward and revved the engine. "All right, let's do it then," he said, and nosed the car out into the street.

The trip only took fifteen minutes via Main Street and then up Ninth to the John Marshall Courts Building. They made a left onto Clay and then a right into the parking lot across from the court. Street parked at the far end away from any other vehicles.

Same laughed, "Little antsy with this new machine of yours, Uncle Cary?"

"Look, it was a big decision to buy this beast. But I couldn't let you get ahead of me with that electric gizmo car. Thought I'd go the other way and use more petrol."

Mitch chimed in, "I think it's so cool that you both have these cars. I can't lose."

Same ruffled Mitch's hair and the boy rolled his eyes at his brother. They crossed the street and climbed the steps of the nondescript red brick building.

Annika had them arrive well before the 9:00 surge of defendants, lawyers, and jurors, so they proceeded quickly through the metal detectors and took an empty elevator up to the third floor. Stepping out, they found her waiting outside the courtroom just as the bailiff came out to unlock the doors.

Annika gave Street a quick peck on the cheek and put her hand on Same's shoulder. Turning her address to Mitch, she said, "Thanks for keeping these guys on time, Mitchell. My first rule for keeping jurors on my side is to respect their time. Always show up before they do, and always be prepared." Mitch nodded seriously, and Annika turned back toward Same with a quick smile. "All right, game on, let's go in."

As they walked in Same couldn't help but admire the interior of the courtroom. It was really quite posh in comparison to the crowded district court where his arraignment and bail hearing had been held. It was certainly cleaner.

Same had never had occasion to appear in one of the criminal courtrooms and he wasn't particularly happy that it was his own trial that was responsible for his first visit. The public seating looked quite comfortable with the seats covered in a blue brocade fabric. The trial area was all in walnut with a metal railing separating the public area from the trial proceedings. The walls were all white and punctuated with portraits of prominent judges from the past. Behind the judge's bench was a free-standing walnut wall with a brass seal of Virginia.

Annika walked quickly up the aisle and turned to the right to deposit her briefcase. She motioned Street and Mitchell to sit in the first row of seats just behind the defense. Wordlessly she took a stack of files from her briefcase and began flipping through them, occasionally scratching new notes over old notes. Same spent some time readjusting the knot on his tie to ensure the dimple fell directly in the middle. A sideways glance and lifted eyebrow from Annika made him realize that he had been at it for a while, and he quickly put his hands in his lap to keep from obsessing over the tie. He caught himself thinking that if stress caused early onset of the disease, he was royally screwed.

As he waited anxiously for the arrival of prosecutor, judge, and potential jurors, Same watched Annika work and forced himself to think back to their strategy session around Street's kitchen table the previous week. Their review of the facts had left them all a bit gloomy. Julie had been strangled between midnight and 2:00 am Sunday morning. Semen matching Same's DNA profile had been found on her abdomen, but there were no signs of rape. Their own retesting of the semen sample had come back showing a match to Same's DNA and they still had no clues about how the sample could have been rigged.

The access logs did not show when anyone had left the floors belonging to the firm, and did not show anyone entering the firm's space after the janitorial crew went through at 9:00 pm Saturday night. Detective Jones had not uncovered, or had not admitted to uncovering, any other leads or evidence, and the State seemed content to proceed based solely on the damning DNA evidence. From what Same could see, they wouldn't need anything else.

"Okay," Annika had said finally, "I know we've been over all this before, but let's go over our strategy again."

"Beg for mercy?" Same asked.

Annika threw him a disgusted look and shifted her address to Mitchell and Street, "There's an old lawyer joke that goes something like this: if the facts are against you, argue the law. If the law is against you, argue the facts. If both are against you, holler and pound the table. Well, we don't have much in the way of facts or law, but I think we can do better than pounding the table.

"Now, I want to come at this thing from two angles. First, I want to force the State to prove their case beyond a reasonable doubt. I want to push them on their procedures for the DNA evidence, and I definitely want to push Detective Jones on his investigation. I'm going to allow Jones to open up the full aroma of his personality to the jury, and then I'm going to hammer him on cross. We don't have any hard evidence against him, but I want to suggest to the jury that he could be involved somehow, and at the least he's an arrogant, unprofessional pig. A juror voting for acquittal is often voting against the State as much as she is voting for the defendant.

"Second, I want to put on a slew of character witnesses to build up your image. Most defendants are repeat criminals and don't want to open the door to character evidence. But the State thinks they have an open and shut case here and they're only putting on a few witnesses. I want to shift this trial so that it's about your character, not your DNA. We'll keep putting on character witnesses until the judge makes us stop. Hopefully that will be freshest on the jurors' minds when they go back to deliberate."

Same found himself watching Mitch as he listened intently to Annika. Mitch seemed to find the process utterly fascinating and had developed a near reverence for Annika, so Same had kept him involved in every aspect of the case as it moved forward. As role models went it was hard to top Annika. The way things were proceeding, she was certainly looking better than a demented older brother slowly rotting in prison.

Same shook his head to clear the morbid thoughts as Annika continued, "Same, we'll reserve you for the end, depending on what transpires. But before all that, we need a good jury. So we're looking for some sweet old ladies with sympathy for our dear, gentle family-man here, and we're looking for some anti-establishment technical types who will understand the State's burden of proof and question the evidence. A guilty verdict must be unanimous, so we only need one juror to hold out on our side. A hung jury is a win for us."

Same was thinking he'd really rather prefer an acquittal and a well-written apology from Detective Jones and the DA, when suddenly his reverie was snapped by the sharp voice of the bailiff.

"All rise!"

From behind the walnut wall emerged the small, bent frame of the Honorable Richard Jefferson Ewell, Presiding Judge of the 13th Judicial Circuit of Virginia. His family was apparently blessed with both fertility and long life, and at eighty-nine years old he was actually the last surviving grandchild of Confederate General Richard Stoddert Ewell of Prince William County. With his hobbled walk heavily favoring the same leg lost by General Ewell during the war, the lawyers practicing before him simply called him the General.

Annika had warned Same before the trial to speak up because the General got annoyed when he couldn't hear. But she also confided with a wink that the General was a bit partial to her. Apparently he lived for tall women and hard-fought battles in his courtroom.

The General sat and opened the file before him, carefully organizing various papers on his desk. With the judge's diminutive stature and hunched posture, Same could scarcely see the man over the front edge of the bench. Finally he peered out into his courtroom. A couple of reporters and students had trickled into the back of the courtroom, and the General's sharp gaze quickly silenced their whispers and shuffling notepads.

The prosecutor's table, still empty, held his eye for a moment. Then he cleared his throat several times, poured a drink from the water pitcher on his desk, and took a deliberate sip.

Finally, nearly a minute after his entrance, he spoke, "Please be seated. Now calling case number 05874, Commonwealth v. Tyler L. Harrison, Jr." Just as he finished calling the case the rear doors popped open again and a middle-aged man came hurrying up to the prosecutor's table, breathing heavily and trailed by fresh-faced and wide-eyed intern. Without looking at the new arrivals, the General turned to Annika. "Ms. Tamm, in the absence of the State to prosecute the case this morning, I would consider a motion to quash the indictment at this time."

Melvin Biggs, the newly arrived prosecutor, stood motionless with a slightly shocked expression. He was a short man, possibly 5'5" on a good morning, and aging not so gracefully into his mid 50's. He was dressed in a slightly wrinkled, ill-fitting suit that did little to hide his expanding waistline. Annika had explained to Same that drawing Melvin on the case was both good and bad. On one hand he was a fair man who took to heart that the prosecutor's task was not to win cases, but to see that justice was done. On the other hand he had an encyclopedic knowledge of the law and couldn't be bested on that front. Annika admitted that she quite liked him and wryly noted that it would be almost a shame to have to demolish him in this case.

Annika raised her eyebrows at Same and rose quickly. "Your Honor, the defense moves to quash the indictment for lack of prosecution."

"In light of his recent appearance, that motion will be denied," the General quickly replied.

Finally turning his address to Biggs, the General welcomed the prosecutor, "So good of you to join us for jury selection, Mr. Biggs. I will expect to see you in my courtroom 15 minutes early for all settings in this case moving forward."

Biggs put on his best apologetic expression. "Absolutely, Your Honor. I'm sorry for my tardy arrival this morning but the elevator..."

The General cut him off with a wave of his hand. "Let's not delay the proceeding any further with apologies. Please read the indictment so that the defendant may enter his plea."

Same caught himself before he cracked a smile. He knew trial courts had wide discretion in the conduct of a trial, but he had never seen that move before. It was amusing when Biggs was on the hot seat, but he knew Annika would be there in her turn.

The charge was read and Same forced himself to make eye contact with the judge and deliver his "Not Guilty" in a strong, clear voice, as if that would somehow convince the General to throw the case out. The jury panel was then called in and Same caught his first glimpse of the ordinary citizens from whom would be selected a jury that would decide his fate.

They filed in slowly, looking around the courtroom hesitantly in much the same way he had when he first walked in this morning. As they sat in their assigned rows on Biggs's side of the aisle, their eyes all eventually came to rest upon Same, wondering what he had done and what kind of monster lurked under that average exterior. Same saw a number of looks that he characterized as curiosity, fear, or mistrust, but none that were particularly sympathetic. Hopefully Annika could do something about that.

The General began with some introductory remarks and general qualifications for service. Two jurors who were no longer residents of Richmond were excused, and the parent of a young infant followed soon after. The floor then passed to Biggs to question the panel. Biggs droned on for an hour about the role of a jury and the importance of considering only the evidence presented on the witness stand, and then determining whether that evidence proved each element of the criminal offense as presented in the charge that would be given at the conclusion of the trial.

When it was Annika's turn, she picked up on Biggs's discussion of the burden of proof. In more concise and less lawyerly language, she engaged the panel in a discussion of what it meant to prove something beyond a reasonable doubt. She noted the variety of standards that were used in different types of cases, from "preponderance of the evidence" to "clear and convincing evidence." In most states, the State only had to prove certain facts by the lower standard of clear and convincing evidence in order to do things like taking children away from abusive parents. But in criminal cases like this, the Constitution required that the State prove its case "beyond a reasonable doubt," the highest standard used in the legal system. Indeed, each element of the offense written in the jury charge had to be proved beyond a reasonable doubt. Finally, she asked each potential juror individually whether he or she could follow the law and acquit Same if they had a reasonable doubt about any element of the offense.

As Same watched Annika work the room, he was reassured to see the connection she developed with the potential jurors. The show she put on was certainly better than Biggs, but Same still had serious doubts about whether her show could beat Biggs's hard evidence.

By lunchtime the parties had concluded their questions, the panel had been excused from the courtroom, and each side had exercised its peremptory strikes on those individuals it felt undesirable for any reason. The first thirteen jurors remaining after peremptory strikes constituted the jury plus an alternate, and the rest were sent home.

The jury of his peers was finally seated in their official seats in the jury box. Same took a long look at each as the General went over final instructions. Annika had chosen well, and it wasn't a bad-looking group. They seemed to have gotten one sweet old lady and three technical types. At the very least they were all paying close attention, and Same supposed that's all he could really hope for.

As the General finally excused the jury for the day, Same couldn't help remembering Jones's words during his interrogation. Thirteen-and-a-half for a jury trial but Same only had thirteen. Well, he had a feisty old General for a judge and twelve decent folks for a jury. He may just have that half-ass chance after all.

Chapter Thirty

On Annika's suggestion they arrived early the next morning to avoid most of the gathering flock of television cameras outside. The murder of a prominent young lawyer, particularly one as photogenic as Julie, had brought out reporters like a horde of locusts. Seats in the courtroom became scarce as 9:00 got closer.

As Same casually surveyed the crowd, he felt like a gladiator in the Roman Coliseum. Sure hope they give me the thumbs-up when the time comes, he thought.

Suddenly the thought vanished. In the last seat on the back row sat the man in the blue blazer. The blazer was missing now but the face was there. Same couldn't pull his eyes away from the man, who simply stared straight ahead.

Same turned to face Street in the row behind the defense table. In a low voice he said, "Uncle Cary, don't look anywhere but straight ahead. There's a guy in the far corner seat behind you. He's the one that was shadowing me a couple months ago. I have no idea what he's doing here, but keep an eye on him."

"Are you sure?" Street replied.

"That's the guy. I'd recognize him anywhere."

"All right, I'll keep an eye on him."

Same shook off his latest case of jitters and turned back to Annika at the defense table. Biggs arrived punctually at 8:45 and exchanged a brief nod with Annika before they both turned to the perpetual lawyer's occupation of flipping through notes in their legal pads. Same felt his stomach seething as he watched the two lawyers calmly flipping their pages. He wondered if this was a habit litigators practiced simply to hide their nerves. It seemed to be working if it was. On the other hand, maybe it was just easier to be calm when it wasn't your ass going to prison at the end of the day. At least it was a distraction from the thoughts of the man in the back of the court.

The bailiff's sharp "All rise!" jolted the proceedings to order. The General hobbled in and enjoyed his usual agonizingly deliberate process before allowing the courtroom to sit. After calling the case and ensuring no pretrial motions were left undecided, the General brought in the jury and the trial began.

The indictment against Same was read before the jury and again he had the opportunity to deliver his most authoritative "Not Guilty." Again he felt little better after doing so.

Then Biggs was up for the State's opening argument. Unlike the painful droning of his presentation during jury selection, Biggs was direct, concise, and brutally effective in opening arguments.

"Ladies and gentlemen of the jury," he began quietly, "this is a very simple case. The evidence will show that Julie Welford was a lovely, energetic young woman who had recently accepted a prestigious partnership opportunity at the renowned Richmond law firm of Hustings and Billings. This wonderful young woman's life was tragically and brutally ended around midnight on the evening of Saturday, June the second of this year, when she was strangled at her desk in the H&B offices.

Fortunately for the cause of justice, there was a clue left at the scene of this heinous crime that led us to the perpetrator. You see, he left a glob of semen defiling Julie's body, and the DNA taken from that semen matches one man."

Biggs paused for emphasis as he slowly extended his arm. Every person in the courtroom held their breath until his arm came to rest, pointing one index finger directly at Same. Boy did his performance come up a notch since jury selection, Same thought. With all eyes on him, Same felt an unbearable urge to move, to straighten his tie, to scratch his face, anything. But he forced himself to keep his shoulders square and his eyes leveled at the speaker, just as Annika had instructed him. He hoped the jury picked up on this body language as much as she believed.

"The defendant, Tyler L. Harrison, Jr.," said Biggs finally, his voice now rising. "The evidence will show that the defendant was an associate at the firm. We don't know for sure why the defendant committed this horrible murder. There is evidence that the recent death of his father and the pressure of caring for his younger brother may have sent him into fits of rage that resulted in his use of violence in his workplace. But make no mistake. The DNA does not lie. The defendant brutally ended this beautiful young woman's life with his bare hands, and then left his filthy semen to befoul her asphyxiated corpse."

The courtroom sat in shocked silence as Biggs caught his breath and slowly shuffled back to the prosecutor's table. Not a sympathetic eye in the courtroom now, thought Same. And it was sharp of Biggs to introduce his care of Mitch right from the start to undercut whatever sympathy value Annika would be able to get from it. Same was beginning to think drawing Melvin Biggs as a prosecutor was considerably more bad than good.

The General cleared his throat and took a sip of water, not bothering to hide the broad smile on his face. Based on the opening salvo this was shaping up to be a particularly good one, and the General was clearly enjoying himself. "Ms. Tamm?" he asked.

Annika stood quickly. "Your Honor, the defense will reserve opening argument until the presentation of our case."

Clearly disappointed, the General continued, "Very well then. Mr. Biggs, please call your first witness."

Biggs seemed disconcerted by Annika's unusual choice to reserve opening. Annika had explained to Same last night that the usual practice was to present the defense theory of the case at the beginning. But in this case their defensive theory may rely on openings presented by Detective Jones, so she wanted to reserve her opening to see what she could get out of Jones before she suggested anything to the jury.

Shrugging off his concern, Biggs stood. "Your Honor, we call Detective Richard Jones."

Right on cue, both back doors slowly opened and in strode the man himself. He seemed to thoroughly enjoy the eyes of the courtroom, and cast a broad smile to several reporters as he strutted to the front. For this occasion he had chosen a beautifully tailored black wool Armani suit with a crisply starched white shirt and solid white silk tie. His white silk handkerchief protruded artfully from his front breast pocket, and he paused for a moment at the witness stand to wink at the court reporter and adjust his hefty sterling silver Bulgari cufflinks before taking his seat. What a piece of work, thought Same. Like a muskox parading down Savile Row.

After Jones was sworn in and provided some simple background on his qualifications and experience as a detective, Biggs got straight to the point.

"On the morning of Monday, June the fourth, were you called to investigate a suspicious death?"

"Yes, sir. I was called out to the offices of Hustings and Billings. We heard some lady got strangled to death."

"Okay, and are the offices of Hustings and Billings within the city limits of Richmond?"

"They sure are."

"Where did you go when you arrived at the office?"

"We went up to the 16th floor, which is the main entry for the Hustings office space, and over to the office of the deceased, next door to Harrison's. I'd been there before for an earlier suspicious death so I knew my way around."

Same and Biggs both stiffened at the nonresponsive and highly prejudicial answer. Biggs cast a nervous eye over at Annika, but she merely continued scribbling notes.

Biggs quickly continued, "Can you describe the scene in the deceased's office when you arrived?"

"You betcha," said Jones with a trademark grin aimed directly at Same. "The lady was lying on her back by her desk with her skirt up over her breasts and only white panties below the waist. Her right leg was bent up under her left. She had bruises on her neck and she was all blue from being strangled." Pointing to Same he continued, "Plus she had this guy's semen on her stomach."

Both Biggs and the General jumped at the last response and turned immediately to Annika. Same and half the courtroom audience could have made the objection to the last statement, but Annika let it slide again.

Same knew it was a dangerous game Annika was playing. By not objecting to inadmissible pieces of his testimony, she could give Jones just enough rope to hang himself. But her failure to object also meant that they wouldn't be able to complain about this prejudicial testimony on appeal, if it came to that.

Hesitantly, Biggs continued, "Um, okay, and just restricting your answers to the facts you observed, can you tell me if you discovered the identity of the victim?"

"Sure," said Jones, "her name was on her ID, which was in a purse on her desk. It was Julie Welford."

"Okay, and in the course of your investigation of the crime scene, did you take any samples of biological materials?"

"Absolutely, I had the forensic techs take a cheek swab from several males who were present at the office that morning, and at the post the medical examiner took a sample from Harrison's deposit on the broad."

Same could feel himself squeezing the arms of his chair to keep from saying anything. Even as much of a bastard as Jones was, making a scene to defend the honor of his friend would not bring Julie back, and it sure wouldn't help to dispel the notion that he was prone to "fits of rage."

The General, looking peeved, cut in suddenly. "Mr. Jones, you will avoid crude references to the victim in this case or I will find you in contempt and stay this trial until you've had the opportunity to enjoy the accommodations at our local jail for an evening. Do you understand me?"

His smirk slightly diminished, Jones nodded affirmatively and the General motioned for Biggs to proceed.

"Okay. So, Detective, what did you do with the biological samples?"

"I had the forensic techs send them on over to the DFS like always."

"And DFS stands for the Department of Forensic Science?"

"Right on, Counselor."

Same caught Biggs rolling his eyes as he turned away from the Detective. At least the prosecutor also realized what a colossal ass the man was. Biggs took a breath and looked at his notes at the prosecutor's table, then turned back to the witness.

"Detective, without getting into the circumstances of the encounter, can you tell me if you had occasion to encounter the defendant earlier this year, prior to the morning of your investigation of Ms. Welford's death?"

The Detective snorted. "You mean when he killed his stepmother?"

The courtroom erupted in gasps and the General literally jumped to his feet behind the bench. "Stop!" he shouted. "Detective, you will restrict your answers to the questions asked. You've been in court before and you know the drill. Get out of order again and you will be in contempt."

Swinging his head to Annika he shouted, "Ms. Tamm! Are you awake over there? Feel free to offer objections to inadmissible evidence at any time you see fit."

Same knew that criminal trial lawyers like Annika were extremely sensitive to evidence of alleged prior crimes, which were almost never admissible at the guilt or innocence phase of a trial. Under ordinary circumstances, Jones's comment could have been grounds for a mistrial. Holding her objections at this point took some nerve.

"Your Honor," replied Annika calmly. "I will certainly defend my client's interests."

The General threw a withering glance at the audience and the twittering among the reporters quickly silenced. He motioned to Biggs to begin again.

Biggs, glancing nervously at Annika again, tendered a final question. "In the course of that investigation, did you discover that the defendant's father had recently died and the defendant's brother was left in his sole custody?"

"Tyler Senior died about two weeks before I bumped into Junior," said Jones, giving Same one of his best shit-eating grins. "Can't say as the old man would have wanted it that way, but Same got custody of his little brother once the boy's mother was out of the way."

The General's face began to get red, but before he could erupt, Biggs quickly turned the witness over for cross-examination. Here we go, thought Same, let the games begin.

Annika popped to her feet and gave the detective a delightful smile of her own. "Mr. Jones," she began cheerily, "let me start by congratulating you on your sartorial taste. That suit is exceptional. Is that Armani?"

A slight flush crept into Jones's face and he stammered proudly, "Yes. Why, yes it is. By the way, sweetheart, it's Detective Jones."

"Ah, of course." She pointedly made a note in her legal pad before continuing. "Did you have that tailored here in Richmond?"

"No, ma'am. I only select my wardrobe from New York, actually."

"Well, I can tell you're a man who takes great pride in his professional appearance." Annika put on a tone Same recognized as mock admiration. "With the cufflinks thrown in I'll bet that put you back a month's wages! I've seen a suit like that go for $3,000!"

"A gentleman wouldn't say, Ms. Tamm, but I can tell you you're a bit on the low end. It was worth it, though, wouldn't you say?" he asked, now positively beaming.

"It was definitely worth it," she said, throwing the Detective a quick wink. "But it's got to make it hard to find proper attire when the department is so stingy. What do they pay you a month?"

"Not nearly what I'm worth, I can assure you that!" Jones laughed.

Biggs could finally stand it no longer and rose to put an end to the banter. "Objection, Your Honor, relevance."

The General agreed, "There seems little relevance for the rest of us indeed, Mr. Biggs. Ms. Tamm, perhaps you would care to move along and reserve the personal conversation for a more private occasion?"

"Actually, Your Honor," said Annika, raising her voice, "Mr. Jones's pride and financial straits are relevant to his motive for murdering Julie Welford."

The courtroom exploded. Reporters scrambled for the door to update their news outlets. A juror midway through a cup of water inhaled and began coughing violently. And clear above the ruckus, standing and leaning red-faced over the rail of the witness stand, Detective Jones roared, "I WHAT? You watch it, lady!"

After considerable pounding on the gavel, the General was finally able to regain control of the courtroom. A conference was called with Annika and Biggs at the bench. Intense whispering ensued, then Annika was allowed to proceed with the warning to watch her step lest she find herself on the losing end of an ethics complaint. Despite his red face and firm tone, Same could see the pleased look on the General's face. This really was turning out to be a fine case after all.

Annika's mock infatuation turned to a cold, clipped professional tone as her cross-examination continued. Pen and legal pad in hand, she moved closer to the witness stand, stared straight into the detective's eyes, and began slowly reeling off her questions.

"Mr. Jones, you have referred to the defendant as 'Same.' Isn't that the nickname used by his family and friends because he shares his father's name?"

Jones, still struggling to get his breathing under control, said in a malevolent bark, "What do you think?"

Annika kept moving. "And Mr. Jones, isn't it true that you investigated Mr. Harrison in connection with the death of Alaina Harrison, Mr. Harrison's stepmother, at the offices of Hustings and Billings approximately two months before Julie Welford's death?"

"I sure did. You interested in hearing all about it now? And I told you before it's Detective Jones."

"Right," said Annika, "Mr. Jones, isn't it true that your investigation ended when the medical examiner reported that the autopsy was consistent with Alaina's accidental death, just as Mr. Harrison described it to you?"

"Yeah, I had to wrap it up, but I'll tell you right now that…"

"Mr. Jones," Annika cut him off, "that was a yes or no question." Her eyes never leaving the detective, she addressed the General, "Your Honor, please remind this witness to listen carefully and just answer my question."

Same was exceedingly pleased to see that Jones's face, having lost any trace of a grin, had now developed a twitch as he tried to keep himself under control. With his own shit-eating grin pointed at Jones, the General instructed the witness per the request of defense counsel. Same felt a smile coming to his own face, and quickly pinched himself to keep his focus on maintaining the serious demeanor Annika had instructed.

Annika resumed, "Now Mr. Jones, isn't it true that during the course of your investigation at the H&B offices, you saw a USB flash drive in Mr. Harrison's office and learned that software valued at approximately $200,000 was saved on that drive?"

The twitters in the audience grew. Jones looked shocked. Biggs looked positively ill.

"Yes," Jones said huskily.

"And Mr. Jones, isn't it true that in your report on Mr. Harrison for the Julie Welford investigation, you noted that Mr. Harrison complained that the USB flash drive was missing from his office that same morning?"

"That's right, so?"

"Mr. Jones, isn't it true that despite it being the only evidence of theft at the crime scene, you never followed up on the missing USB flash drive during your investigation?"

"You're so right, because we had your boy's semen on our goddam victim!" the Detective spluttered.

"Ah, right," said Annika slowly, pausing for effect and moving her voice lower, "and Mr. Jones, isn't it true that you were the one who ordered the sample collected from Julie's body, and you were the one that ordered the sample collected from Mr. Harrison's cheek, and you were the one that ordered where that material would be tested?"

The Detective didn't answer, unless you counted the twitch under his right eye as an affirmative.

Annika continued, "Mr. Jones, isn't it true that during the Alaina Harrison investigation, Julie Welford asked you to leave the premises because you had failed to obtain a search warrant?"

"We only left because that woman started spouting lawyer-talk about..."

Annika cut him off again. "It's a yes or no, Mr. Jones."

Jones couldn't restrain himself any longer. Leaning forward over the witness stand he pointed a fat finger at Annika. "It's Detective Jones, goddam it! I've done more shit work to earn that title than your lawyer ass could ever imagine."

As the General scrambled for his gavel, Annika looked at the jury. "It seems you've been doing some work outside your job description as well."

Biggs jumped up with a loud objection as the General pounded the gavel. "Detective Jones!" yelled the General. "My lawyer ass now finds you in contempt. That will be a fine of $200. In the interest of actually proceeding with this case, we will hold the incarceration for your next offense. Ms. Tamm, any more sidebar comments like that and you will be joining the detective."

Taking a few deep breaths, he turned to the jury. "The jury will disregard the last comment made by counsel and remember that evidence will only come from the witness stand."

Annika quickly continued. "I have only a few more questions Your Honor." She turned back to Jones. "DETECTIVE Jones," she said, her emphasis drawing a stifled laugh from the jury box, "isn't it true that in front of several other employees of H&B, Julie Welford stood on a box of files to mock your actions and put her face no more than six inches from your own while she demanded that you leave the premises?"

Jones was clearly ready for the end of this ordeal. "Yes," he said quickly.

"And did I hear you correctly that when you entered H&B to investigate the death of Julie Welford, you proceeded directly to the 16th floor because, and I quote, 'you knew your way around'?"

"Yes."

"One last question," said Annika, as she finally returned to her seat. She took a long look at her note pad, and finally looked up. In a slow, calm, perfectly level voice, like a matador gracefully thrusting the final sword, she asked the question everyone desperately wanted.

"Detective Jones, isn't it true that you killed Julie Welford?"

With the jury's eyes glued to his face, the detective's hissed negative was immediately belied by the massive twitch under his right eye.

Same could have stood up and cheered.

Chapter Thirty-One

The General recessed for lunch after Detective Jones was released from the witness stand to lick his wounds. It was still mid-morning, but he could sense that the jurors needed a break after the morning's theatrics to collect themselves and focus on the technical evidence to follow.

The spectators began to file out. Agent Tatum, having shed his blue blazer for the more casual apparel of a reporter, smiled to himself as he stood and turned to leave. Suddenly he stopped in his tracks. Standing against the opposite wall was Ivy Legal. They spotted each other at the same time.

Ivy Legal made the first move toward the door. Tatum hastened in pursuit and followed him into the stairwell without comment. When they were outside, Ivy turned. "Tatum, what are you doing here? I instructed your director that you were to be removed from this situation."

Tatum smiled, "I don't think you instruct my boss. As it happens, I'm taking a couple days leave to watch this spectacle. I'm curious whether my plan ended up working. You going to shoot Harrison in the courtroom? It'd be rather messy."

"Too bad we have to go through the metal detector. At least I could hit him." Ivy Legal didn't wait for a response, but walked quickly down the steps.

***

With the case going so well, Street took the opportunity afforded by the recess to treat Annika, Same, and Mitch to lunch at the Commonwealth Club. The large red-brick building, originally the site of a home, had been a gentleman's club since the late eighteen hundreds. Amazingly it was still for gentlemen only. There had been one attempt to break the gender barrier, but when she was told there would only be one dressing room, the applicant dropped her bid for membership.

Same loved the club and wrangled an invitation out of Uncle Cary whenever he could. Mitch's appreciation for the place had been expressed in simpler terms: "All those portraits of the old dudes are awesome."

After they were seated in the upstairs dining room, Annika had her hands full fending off excited questions from Mitch, who was positive he had observed several critical facial expressions on jurors that indicated they were pulling for Same. Street and Same were feeling pretty chipper as well after the detective's meltdown. When Mitch finally settled down enough to take a bite of his BLT, Same took the chance to get some words in edgewise.

"That was brilliant this morning, Tamm. I think you definitely won some hearts and minds. You're worth every penny."

Annika laid down her fork. "Don't be ridiculous, Same. I'm not billing for any of this." She paused and frowned. "And in any event, this case is far from over. Their next witnesses are probably the medical examiner and then the DNA analyst. Jurors will often believe whatever an expert witness tells them, and they'll especially follow a DNA expert. If the State can trot out an expert to say 'DNA match,' the jury shuts down and convicts."

Same chose not to let this dose of realism rain on his parade. "Well, in any event you got us off to a swell start. I say we have a toast to fine friends and a fine morning, and may we have many more outside of a prison visitor center!"

Raising his iced tea, Street joined in. "I'll drink to that, sir!"

"Here, here!" cried Mitch.

Annika couldn't help but laugh at the oddly buoyant little family. "All right," she said, "here's to us."

Lunch passed pleasantly with laughter and some jokes at the expense of Detective Jones, but all too soon it was time to make their way back to the courtroom for the trial to resume. After the short drive back to the courthouse, they pressed through the cameras and metal detectors and soon found themselves back in the hushed venue of the General's courtroom.

Court was called to order at precisely 1:30 and the jury was promptly brought in. Biggs called Claudine Freely, the medical examiner, as his first witness of the afternoon. After establishing her qualifications and official position, he asked, "Dr. Freely, you had the opportunity to examine the remains of Julie Welford?"

"Yes, the examination and autopsy took place on the Monday that the body was discovered. I did the initial exam and Dr. Winston Marley did the actual post."

"Would you explain your findings to the jury?"

"The pertinent findings were that of strangulation, manifest by petechiae over the skin of the face. The face was also edematous — swollen in layman's terms. Also present were areas of bruising on the neck.

There were three distinct areas on the back of each side of the neck and a larger one to the front. This was consistent with manual strangulation. In this case there didn't appear to be an impression made by a fifth finger.

"There was also a semen deposit on the lower abdomen of the deceased, but no other signs of trauma on the initial examination. Later Dr. Marley called for me. He showed me evidence within the vagina that there had been recent intercourse. These were consistent with consensual activity."

Biggs asked a few more mundane questions and then turned the witness over to the defense. Annika had no questions and the witness was dismissed.

Same was surprised when Biggs called Robert Nichols next, but he looked over to find Annika merely nodding. Bob was Julie's boyfriend. He was going to be one of their star character witnesses, testifying that he knew Same and didn't believe he would have committed the crime. Then it occurred to Same that Biggs was shrewdly undercutting their case by introducing the potentially exculpatory evidence himself so he'd have a chance to put his own spin on it before Annika got the chance.

After he was sworn in, Nichols took his seat in the witness chair and identified himself. Biggs then approached the stand and asked, "Mr. Nichols, did you know the deceased, Julie Welford?"

"Yes, yes I did."

"And how long have you known her?"

"Almost three years."

"Mr. Nichols, what was your relationship with Julie?"

Nichols looked straight at the jury. "Julie and I had dated for three years and were planning to announce our engagement to our families in the fall." He choked up and paused. "We had a beautiful relationship."

Biggs didn't seem to be bothered by the emotion. "And when was the last time that you and Julie were intimate?"

"Saturday afternoon before she left to go to the office for a client emergency that night."

"When you say office, you mean Hustings and Billings?"

"Yes."

"Mr. Nichols, I realize this is intensely personal, but did you and Julie engage in vaginal intercourse that afternoon?"

Nichols leaned forward slowly. "Yes."

Biggs turned toward the General. "No further questions, Your Honor."

The General turned to Annika, "Ms. Tamm?"

Annika paused to think for a moment. Biggs had nicely steered the emotional weight of Nichols's loss in his favor, at the same time explaining the medical examiner's findings. Better to get some space before presenting his support for Same's good character.

"No questions, Your Honor," she said. "But we reserve the right to recall this witness during the presentation of our case."

"Very well," said the General, "then let's move along. Mr. Biggs."

Biggs then called Penelope Rodriguez, the DFS analyst who had run the samples provided by Detective Jones. On direct examination, Biggs took her through a thorough discussion of the principles of DNA analysis, error rates, and other general background on the processes used by the lab.

Delving into specifics, Rodriguez then testified that she had received two samples of biological material, one taken from the substance on the victim's body and one taken from the defendant's cheek swab. The sample from the victim's body contained a female and a male DNA profile. A female DNA profile was often found in sexual assault cases from the skin or fluids of female victims from which the tested substances were removed. The male DNA profile was compared to the profile derived from the defendant's cheek swab, and the defendant could not be excluded as the donor of the male DNA profile. The chances of someone else donating the male DNA profile were on the order of one in trillions.

As Rodriguez's testimony continued, Same watched the faces of the jurors and grew increasingly worried. Annika was right, they were buying it hook, line, and sinker. And why wouldn't they? After all, whatever feelings they might have about Detective Jones, how in the hell could he have faked a DNA test?

When it came time for cross-examination, Annika had little luck recreating her magic from the morning. She poked around Rodriguez's qualifications, the lab's accreditation, the chain of custody of the biological samples, and the procedures for preventing cross-contamination of samples. Rodriguez was calm, professional, and unflappable during cross. Annika had to settle for little more than emphasizing that Rodriguez had only tested the substances that were sent to her, and had no idea how technicians at the crime scene had handled them before they were sent.

Eventually Annika passed the witness and Biggs stood to call his next witness. "Your Honor, we call Ms. Molly Rose."

Same jolted up straight. What the hell were they calling Molly for? Annika was planning to call her to describe Same's shock at finding the body. Same's distress was doubled as he caught Annika staring at him, wondering exactly the same thing. With a sinking feeling clamping down on his stomach, Same managed a weak shrug as the rear door opened.

The time Molly had spent making her entrance memorable had clearly paid dividends. She had somehow managed to find a look between sexy lawyer and nineteenth-century brothel. Same wasn't aware that such a look existed, but he had to admit she wore it phenomenally well. But what was she doing as a state's witness?

After directing a flirtatious look at the General, Molly was sworn in and Biggs began his examination.

"Ms. Rose, are you acquainted with Tyler Harrison, Jr.?"

"Yes, sir," said Molly sweetly, "I was his temporary executive assistant at the law firm of Hustings and Billings until his regular secretary got back from a leave of absence because she was hurt real bad in a car crash a few months ago that left her with a broken leg and some other injuries and…"

Biggs cut her off. "Ms. Rose, I'm sorry, but if I may interrupt. We must follow a question and answer format for this examination."

"Ma'am," added the General, unable to resist addressing such a lovely creature, "we certainly do want to hear what you have to say, but counsel is correct, please do limit yourself to answering his questions."

"Oh yes sirs," said Molly, quickly lifting a hand to her mouth, "I'm so sorry. I promise to listen very carefully."

"Don't worry about it," said the General with a smile, "Mr. Biggs, please continue."

Biggs took another look at his notes and asked the next question, "Who did you initially work for when you were hired by the firm?"

"Well I worked for Mr. Harrison from day one," she said with a pretty smile directed to Same. "And I also worked for Ms. Welford before she… before she…" Molly's testimony stopped suddenly as her lip began to tremble and tears welled up in her eyes. Waving her hand to fan her face, she finally came out with it. "Before she died," she wailed, and the tears burst forth.

Oh crap, Same thought to himself. Anyone on the jury who hadn't emotionally connected with Bob Nichols was now ready to hang whoever caused this pretty young secretary such pain. Biggs fetched a box of tissues offered by the court reporter and after a few minutes of dabbing and sniffling, Molly seemed able to continue.

"Now, Ms. Rose, are you okay if I ask you some more questions?"

"Oh, yes sir, I'm so sorry again. I will try my very best."

"Okay, we'll go slowly and take any time you need to answer the questions. Now, to be fair, you did not want to come here to testify today, did you?"

"No, sir," said Molly, and delicately dabbed at her nose with a fresh tissue. Annika stiffened as the questions took a turn toward inadmissible territory, but decided to see what Biggs might be up to before cutting off the line of questioning.

"And what did you tell me about why you didn't want to testify?"

"Well, because I just know that Same would never, ever do anything like that. He just wouldn't," she said, with a wide, teary-eyed smile at Same. "He was a very kind, sweet boss and a kind, sweet man and he just wouldn't do something like that."

Despite the praise, Same felt the knot tightening in his stomach. What was this about? Was Biggs just undercutting more of their character evidence by presenting it himself? He sensed stillness beside him and noticed that Annika had stopped scribbling notes and was staring intently at Molly. What was Biggs up to?

Biggs continued, "And were you aware of anything other than a professional relationship between Same and Julie?"

"No, sir," said Molly quickly. "They were just colleagues."

Biggs took a long pause and then quietly dropped the bombshell. "Ms. Rose, have you had sexual relations with Mr. Harrison?"

Annika was shouting "Objection" before the word "sexual" had left Biggs's lips, but the question was out. Again the courtroom exploded in motion and sound, this time unabated by the General's pounding gavel. Same slumped slightly in his chair and put his hand to his forehead. Apparently Molly hadn't been able to keep their little secret from the prying of the DA's office. His loss of composure earned him a hard, subtle fist in the shoulder from Annika, and he quickly straightened up and raised his eyes to meet Molly's on the witness stand. When she saw him looking at her, she quickly averted her eyes and turned a wide, frightened look to the General.

As the courtroom gradually subsided, the General ceased his pounding and barked, "Counsel, up here, now!"

Annika and Biggs quickly approached the bench. The discussion was conducted in fierce whispers to keep the jury from hearing, but the intensity was clearly communicated by Annika's violent gesturing. Biggs appeared to be making careful, planned points, but of course he knew this objection was coming.

Annika had been taken completely by surprise and Same knew it was all his fault. He knew this would look bad, but Same was sure in the aftermath of their encounter that Molly would do anything to keep it a secret. Underneath he was candid enough to realize that mostly he hadn't wanted to tell Annika that he had a fling with a temp secretary.

As the bench conference broke up, the body language said it all. Annika walked back to the table and sat quickly, her eyes never connecting with Same's. He leaned over to whisper that he was sorry, but she simply scribbled on her notepad without expression. As Same straightened up, Annika tore a page out and turned her eyes back to Molly as she pushed the note over to him. "You're an ass," was all it said.

Out of the corner of his eye, Same caught a glimpse of Mitch leaning into Uncle Cary, who had an arm wrapped around the boy's shoulders and a stony look on his face. Same leaned back upright and took a deep breath as he turned forward. Finally, rock bottom.

The rest of the afternoon was miserable. Biggs led Molly through a detailed description of their "courtship" and sexual encounter at the office. The State's theory, which would undoubtedly become painfully clear during their closing argument, was that Same had a pattern of seducing attractive women he worked with. His motive in killing Julie may have been to keep an affair with her secret from his new flame Molly.

Annika did her best to limit the damage with frequent objections, but there was little she could do. All the jurors saw when they looked at Same now was a rich lawyer scumbag who hadn't waited a week before seducing this innocent wide-eyed secretary. And he did it in an office next door from where another young, pretty lawyer was found dead, with Same's semen on her body.

***

The afternoon had worn late by the time Biggs tendered the witness for cross-examination, so the General recessed until the morning. Ivy Legal was pleased with the way things had gone. He quietly eased out of the courtroom and went to his car. He took his cell from the glove box and phoned his office.

When she heard his voice his secretary screeched, "Where the hell are you?"

"I'm in Richmond. What's the matter with you?"

"The Chief has called four times. He wants to see you this afternoon."

Ivy looked at his watch. "Tell him I'll be there at 6."

Mercifully traffic was fairly sparse and he arrived at his office at the stroke of 6:00. His secretary placed a forefinger over her lips and pointed to his office.

He walked in and feigned surprise that his visitor was present. "Mr. Crist, you're here already. Sorry I wasn't here when you arrived."

Crist's response was clipped, "Dr. Sebarius, I understand you were in Richmond and therefore, I assume, at the Harrison trial."

"That is correct."

"May I ask why in the name of God you were there?"

Sebarius was surprised by the question, but decided to be forthright. "I wanted to witness that bastard's humiliation personally."

"This was not your wisest decision. If anyone recognized you, it will obviously lead to awkward questions about our interest in the case."

Sebarius decided not to bring up the fact that Tatum was at the trial too. "No one recognized me. What's the problem?"

Crist was growing more irritated, "Your inability to recognize the severity of the risk seems indicative of your poor judgment. We brought you down from Boston for your expertise in healthcare systems, not black ops."

Sebarius interrupted, "Eliminating these ignorant pockets of resistance is the only way to buy time to install the system we're trying to create. Our system will be successful, and you and I both know it is the only way to keep this country from going bankrupt. If I have to explain it to you again I will."

It was like Sebarius had sprinkled salt on Crist's open wound. "I don't need you to lecture me…"

Again Sebarius cut him off, "If FDA keeps approving drugs that crush CMS budgets, we're just shooting ourselves in the foot. CMS has to be able to incorporate its cost-benefit analyses directly into FDA efficacy analyses. Once we work out the kinks in the process with the first few drugs, we'll have a coordinated system that won't be slowed by these minor hiccups."

Crist stood and moved behind his chair to place it between him and the rabid doctor. "You're preaching to the choir. What I'm talking about is the way you brought in the FBI and created this current mess."

Sebarius's tone ratcheted to manic. "Maybe you should be visiting with the idiots at the FBI. Their people have screwed it up time and time again and …"

This time it was Crist who interrupted, "Dr. Sebarius, this is information I don't want to know."

"Ah, Pontius Pilate, you want the deed done, but don't want to be involved. Well, I didn't order any innocents killed."

"Sebarius, just shut up. I don't want to hear any more of this shit."

"You don't want to hear it, then take yourself back to Chicago. The politics are dirtier than this in your home town. I don't need you to tell me what to say and not to say. Are you joining the sanctimonious? Joining the people defending the spending of our last dollar on pointless medical care? As I've told you before, it's not as if we haven't had death panels all along. Why are you people so stupid that you don't understand that this is exactly what we've been doing for decades? We have limited funds, and we have to decide who gets covered, what treatments get covered and how much we cover. People outside those coverage limits tend to die. That's a death panel. This is nothing new, it's just more efficient now. Why can't you morons see that we save more people's lives by doing this? It's the same thing as the triage in any ER on any busy night. You can't work on everybody, so you deploy the resources you have in the best way to protect as many as possible. You know everything I've said is true, but publically you want to opt out."

At that point Crist only wanted to put some space between himself and the raving lunatic in front of him. As he moved quickly toward the office door, he said, "I hear you, Doctor. I get it. Just take it easy and I'll be back with you shortly."

With that Crist promptly exited the office and jumped on the next elevator, where he phoned his chauffer. When he was safely ensconced in his car, he placed a call to his boss.

"Sebarius has to go. He is certifiable. I'm going to ask for his resignation. If necessary later we can spin it on him acting as a political zealot gone over the edge."

After a clipped affirmative, Crist hung up and took a deep breath. His next call was back to Sebarius. He got right to the point, "Dr. Sebarius, my superiors have requested your resignation. Please deliver it by courier by ten tomorrow morning."

"You'll have it." The phone went dead.

Crist was expecting further rants, and sat staring at his phone with pleasant but uneasy surprise.

For his part, Sebarius stood looking out of his window toward Constitution Avenue. He had enjoyed the power he wielded from this office and was quietly furious that the fools above him couldn't see the necessary value of his work. As he adjusted his bow-tie he said softly to himself, "Well, Mr. Harrison, maybe my replacement will play footsy with the drug companies. Maybe they'll break our bank with their in-effective drugs. But you will not add to our deficit with your damned dementia."

He sat at his desk, wrote the resignation as an email and hit send. He then gathered a few special mementos from his credenza and placed them in the raincoat he removed from the office closet. It wasn't difficult to carry the small bundle. He walked out without even a glance toward his secretary.

In the garage he dumped the bundle into the trunk of his car. At the street he sat for a few moments contemplating which way to turn. Moments later he headed back for Virginia.

Chapter Thirty-Two

The mood had turned 180 degrees from lunch as Street drove Same, Annika, and Mitch back to his house to talk strategy. The adults had each settled in around the kitchen table with tall glasses of Talisker, neat. Street polished off his first glass with a quick toss and reached to the bottle for a refill. Only when another three fingers had risen from the bottom was a word finally spoken. "Well," said Mitch, "that sucked."

Same didn't look at Mitch but just stared out of the window. He was worried about prison and worried about Mitch, but more than anything else he was just deeply embarrassed.

He turned from the window, picked up his glass and took a strong swig. He found little solace as the liquid slowly burned down to his stomach. Annika still hadn't looked at him and he couldn't think of what to say that would properly apologize to her for screwing up the case. She just stared forward, seemingly fixated on the center of the kitchen table.

Uncle Cary broke the renewed silence. Slapping Mitch's shoulder he said sharply, "Lesson two if you want to be a defense lawyer, Mitch, learn your clients will lie to you."

Same rolled his eyes, "Okay, okay, okay!" He couldn't stand their disappointment anymore. "I did it. I slept with her. We went out for a drink, I had too much, and it happened one time. It was definitely wrong and it never happened again. I'm sorry guys, I know I screwed up and I should have told you, but she acted like she would never talk about it and I didn't think it was relevant to the case."

"Not relevant?" Annika scoffed. "Ha, you really didn't pay much attention in Evidence."

Turning to Annika, Same said, "Look, Tamm, I know, okay. A big part of it was that I didn't want you to think that this was what I had turned into since we'd been apart. I know that's stupid, but that's why I didn't tell you."

Annika kept staring at the table. "Oh, I get it. I don't really care on a personal level. We haven't been together for seven years. It was just stupid to let our case get blindsided in the middle of a trial."

Street, a little warmed up by the Scotch, cut in quickly, "Well she may not care on a personal level, but I certainly do." He pushed back his chair and stood up. Pointing to Mitch he raised his voice, "Are you trying to tell me that shortly after both of his parents died, while you were entrusted with the care of this boy, you were not only getting him shot but also running around chasing skirts all over Richmond? What the hell is wrong with you, and don't give me any of that FTD shit! This is not dementia, this is about you not being man enough to control your little weenie and tend to your responsibilities."

"Jesus, Uncle Cary," said Same. "You wanna not have this conversation right in front of him?"

"To hell with that," Street yelled, smashing his fist down on the table. "Your ass is going in the slammer, so he's going to need to be an adult as of tomorrow. He's going to need to know the consequences of running around town sticking your dick in anything that'll hold still!"

Same saw the scared look in Mitch's eyes and it drove him to his feet. "Listen, old man, I've had about enough of your crap. Not taking care of my responsibilities? I just spent the last year of my life by my father's side as he died in front of me. I've been taking good care of Mitch while all this shit has gone down. We've been shot, I'm being falsely accused of murdering one of my best friends, and I've got the FDA all over my ass for trying to save a drug that might cure this damn disease. The only place my 'little weenie' has been for over a year is in that damn secretary, and that was one time, so why don't you get off my back!"

Street and Same stood eye to eye, both men breathing heavily now and struggling to keep a handle on their emotions. Mitch had squeezed himself as far away from the two as possible and sat hunched over with his head buried in his arms. Annika was still staring into the center of the table, seemingly in a catatonic trance. Finally, his eyes still locked on Same's, Street slowly reached an arm out to set his drink on the table. "I'm going to get some air," he said huskily, and turned to move toward the kitchen door.

He froze as Annika suddenly woke. "That's it," she said.

"What's it?" asked Street quietly, still facing the door.

"I've got it," she continued, a smile building on her lips.

"You've got what, exactly, Annika?"

Grinning broadly now, she jumped up out of her seat and grabbed Street and Same each by a shoulder. "Sit," she said, pushing them both to their chairs. They hesitated for a moment until the smile left her face. "Now!" she ordered, and they sat.

Mitch's face finally rose from his arms and all three could see the wetness in his eyes. Annika turned toward the window. "Mitchell," she said sharply, in her best law professor tone, "You will recall that we got a sample of the substance on Julie's body tested by Uncle Cary's friend at the private lab to double-check the State's results, correct?"

"Correct," said Mitch, wiping his eyes.

"And what results did we get back?"

"The lab said that Same's DNA was a match."

"A match to what exactly? Be precise."

"Um," Mitch hesitated, "a match to the male DNA profile?"

Annika pointed at him. "Correct, sir." Looking back to the window, she continued the examination. "And what did Rodriguez testify to today?"

Mitch began to catch on and tried to be precise. "That Same could not be excluded as the donor of the male DNA profile."

"Exactly," said Annika, "I see you were paying attention. Now, to whom did Rodriguez say the female DNA belonged?"

"She said it matched the victim, Julie."

Annika whirled to face him. "Oh really, Master Harrison. Is that what she said?"

"Um, I think so," stammered Mitch.

"Think harder," said Annika, moving behind him and putting her hands on his shoulders. "She certainly left that impression on the jury, but what did she say?"

"Um," Mitch said, and thought for a few seconds, his brow furrowed. Then he popped up straight. "Oh, I got it, yes. She said that there was a female DNA profile and that a female profile often comes from the victim's skin."

"Exactly!"

"Oh, I get it, I get it! That's it!" shouted Mitch. He and Street both began smiling, and Mitch threw up a hand which Annika slapped in a high five.

Same was still mystified, and more than a little annoyed that his nine-year-old brother had caught on before he had. "You get what, Mitch? How does this help us?"

With an exasperated look, Mitch explained, "Dude, it's simple. Nobody ever tested the female profile. They just thought it would be Julie, so they didn't try to match it to anyone. But it could be the real killer."

"And if you're now telling us the truth about where your little weenie's been," said Annika with a wry look to Same, "that points straight to our sweet, innocent, Miss Molly Rose."

Same rocked back, absolutely stunned.

"Same," said Annika, pacing the floor, "it all fits together. I was watching that woman like a hawk all afternoon because something just wasn't sitting right with me. The act of the sweet, fragile, little bird is just a little too perfect and stereotypical to be really believable. People are complicated, and in my experience witnesses only fit stereotypes that nicely when they are practiced liars putting on a show."

Same started to protest but Annika held up a finger. She was on a roll. "Think about it, Same. She arrived at the firm just after the Ardmore incident and your secretary's 'accident', right? She also has access to the building, so no forced entry necessary and she wouldn't be on the visitor logs we got."

Glancing at Mitch, she continued, "So, tell me honestly, when you were with Molly, did you use a condom?"

Same flushed. "Uh, yes, I did," he said. Not exactly a topic he was ready to discuss yet with his little brother, but he supposed it was all coming out at the trial tomorrow anyway.

"Okay, there we go," said Annika. "Where did you throw it away?"

"Um, well actually, I'm not really sure. I guess she kind of took it off me."

"Bingo!" she said, holding up her arms. "We got her." Annika then gave him a hard look. "By the way Same, the phrases 'um', 'well', 'I'm not sure', and 'kind of' are now banished from your vocabulary. We'll almost certainly need you to testify tomorrow, so you need to get over your embarrassment and come right out with it."

She paused for a moment, and looked over to Street. "Okay, here's what we need to do. Same and I need to prep for his testimony tomorrow. Direct will be straightforward, but cross-examination can be brutal and we need to go through everything Biggs might ask and work on our delivery. Cary, can you get your friend at the lab to run an emergency profile tonight and be available to testify sometime tomorrow afternoon?"

"You bet," said Street, already starting the coffee percolating for what was shaping up to be a very long evening. "Dr. O'Reilly is a dear friend from way back. It should be no problem."

"Good. We need a sample of Molly's DNA to compare to the female profile that the lab already has."

Same piped up, "The office. She spent hours on her hair and make-up at her desk. She kept brushes in the bottom drawer on the left side of the desk. Any gray hairs will be Carol's, but you should be able to find some blonde hairs in there from Molly. The only problem is getting in past the security guard."

"You don't worry about me, Junior," replied Street. "This old man has a few tricks up his sleeve yet. I've never met the security guard that couldn't be bypassed by a doctor with his medical bag responding to chest pains from his bigshot lawyer client."

Same couldn't help laughing. "Are you serious, Uncle Cary, have you done that before?"

Street smiled slightly as he turned back toward the coffee pot. "You young ones just tend to your business and don't worry about this old man. He'll hold up his end of the deal, assuming he's not too old and tired to make it to your trial tomorrow morning."

Same rolled his eyes. He was going to be paying for the "old man" comment for a while. Maybe a sizeable bottle of interesting scotch would do the trick after this was all over. If it ended well, that is.

Chapter Thirty-Three

. . . .

Same woke the next morning as sunlight began streaming in Street's living room windows. He and Annika had sent Mitch to bed around ten and had worked on potential questions and responses into the dead of night. Their last call to Street revealed that he had a few "delays" in obtaining the DNA samples from the office, but was finally on his way to the lab. Excited but exhausted, they finally just grabbed a couple blankets and each crashed on one of the two overstuffed sofas in the living room.

Same sat up on his sofa and looked over at Annika. She was buried under a blanket, only her peaceful face poking out. Before they turned in she had changed into a t-shirt and sweatpants laid out by Uncle Cary before he left. As she settled into her sofa, Same couldn't help but notice how lean and athletic she remained after years of practicing law. Same's workouts had been more sporadic than he liked, but with her iron discipline he was sure she was still religious about her 5:00 am five mile runs.

Letting her slip away had to be one of the dumbest moves of his life. He recognized now that it was less out of any noble motive to spare her from involvement in the disease, and more along the lines of destructive self-pity. It hadn't taken him long to realize how much he missed her, but his pride had kept him from trying to reconnect as the years went by. Good old pride, it will freeze you to death!

The process of being arrested, jailed, and tried had certainly done away with much of that pride. Maybe if they won this thing he should take another shot. Mitch would be for it, that was for sure. Same realized that he probably wasn't a very attractive prospect with the giant bulls-eye that seemed to be on his back, but maybe Annika would agree to an ethics-violating date with her client after a successful verdict. What the hell, it wouldn't hurt to ask anyway.

He suddenly realized that she wasn't asleep anymore, and her deep blue eyes were watching him quietly. She smiled the tight, ironic smile that she always did when she poked fun at him and asked, "You're not contemplating how to add a third onto your string of murders of the women close to you, are you?"

"Uh, no," said Same, with a smile of his own, "I still need you for a bit longer."

The alarm they had set the previous evening suddenly began beeping insistently. Seven o'clock, time to face down all those accusing stares once again, thought Same. But this time, hopefully, Uncle Cary would have their ace in the hole.

Annika sat up on her couch and reached for her phone to dial Street just as Mitch walked in and jumped under Same's blanket. Annika switched the phone to speaker and Street's voice soon boomed cheerily into the living room.

"Well, good morning, my young friends. How did you all sleep?"

"We slept well, Cary," replied Annika. "How about you? You must be exhausted."

"Running on adrenaline and enough coffee to kill a lesser old man," laughed Street. "But we got the results. You were right, the female DNA is none other than the lovely Miss Molly Rose!"

"Yes!" shouted Mitch with a fist pump. He jumped off the couch to give Annika a high five.

"Fabulous," said Annika. "Will Dr. O'Reilly be available to testify this morning?"

"In the car with me right now. Factoring in traffic, I think we should be to the courthouse sometime around nine-thirty."

"Excellent. We will have started by then, but when you get there, give me a call to give me a heads up. Then hand me the results when you walk into the courtroom."

"I've got them in an official lab envelope, does that work?"

"Perfect. Okay, drive safe, we'll see you soon."

Annika shut her phone and they quickly got dressed and headed downtown. The pack of reporters outside the courthouse had grown, and grown hungrier. After yesterday's fiasco they could smell blood and they were eager to get Same's last statement as a free man. They wouldn't get another bite at him if he was convicted today and led away from the courtroom to prison.

They pressed quickly through the reporters and cameras and arrived at a steadily filling courtroom. They exchanged nods with Melvin Biggs as he walked in at precisely 8:45. Annika started scribbling away furiously as Same sat with his arm around Mitch in the row behind the defense table.

As the clock crept closer to nine, Same leaned over to Mitch. "Hey, buddy," he whispered, "things are looking good right now, but you never can tell what will happen in a trial. If things don't go the way we want today, I may have to go away for a while. You understand?"

Mitch nodded solemnly, so Same continued, "But we have the new evidence now so we should be able to fight it even if I am convicted. You know how much I love you and you know we'll always be a family, so you keep your head up and you do what Uncle Cary tells you and I'll see you again when we finally beat this thing, okay?"

Mitch didn't nod this time but just wrapped his arms around Same's neck and squeezed. Same wished he could hold him like that forever, but their embrace was interrupted after a few seconds by the entry of the bailiff. Same quickly moved around to the defense table as the bailiff called the courtroom to order. All right, thought Same, now let's see about that half-ass chance.

After the General's usual entrance, Molly Rose was recalled for cross-examination. The reporters tittered and scribbled notes as she paraded down the aisle, again having nailed that unusual combination of professional and late evening attire that Same now thought of as her bordello-esquire look. Same watched her in a new light as she threw him a vacant smile on her way past to the witness stand. Same smiled back. She had no idea what she was walking into.

Annika spent the first fifteen minutes of her examination essentially killing time — going over some of Molly's answers from yesterday and filling in a bit of her probably fabricated professional background. Molly, or whoever she was, seemed quite comfortable on the stand today and answered all of Annika's questions directly in her sweet, mild-mannered tone.

At 9:20 Annika's pocket buzzed. She quickly reached in to silence her phone and Same could see the slightest trace of a smile as she lowered her eyes to take a quick look at her notes. "So, Miss Rose," she asked finally, "you testified yesterday that your sexual encounter with

Mr. Harrison was unexpected, is that correct?"

"That's correct, ma'am. It just kind of happened, I guess."

"But you did have a condom with you that he used to protect the two of you, is that correct?"

Molly began to look a bit unsettled, and shot a quick glance to Biggs at the prosecutor's table. After a pause she answered, "Um, yes ma'am, we used a condom. But, um, I think it was Same's if I'm not mistaken."

"Ah, okay," said Annika, "and do you recall what you did with that condom after the sexual encounter was over?"

Molly shifted in her seat and shot a more pointed look at Biggs, and he jumped quickly to his feet. "Objection, Your Honor. I don't believe this line of questioning has any relevance. Counsel is simply badgering this witness by prying into embarrassing personal details."

"Your Honor, may we approach the bench?" asked Annika. The General waved them in and Annika and Biggs approached. Before they reached the bench, the back doors quietly opened and in walked Street, accompanied by a striking woman with porcelain skin and fiery red hair. To Same's eye she was in her late 40's, and he guessed she must be Dr. O'Reilly. He had assumed the doctor was a man, and wondered now just how dear this "dear friend" was to Uncle Cary. The man had quite a lot up his sleeve, it seemed.

Dr. O'Reilly slid into an empty spot along the wall at the back, and Street proceeded up the aisle to lay a large envelope on the defense table. At the bench, Annika quickly turned to the General and said, "Your Honor, on second thought we will withdraw that last question."

She walked quickly back to the defense table and slid several pages out of the envelope, pretending to read each page. As the seconds ticked by, Same could see both the General and Molly growing more impatient. Same bit his cheeks to keep himself from giving anything away by his facial expression, but couldn't wait for Annika to blow the lid off this thing. She didn't disappoint.

The General cleared his throat. "Ms. Tamm, do you have further questions for this witness?"

Annika looked up from the papers. "I should say so, Your Honor." Turning to Molly, a confused expression on her face, she asked, "Miss Rose, this has me a bit befuddled, but can you explain to me why your DNA was in the semen on the victim's body?"

The courtroom froze, dead silent, and Same could have sworn it took a good three seconds before the first realization hit. From one of the reporters in the back, it came as clear as day, "Holy Shit!"

Pandemonium erupted again. The General began pounding his gavel in futility as Biggs leapt to scream an objection, reporters dove for the exit, and Annika's sweet old lady juror started repeating "Oh my heavens, oh my heavens, oh my heavens!" Above the ruckus Molly finally burst into tears and began sobbing loudly.

By dint of persistence the General's gavel finally won out. When a measure of order had returned, the General began barking orders. "Bailiff, you will remove the jury. Officer," he said, pointing at a uniformed officer at the back of the courtroom, "escort the gentleman who shouted that profanity from my courtroom." Pointing toward another officer he said, "You, sir, escort this witness to the restroom so that she may compose herself."

When the commands had been carried out, and Molly's sobs finally died out down the hallway outside the courtroom, he finally shouted, "Counsel, up here, now!"

When the conference convened at the bench, Annika took over immediately. "Why don't I explain the foundation for that question, Your Honor?" she asked.

"Yes, why don't you, Ms. Tamm," said the General. "Perhaps you'd also like to have a moment to take a passing glance at Code of Professional Responsibility and the Rules of Evidence before you do?"

"Oh, Your Honor, you know me better than that," she said with a smile. "I just received a report from the private lab we used to check the State's DNA results. The first time around, neither of us bothered to try matching the female DNA, assuming it would belong to the victim. Based on a hunch, I had my investigator collect a known DNA sample belonging to Miss Rose last night. He and my DNA analyst are present to testify. From the information I was just handed, it turns out that the female DNA profile in the semen sample is a match to our sample from Miss Rose. And as you just heard, my client's semen was collected just the night before the murder in a condom likely covered in Miss Rose's DNA."

"Ms. Tamm, I must profess my hearty skepticism that you were just now informed of this in such an artfully staged manner," said the General, "but nonetheless, Mr. Biggs, what say you?"

Biggs stood silently, processing what had just happened. "Mr. Biggs!" said the General forcefully.

"Yes, Your Honor," said Biggs, waking from his trance. "Uh, well, based on counsel's representations, if she lays a proper foundation we won't object to the question."

Annika jumped in again, "Mr. Biggs, perhaps I might proffer the testimony of Dr. Street and my DNA analyst now that we are outside the presence of the jury. If you find the testimony credible, we will offer a motion for a continuance of the trial for several days to allow you to confirm the DNA findings and investigate Miss Rose's involvement further."

Biggs thought for a moment. Finally he straightened up and addressed the General. "Your Honor, in the interest of justice and in light of this newly discovered and potentially exculpatory evidence, I think Ms. Tamm's suggestion…"

Biggs was cut off as loud voices began to be heard behind the side wall and the side door of the courtroom suddenly banged open. The officer tasked with escorting Molly, now red-faced and panting with exertion, walked quickly to the General and whispered urgently in his ear. The General's face progressed quickly past the shade of red worn by the officer and finally ended on an unhealthy purple. Standing up to his full height the General shouted, "That tiny little woman overpowered you? You find me that witness! You get out there and you find her!"

The officer hastily retreated and the General slowly sank back into his seat and poured himself another glass of water. He took a long sip and his face began subsiding to a color more conducive to prolonging his tenure on the bench. Both Annika and Biggs remained motionless, afraid to move for fear of attracting his wrath.

Finally, after a slowly lengthening series of deep breaths, the General addressed the entire courtroom. "Ladies and gentlemen. At this time the trial is continued on the court's own motion until Monday morning of next week so that the presence of an essential witness may be secured and the parties may conduct further investigation into evidence that has just arisen."

He then turned his eyes downward to address the lawyers. "Counsel, we will hold a conference in my office at 9:00 am on Friday morning to determine the scheduling of witnesses moving forward and to entertain any motions that may be appropriate at that time. Mr. Biggs, you will report at 8:45 as usual. Mr. Harrison," he said, looking at Same, "your presence will not be required at the conference on Friday. If I do not see you again, good luck to you, sir." That set off a buzz among the reporters and the General's gaze finally returned to them, "Ladies and gentlemen, court is adjourned."

He banged his gavel with particular emphasis and the bailiff ordered them all to their feet. As the General slowly limped out of the courtroom, Same could swear he heard the old man chuckle.

Chapter Thirty-Four

The door closed behind the General, and Same turned just in time to catch a nine-year-old cannonball plowing into him. Mitch squeezed him with a vice grip around his waist, and Same didn't even bother to try to check the flow of tears as he held onto his brother. They had both been through so much over the past few months. It looked like Fortune's wheel was finally beginning to turn in their favor.

Same looked up through blurry eyes to see Annika making final arrangements with Biggs. She shook Biggs's hand a final time, walked back to Same, and wrapped her arms around his neck. Same held on to both of them for dear life.

Drs. Street and O'Reilly finally made their way from the back of the courtroom through the stream of departing reporters. "Congratulations, Counselor," Street said loudly as they approached. "So is that it?"

He stuck a hand out to Annika and Same was shocked to see the "Snow Queen" quickly wipe away a tear as she straightened up and reached out to accept his hand. "All except the formalities. The prosecutor says the State won't move forward with the case if their testing results match ours and they can't find Molly. So our hearing Friday should result in a quick dismissal."

"Thank God," said Street, turning to wrap Same in a giant bear hug. "Congratulations, kid."

After a few seconds Street pushed apart. "But I'm forgetting my manners. Let me introduce you all to our saving grace, Dr. Bridget O'Reilly."

Dr. O'Reilly stepped forward and extended a long, elegant hand. "Congratulations to both of you. I'm Bridget."

Both Same and Annika jumped to pump her hand and thank her profusely for the work she had done overnight and making the trip down to Richmond. "Bridget, I'm terribly sorry that we brought you all the way down and then didn't need you to testify after all," said Annika. "I will pay all your fees for testing, trial prep, travel, and anything else just as soon as you have a chance to tally them up."

Street's elegant friend waived her hand. "Don't worry about it, really. It was just a favor to a friend." She looked at Street. "Besides, Cary has promised to show me around the city for the afternoon and take me to The Hard Shell for seafood tonight. Now that you'll all be free for dinner," she said with a wink to Same, "why don't all three of you join us for a little celebration?"

"Okay, sounds great," Same replied, looking over to catch a nod from Annika.

"Perfect," said Street. "You three go enjoy the afternoon. Meet at the bar at 6:00 or so and I'll try for a reservation at 6:30. I'll give old James Lance a call too. That kid could always use another meal, and he's been texting me nonstop to get updates on the trial. He's got a flight in from Paris getting to DC at noon, so he should be able to make it."

They chatted for a few more minutes and then prepped themselves for the swarm of reporters that would descend on them at the courthouse steps. On Annika's instruction, Same said only that he was glad the prosecution would have the opportunity to investigate some new evidence, and was confident that evidence would exonerate him. Then they left the disappointed swarm to feast on Biggs.

The rest of the afternoon was the happiest Same could remember. They left the itinerary up to Mitch, and consequently soon found themselves playing football at Byrd Park overlooking Swan Lake. It was a warm September afternoon, and they caught more than a few surprised looks from passing joggers as the well-dressed threesome shed what clothes they decently could to chuck a ball around one of the empty fields. Same couldn't help but admire the easy, flowing athleticism of Annika's movements. She hadn't lost a step since they first met nearly a decade ago, and he found her glance and her laugh to be just as infectious now as he remembered from law school.

Lunch was hotdogs, gigantic tubs of popcorn, soda and a matinee at Bowtie Cinema. After devouring his hot dog in near record time, Mitch sat transfixed on the front of his seat. Same leaned back and let the movie float past, content simply to savor Annika's closeness and the resilient spirits of his kid brother.

Halfway through the show, he suddenly felt Annika's fingers intertwine with his on the armrest. His stomach flipped and was suddenly filled with the kind of butterflies he hadn't felt since he was a teenager. He glanced over at her. Her eyes remained glued to the screen, but he could see the faint edge of a smile on her face. When the credits rolled Same couldn't remember a single thing that had happened, but he knew he would always remember it as the best damn movie he had ever watched.

By the time the movie ended the afternoon had grown late and they headed straight for The Hard Shell. Street, Bridget, and James Lance had already arrived by the time they got there, and they quickly settled into quiet corner table where Street had champagne waiting.

The crab cakes they ordered for appetizers were delicious, and as his second glass of champagne dwindled, Same finally felt completely relaxed for the first time in months. He watched Annika as she fended off more questions from Mitch and congratulations from the others. When their eyes occasionally met he saw the light that he remembered so clearly from their days in Williamsburg. Thinking about her hand in his at the movie theater gave him butterflies again, and he smiled at how young he felt all of a sudden.

Lance caught the smile during a lull in the conversation and quietly addressed the table, "I'm sorry I couldn't be there with all of you at the trial. One of my French government clients was losing secrets like it was going out of style and I don't think they would have let me out of the country until I fixed the problem. But, Same, buddy," he said, nodding to Annika, "it sounds like you had one hell of a lawyer on your team."

Annika laughed, "Why thank you, James. I wasn't so bad, if I say so myself."

Same couldn't stop watching the sparkle in her eyes as the maitre d' approached the table. "I believe it is a birthday for Mr. Harrison?" he asked with a smile.

Same quickly straightened up. "Er, yes. Actually in a few days. How did you know?"

"Ah, a friend of yours dropped this birthday card off for you at the desk."

The smile left Same's face immediately. "I'm sorry, sir, is there a problem?" asked the maitre d', worried. "I shall dispose of it immediately."

"No, no," Same interjected, forcing a smile back to his face. "It's just a surprise, that's all. Thank you for delivering it."

The maitre d' gave a half-hearted laugh and quickly hurried away after handing the card to Same. The table was dead quiet and all eyes were glued to Same as he quickly tore open the card. Inside an ordinary birthday card was a short message. After reading it once, he cleared his throat and read it aloud to the group. "Dear Same, congratulations on your case. I organized certain operations involving you until I learned why you were being targeted. Now those behind the operations have relieved me and my agency of our involvement. Sorry for the mess. Call me if you want to burn the bastards. And happy birthday. B.T."

Same looked up to find five pairs of eyes staring at him in shocked silence. "There's a DC area code phone number here."

After a few more seconds of silence Street finally spoke up, "Well, it looks like you've got another Deep Throat. One who tried to kill you this time. Lovely."

Annika looked pensive and pointed her fork at Street. "But before he knew why he was being asked to do it. He's probably with FBI or DEA or Treasury or somebody else that HHS needed for hired muscle. Molly certainly didn't set this process in motion, and whoever was giving B.T. orders is still out there and probably still sees Same as a threat."

The table fell silent for a few moments as the reality of Annika's statement set in. "But I do have a suggestion, if you want my opinion," she said quietly, looking down and tracing the rim of her glass with her index finger.

"By all means, pray tell," said Street.

Annika looked up. "Well, it strikes me that the powers that be may be more open to negotiating now that they have failed at their attempts to play hardball and left a few loose ends out there. I say we go straight to the top and talk to the two directors in the email you hacked."

Same raised his eyebrows. "So we just give them a call and say, 'Hey, there, let's chat about your murder plots?' There's no way we're getting anywhere close to these people, let alone convincing them to come meet with us."

"You're right, you're right," said Annika, tracing her champagne glass again. "But they would probably respond to an emergency request from each other. You hacked their email before, why not do it again? Send each a quick email from the other saying that the Nanotine situation is desperate and they need to meet for damage control. Set the place, and you and I drop in when they meet."

Same looked at Annika for a few moments then over at Lance. "Feasible?"

Lance shrugged. "I don't see why not. If you're meeting them in person, it won't matter if I leave a trail they can find once they discover their email has been hacked."

Street cut in quickly, "But why do you think they're actually going to listen to you?"

"Agency heads are political creatures," Annika responded. "They may be playing some game involving money or policy, but ultimately their careers and their prestige are the most important things to them. Give them a way to salvage that, and I think they'll be willing to deal. You'll have to give up revenge and justice, for now at least, but I think you can salvage Nanotine and get the target off your back."

All eyes turned back to Same, waiting for him to speak. The phrase "burn the bastards" in the birthday card certainly had a ring to it after the murder of Julie and the attempts on his own family and the Watsons. But this was no movie. The little guy usually lost in real life. If he had a chance to protect his family and get Nanotine back on track for the thousands of people who needed it, that was as much as he could really hope for. For now, as Annika said. The wheels of justice would turn slowly, but maybe Richmond PD could turn up Molly and the real killer independently.

"Okay, let's try it," he said. "If it doesn't work, we contact B.T. and burn 'em to the ground."

"Fantastic!" exclaimed Bridget. She looked over to Street with a wry smile and rested an elegant hand on his arm. "Your friends are exciting, Cary. You've got to have me down to Richmond more often. We haven't even reached dinner and we're already bringing down federal agencies!"

"Ha!" exclaimed Lance. "I would have thought driving with Dr. Street would have been all the excitement a person could handle. I think I left claw marks on the dashboard during our last trip."

"Cary does find a way to make things exciting," she said with a wink to Street, "even the wait for the centrifuges to spin the DNA last night."

Street spewed scotch back into his glass as his face turned a deep red. Bridget let out a delightful laugh and Same's jaw just about hit the table.

"What did you guys do while you were waiting?" asked Mitch quickly.

"Ahem," coughed Street, mopping his mouth with the napkin, "We played some cards to stay awake."

"Well, that doesn't sound very exciting," Mitch replied, clearly disappointed.

"Maybe cards will be more interesting when you get older," said Street quickly. "Thank God, here's dinner." Bridget laughed again as the waiter arrived with steaming plates.

Dinner was excellent, as always at The Hard Shell. Details of the email and the meeting with the directors were ironed out. No time would be wasted—Lance would send the emails tomorrow afternoon and the meeting would be on for Saturday night. The group agreed to reconvene on Sunday night at Street's house for a birthday dinner for Same, and, if all went well, a toast to the successful negotiations with the directors. Maybe it was just the champagne, but Same found himself growing more and more hopeful that the whole affair might be nearing a happy conclusion.

Chapter Thirty-Five

The negotiations with the directors turned out to be shockingly easy. Dr. Mendelson with CDER arrived first at the bar of the Grand Hyatt Washington and chose a dark table along the side wall. Annika and Same kept up a flirtatious conversation at a corner of the bar until they saw Dr. White from CMS come storming in approximately ten minutes later. They waited to approach the table until it was obvious from their heated discussion that the two women had figured out the email hack.

Same decided to come out strong. Sitting down at their table, he ignored their surprised looks and laid down his trump card. "Good evening, ladies. Your people have killed my friend and made several attempts on my life due to my questions about Nanotine, and I have an inside man who will testify to it." Maybe he was exaggerating B.T.'s willingness to help, but what the hell, how would they know? "I don't need explanations and I don't intend to go public if you meet three very easy demands."

He waited in silence for their reaction. Neither woman moved. Finally, Mendelson looked over to White, who shrugged and leaned back in her chair. Mendelson then turned back to Same, "How much do you want?"

"Not money, Doctor, just peace of mind. I want Nanotine back on. I want any action or watch on my family and Sally Watson called off. And I want any future decisions on drug trials to be performed without illegal CMS input. Remember my man on the inside and my ability to monitor your communications. I'll let you discuss this offer. I'll be at the bar when you're ready."

Same slowly walked back to the bar and stood beside Annika where he could watch the directors huddle, whispering fiercely. It took no more than a minute before Mendelson raised her head and motioned to Same. She leaned in close as he sat down. "You've got a deal. You can have Nanotine, and we already sacked the guy who authorized the hits on you. That stuff didn't come from Dr. White or myself."

"I'm sure the direct orders didn't come from you, Doctor, but I can guess how that game is played."

"Whatever, Harrison, now you listen to me. You are in the middle of a process that is much bigger than you or us or any one disease. CMS asked FDA to stop trials because Nanotine halted but didn't reverse degeneration, thus potentially leaving hundreds of thousands of middle-aged, otherwise healthy individuals who would need full-time care for perhaps another thirty or forty years. The cost of that care would be enormous, and would ultimately be borne by Medicare and Medicaid, leaving less money for the millions of other people who depend on those programs. This system does a lot of good for a lot of people. You just take some time to think about unintended consequences if you ever get the itch to meddle around in our business again."

"I will most certainly will be giving that thought, Doc," said Same, rising. "Good night, ladies."

He left the two directors staring at each other across the table as he walked out into the evening air with Annika. He quickly relayed the conversation and then they walked in silence to the train station. Annika seemed wrapped in thought.

Finally Same asked, "So, what do you think? You think they'll keep up their end?"

"No," she said, and smiled. "I think they'll leave you alone and re-approve Nanotine, but after they figure out whoever B.T. is, I'm betting they'll go back to their old 'cooperation.' But that's a different fight for a different day. Besides, you never know, the police may be able to get to them through Molly Rose. We may as well wait to see if anything comes of that."

Their spirits gradually picked up on the train ride back down to Richmond. As they described the meeting to Street on the phone, they came to the conclusion that the outcome was really as optimistic as they could have hoped for.

On Sunday afternoon they arrived at Street's house to find Lance in the kitchen recounting to Street and Bridget's amusement the highlights of his work with the French government. From the jovial mood in the kitchen and the look of the bottle of Talisker in the center of the kitchen table, he must have arrived at least an hour ahead of them.

After a round of congratulations and hugs, Street began carefully crafting his special seasoning for steaks while Bridget prepped onions and asparagus for the grill. Same was amused to see how often one would "accidentally" bump or brush the other as they made their way around the kitchen. Mitch had grabbed a week's worth of Uncle Cary's newspapers and was hungrily devouring all the comics he had missed during the trial, occasionally reading out funny lines to Annika and James.

For Same's part he simply leaned back against the wall and breathed in the whole scene. It was hard to imagine a better group of friends and family than this. The events of the past few months had locked him in a mindset revolving around death and deterioration. To beat the murder charges, to build a truce with the directors, and to feel that ray of hope with Annika was like waking from a horrible dream.

The silent entrance of an uninvited guest brought him abruptly back to the present. Out of the corner of his eye Same noticed him simply standing in the entrance to the kitchen. He was tall and thin with carefully combed silver hair and was dressed like a law school professor with a tweed jacket and dark bow-tie. Same recognized trouble by the black leather gloves he wore in mid-September, but his most frightening features were the icy blue eyes with which he calmly surveyed the room.

Same gave an involuntary start as he caught sight of him, and quickly shrugged himself off the wall. "Hey, bud, excuse me, who the hell are you?" he said loudly.

The rest of the kitchen froze as they looked up and followed Same's gaze. Oh, shit, Same thought. How stupid. He had foolishly allowed himself to get wrapped up in the moment. Now his whole family might be paying the price.

The man held up a hand. "Mr. Harrison, please allow me a moment to introduce myself. I'm Dr. Sebarius and I serve my country within the Department of Health and Human Services. That is, I did until this past week."

"What agency in HHS?" asked Same, letting the "serve my country" slide.

"My precise position is unimportant, Mr. Harrison. Suffice it to say that I was given the unique opportunity to facilitate the cooperation between agencies to save our great nation from financial ruin. My reason for being here is simple. I want to apologize for the bumbling antics of the FBI in the Welford affair."

"Wait a minute," said Same. "You're the guy who got fired by Dr. Mendelson, aren't you? Are you telling me that you started all this in motion and I'm supposed to accept your apology that your people shot us and killed my friend?" He began slowly moving toward the man and he could feel his anger rising. "You gotta be fucking kidding me."

"No, Mr. Harrison, I would say fucking killing you would be more appropriate, although that is rather a crude way of saying it, especially in front of ladies and a child." With that Sebarius smoothly produced a compact black pistol with silencer from a shoulder holster underneath his tweed jacket.

"Mr. Harrison," he said calmly but with authority, "you will kindly take several steps back to where you started. I see you're a bit surprised by my little toy. Virginia is such an accommodating state. I was able to stop by Green Acres gun shop on my way down from Washington. Just walked in, made my purchase and out I went. So very convenient and not even a background check. Not that that would have been a problem, but it would have been an irritating delay."

Same saw the barrel aiming steadily into his forehead and stepped back. Just wait, he thought to himself. Play along. Wait for the right moment.

As Same stepped back he saw Lance slowly set down his glass. The man caught the movement as well, and without moving his eyes from Same, pointed his left hand at Lance. "Mr. Lance, if you move toward me, I will shoot Mr. Harrison. It's convenient for everyone that I find you here as well. If you please, sir, you and Ms. Tamm will take the boy against the counter where the good doctors are standing."

Same could see Lance's massive fists clenched tightly, but he and Annika did as they were instructed. Same was now on the south wall of the kitchen while the other five were against the counter on the north wall. A countertop for seating extended into the center of the kitchen from the east wall and separated Same from the rest of the hostages. The only entrance and exit was in the southwest corner, which the man now blocked.

"Now," he continued calmly, his eyes and the pistol's aim never leaving Same's face, "I am offering an apology only for the mistakes of the FBI, who are not 'my people' as you stated. My own investigation suggests that the semen sample was meant to place you in a house of child prostitution, but the FBI's incompetence in collecting the sample from the ladies room in your law office resulted in the unfortunate death of your colleague. You see, I too am a victim of their incompetence, as I was asked to resign from my position because of it."

Sebarius's eyes open wider as he continued, "I wanted to take a reasonable approach. I wanted to make this turn out right for our country. But now you have left me with nothing to lose. All of you have contributed to my loss of position and respect."

Street couldn't contain himself any longer. "Perhaps you could have tried this reasonable approach first before the shootings, kidnappings, and the murder of an innocent young woman?" Street asked, his voice rising angrily. He reached for his glass of Scotch, took a long pull, and sloshed it back on the counter.

Sebarius's smile froze and turned malevolent as he swung his weapon to point at the doctor. The sudden movement drew a muffled gasp from Mitch, who had been slowly pushed behind Bridget as Sebarius talked. Sebarius said icily, "Don't get restless, Dr. Street. The consequences will be quick and severe."

Street harrumphed, took another drink, and sloshed his scotch again as he returned the glass back to the counter. Turning his attention and the gun back to Same, Sebarius continued after a moment, "I'm not sure what consolation it offers, but Ms. Welford was a most unfortunate unintended casualty. Let's call her collateral damage. My condolences, she sounded like a wonderful young woman."

Same could feel his blood pressure rising at Sebarius's faked sympathy for Julie. He was now positive that the man was actually insane and was intending to execute every single one of them.

He found himself considering the dynamics of rushing a man with a gun pointed at his head from eight feet away. The weapon appeared to be fairly small caliber, though Same was no expert. He remembered the story of the British colonial soldiers having to switch to higher caliber ammunition in the late 1890's to bring down charging tribesmen who were hopped up on pride and rage and various drugs.

Pride and rage would have to do for Same.

If Sebarius shot him in the head it wouldn't matter what caliber his gun was, but if he could get that gun pointed somewhere else, he bet Sebarius could only get off one or two shots to his body before Same reached him. If he could just get to him, he could at least interfere with him long enough for Lance to come clean up the rest.

Lance was the next closest to Sebarius at about twelve feet, and from the tension he could see in Lance's body, Same knew his friend was more than ready to bring the pain. He just had to buy more time, get Sebarius distracted, and be ready when he let his aim drift again.

"Sebarius, or whoever you are," said Same, "your intent to only frame me for having sex with child prostitutes is no consolation for the death of my friend, believe it or not, so let's cut the bullshit. You ass-clowns decided to play God with Nanotine rather than do the jobs required under the law, and now you're sorry that you weren't able to hush it up?"

Same was trying to goad him, but Sebarius just laughed. "That's ridiculous, I was doing my job, Mr. Harrison." His laugh died out and now was replaced by a vicious sneer. "You see, I'll be doing all of you a favor. If things didn't end tonight there would just be a continuation. Our government will not simply fold and let this drop. Your friend Mr. Lance will spend the next twenty years in the federal penitentiary for his little stunt at FDA headquarters and you will not…"

"Blah, blah, blah, blah," cut in Street, taking a step forward to retrieve the Talisker from the kitchen table. "Sonny, why don't you run back up to Washington and let them know that the average citizen isn't going to sit on their thumbs while the beltway group plays God."

Sebarius's eyes fixed on Street as he continued, "And you Dr. Street, you're so pure. You play God on a daily basis but start preaching when someone proposes a simple but necessary solution to an awkward problem."

"Listen here, boy," slurred Street, pointing with his glass of scotch, "why don'tcha take off your pretty little bow-tie and let me whip your skinny little ass for you?"

Street's slurred words snapped the last thread of restraint in Sebarius's diseased mind and he jerked the gun toward the doctor. That was all the opening Same had been waiting for. Dropping his shoulders down low in front of his body, he drove through the balls of his feet like a sprinter leaving the blocks. He had gotten one full step when he felt the first bullet slice through the top of his right ear and crease the back of his deltoid muscle. He was pleasantly surprised at how little it stung with the massive amount of adrenaline now flooding his bloodstream.

As he planted his left foot to accelerate through Sebarius, he felt the second bullet kick hard against the inside of his thigh. His foot skidded out from under him. His hurried right step wasn't quick enough to compensate, and he began falling as he angled toward Sebarius's feet rather than his torso.

For his part, Sebarius showed remarkable dexterity. As Same plunged toward his feet, he leapt to avoid him like a shortstop dodging a hard slide into second base. Same hit the ground on his side, arms flailing to make contact with Sebarius's feet and throw him off balance. His journey ended abruptly as his head connected with the corner of the wall at the kitchen entrance, and his world suddenly showered white stars and went black.

Sebarius's aerial display was cut short abruptly by a sickening crack. His eyes on Same, Sebarius never saw James Lance. In a classic form tackle, Lance drove his thick forehead directly through the thin man's sternum while wrapping up with his arms. Scooping Sebarius's lower body upwards, Lance extended his legs and drove the man's top half down to the floor as their momentum carried them out of the kitchen and into Street's dining room.

The floor in the dining room wasn't carpeted, but it wouldn't have mattered. Nearly three hundred accelerating pounds of battle-hardened muscle speared Sebarius's cracked chest into the floor, crushing his heart. His head whipsawed backward into the floor, fracturing his skull and making a soft thud on the hardwood like a rolling pin hitting wet bread dough. The bow-tie, miraculously, was preserved perfectly in place. But as Lance could tell from Sebarius's bloodshot, protruding eyeballs, death was instantaneous.

***

Same awoke to blurred voices and shapes hovering around his midsection. This could be bad, he thought to himself, best just to close my eyes again. A sudden excruciating pain in his left groin brought his eyes wide open and consciousness flooded back. He recognized that he was lying on Street's kitchen floor and that Street, Bridget, and Annika were struggling to get his pants off while Mitch was holding his hand and Lance was yelling on the phone in the living room. Happily, Sebarius was nowhere to be seen, but goddam his crotch hurt!

As he started to sit up, Mitch shouted happily, "He's waking up!"

"Same, lie down!" shouted Street. "Annika, you keep his shoulders down. James!" he shouted, "I need some exposure here."

Same brought himself up on his elbows and looked down in time to see Lance insert two fingers into the bullet hole in his trousers. He ripped the fabric as if it was tissue paper. The thigh was covered with blood and continued to bleed in spurts with each beat of his heart.

Street tried to stem the flow with his thumb, which brought a shriek from Same, "Holy shit, Uncle Cary, that hurts."

Street yelled just as loud, "Shut the fuck up and lie back. If there's ever been a time for your self-hypnosis it's now."

"I can't. It hurts. What is it?"

Same could see Street's hands moving quickly as he said, "Afraid that bullet hit a big vessel, maybe the femoral artery. You want to save this leg and more importantly, you want to live, do what I taught you at William and Mary. Relax yourself and help control this bleeding. With your blood all over me you better not have picked up something from Molly that won't wash off. Now get on it, do your part."

Same laid his head back and struggled to focus on his breathing as Street barked orders. "Mitch, run up to the linen closet and get two washcloths."

Mitch took off and was back almost before he left.

"James, get his belt." Street removed his thumb, folded a washcloth as small as he could, and reached up on the kitchen counter to grab a small, round pepper shaker. "This will work just lovely. We'll get pressure with no sharp edges to cut anything else."

He placed the shaker in the wound with the cloth on top and then the second cloth. With Lance's help they ran the belt under the buttock, over the hip and down over the pack. Lance tightened the belt until Street said, "That'll do it. Much more and you'd amputate his leg."

Street sat back on his haunches, "That all we can do for right now." He stood and went into the library and returned with a blood pressure cuff and stethoscope. He took Same's pressure and shook his head. Same was paler than a freezing witch and diaphoretic with profuse sweating.

The rescue squad arrived and announced they would take over. Street gave them a twenty-word history and then ordered, "Start an IV and move him as quick as possible."

The EMT didn't reply, but took a BP cuff from his kit.

Street was incredulous, "He has a cuff on his arm. A minute ago his BP was 88/40."

The second tech started to loosen the tourniquet. Street yelled, "Don't loosen that yet. He's lost a bushel of blood, look at the floor. You try to take that belt off and I'll break your hand. I'm a physician and will assume responsibility. Your partner has the IV going, now get him out of here. I know all about the need for circulation, but if he dies from hemorrhage he won't need the leg."

***

When Same came around again he found himself in a bed, staring straight at a heart rate monitor with a clock reading 1105. He lay still and tried to fill in where he was. Next to the monitor was an IV pole with a bag of blood and a large bag of Ringer's lactate solution hanging. He traced the tubings down to his arms. As his focus lengthened he saw more medical equipment and finally noticed the railing on the bed.

Oh shit, he thought, he was in the Medical College hospital, and in a room just like his dad's! Was he already at the last stages of FTD? Were they about to pull the tube?

He turned his head in a panic and suddenly caught sight of Mitch and Annika reading in a chair by a window with Street standing beside them. The memories came back in a rush. The botched charge at Sebarius, the emergency work on the kitchen floor, the arrival of the paramedics. Christ, he was going to have to stop winding up in this damn hospital.

Just then Lance and Bridget walked through the door carrying coffees and large birthday cake. "Hey! Look who just woke up when the food arrives!" Lance exclaimed.

Annika and Mitch jumped from their chair and all five crowded around. Street put two fingers to the pulse on Same's wrist. "How are you feeling? You lost quite a bit of blood."

Same took a few seconds to enjoy the sympathy from all their concerned looks. When it would just be too selfish to hold out any longer, he finally replied, "Well, a little embarrassed to be honest."

"Embarrassed?" asked Street, "What do you have to be embarrassed about?"

Same looked up at the ceiling. "Just embarrassed that I missed that Sebarius asshole by so much after I had to teach James how to tackle during his junior year at William and Mary."

Lance burst out laughing. The others quickly joined in, relieved to hear him in good enough spirits to be teasing Lance again.

"Dr. Street, call the nurse," laughed Lance, "this man is clearly hallucinating!"

Same even found himself chuckling, but stopped as he discovered the growing pain in his groin. Come to think of it, there was a lot more than just his groin that was hurting.

"But dude, seriously," said Lance, "that may have been the single worst tackle I have ever seen. You didn't even touch the man!"

Street couldn't help but chime in. "You took your sweet time going for it too," he said. "If I had to drink another glass of scotch to keep his attention, my breath would have knocked him over. And then you had the gall to bleed all over my damn kitchen."

"It wasn't the drinking that tipped me off to your game, Uncle Cary," Same retorted. "Lord knows that's not unusual. It was the sloshing on the counter. I don't think I've ever seen you let a drop of the Talisker go to waste."

"Here's to that," said Street, raising his coffee cup in a mock toast.

Annika raised her cup. "And here's to our Same taking a bullet for us and having the good grace to come out alive," she said. They all raised their cups in a salute.

"Thank you, thank you," said Same, raising his arms. "But what happened to Sebarius?"

The group quieted and looked silently at Lance, who looked at the floor and scratched his jaw. Street jumped in after a few seconds. "Umm, well, let's just say that James ended him abruptly."

Same turned and put his hand on Lance's arm. "Thank you, James. You saved my family, man. Thank you."

"Well," stammered Lance, still looking at the floor, "You're welcome, but I wouldn't have gotten to him if you hadn't drawn his fire. I think it was a team effort." He looked up with a smile. "At any rate he's gone now."

"Yeah, he's gone now, but how many others are there like him?" asked Same. "What else are these regulatory agencies going to be coming up with in the name of protecting the health of the public?"

Street scratched his head, grinned and said, "Knowing you, you'll probably be right in the middle of it. But for now I paid good money for this cake and James probably had to bribe somebody to bring it in, so let's fire it up."

Mitch and Bridget carefully placed thirty-three candles into a chocolate cake with cream cheese frosting, then lit each one before a beautifully out-of-tune rendition of "Happy Birthday" commenced.

"I'm going to need a little help blowing the candles out, Mitch," said Same. "You think you can do the honors for me?"

"Yeah, but you gotta make a wish first, dude."

Same closed his eyes for a moment, then opened them again and put his hand on Mitch's shoulder. "All right, buddy, hit it before the fire department gets called."

Mitch did the honors with great gusto, then turned back to Same as Lance began cutting the cake. "What did you wish for?"

"Nothing."

"Nothing?"

Same laughed and looked around at his family. "Couldn't think of anything else I could want."

Acknowledgments

We would like to express our deepest thanks to Alan Dow, M.D., Assistant Dean, MCV/Virginia Commonwealth University for his guidance; Christine Fuller, Professor and Director of Neuropathology and Autopsy Pathology, MCV/Virginia Commonwealth University for her patient teaching; Joann Bodurtha, Professor Pediatrics and Genetics, MCV/Virginia Commonwealth University for her advice and shared laughs; Chistopher Renjilian, M.D., for guidance at the University of Pennsylvania; Lt. Shawn Marshall, City of Richmond Sheriff's Department; John Schilling, Esq.; Judge M. Hannah Lauck, for reading and advice; Judge Walter W. Stout for his advice and direction; Shannon Wolford, for reading and comments; Susan Dickinson and Sharon Denny, Association for Frontotemporal Degeneration, for reading and comments; Anne Ward, for reading, editing and eternal patience; and Susan, Trevor, and Margaret Eissler for reading, assistance and encouragement.

FRONTOTEMPORAL DEGENERATION (FTD)

FTD is a disease process that affects the frontal and temporal lobes of the brain. It causes a group of brain disorders that are characterized by changes in behavior, personality, language, motor skills, and executive functions.

FTD at a Glance

- The average age of onset is 56 years.

- Many diagnosed with FTD are at the height of their professional careers and still have children at home.

- Life expectancy averages 8 years from the start of symptoms, but ranges from 2-18 years depending on the specific disorder.

- FTD accounts for 10-20% of all dementias and is nearly as common as Alzheimer's disease in people under 65.

- Clinical diagnoses include: primary progressive aphasia (PPA), behavioral variant frontotemporal dementia (bvFTD), progressive supranuclear palsy (PSP) and corticobasal degeneration (CBD).

- Because FTD has not been well understood it is difficult to know with certainty the number of people affected.

- 50% of cases have some family history, but researchers have only identified definite genetic mutations in 10% of cases.

Language problems include loss of fluency in speech, understanding, reading, and writing. Some people become hesitant in their speech and begin to talk less, but appear to retain the meaning of words longer. Others experience a deterioration of vocabulary and recognizing objects, but retain the ability to produce fluent speech.

Behavioral symptoms include loss of empathy and inappropriate social behavior. People become less involved in daily activities and withdraw emotionally. Unusual behaviors also include swearing, overeating or drinking, impulsivity, repetitive behavior, or deterioration in hygiene. The person may show little awareness of behavior changes and little concern for their effect on others. The person may also spend excessively or take financial or legal risks.

Motor symptoms include decrease in movement on one side of the body and muscle rigidity with tremor, problems with gait and balance, or inability to coordinate eye movements.

Damage to the brain's frontal and temporal lobes affects complex thinking and reasoning, impacting a person's ability to plan and execute activities. Symptoms include distractibility, inflexibility, apathy, poor judgment, and abrupt mood changes. Memory is usually preserved for a while, but some patients have impaired memory early on.

Diagnosis and Treatment

Obtaining a diagnosis is a difficult process because symptoms start slowly and can resemble several other neurological and psychiatric disorders. Bipolar disorder, depression and Parkinson's disease are common misdiagnoses. At this time there is no single test that can confirm a diagnosis of FTD. Diagnosis requires a comprehensive evaluation including medical, neurological, and neuropsychological tests and brain imaging.

The pace of research into FTD is increasing rapidly. Scientists are energized by advances in understanding these disorders and the first drugs for FTD are entering clinical testing. It is a time of great activity and great hope.

Funding for continued research is critical. Participation of patients and families in studies is essential. A cure will only be found through expanding partnerships between families and physicians, scientists and funders, and policy makers and the public.

The Association for Frontotemporal Degeneration (AFTD)

AFTD is a not-for-profit organization created in 2002 to advocate for people who live and work with FTD. AFTD's mission includes promoting awareness; providing information, education and support to people diagnosed with FTD and their caregivers; educating health professionals; and funding research into treatments and ultimately a cure.

For more information visit WWW.THEAFTD.ORG.